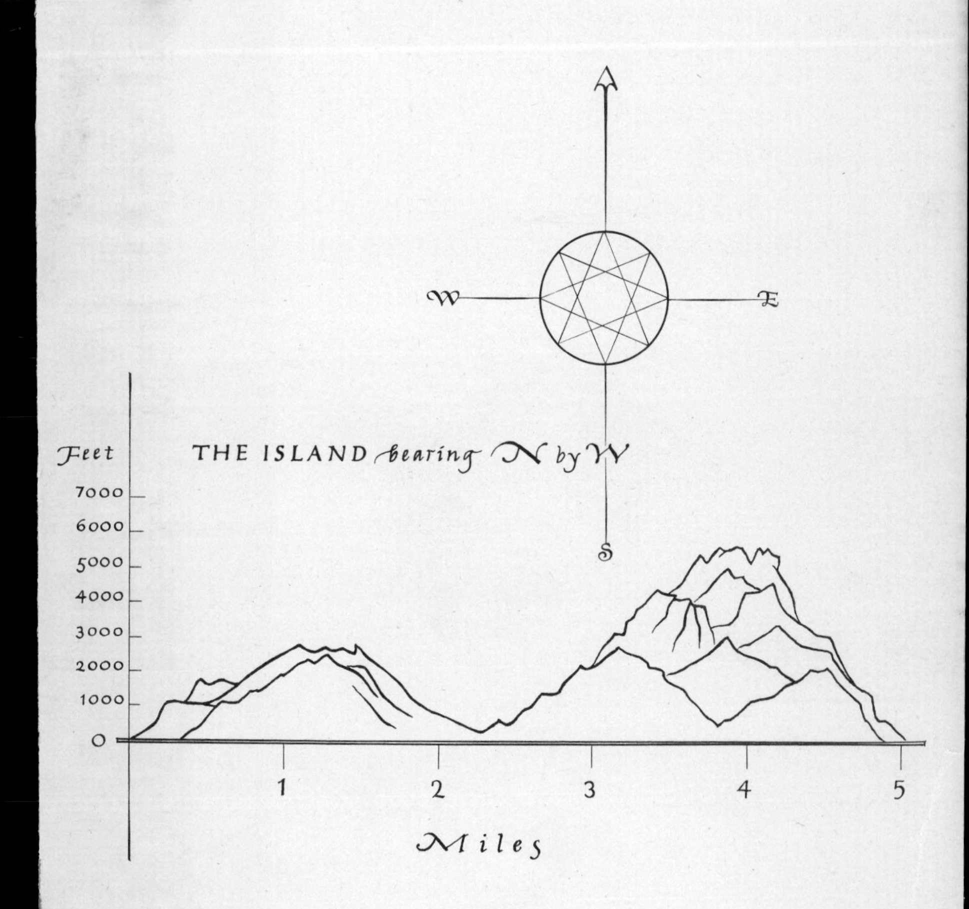
W
E
S
Feet
THE ISLAND bearing N by W
7000
6000
5000
4000
3000
2000
1000
0
1
2
3
4
5
Miles

LOST

ISLAND

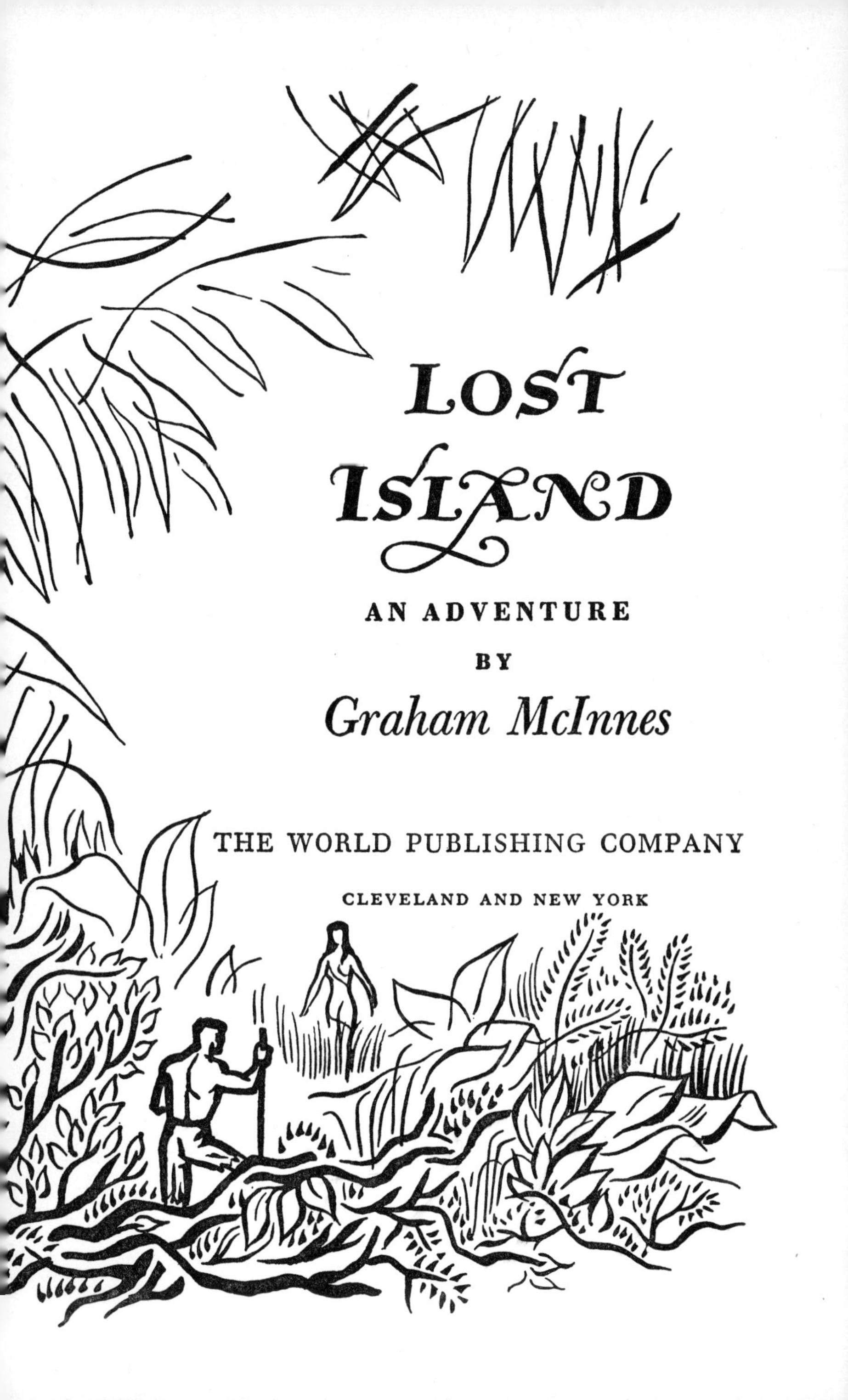

LOST ISLAND

AN ADVENTURE

BY

Graham McInnes

THE WORLD PUBLISHING COMPANY

CLEVELAND AND NEW YORK

Library of Congress Catalog Card Number: 54-5349

FIRST EDITION

HC 554

To my brother Colin

In memory of the Coral Island of our boyhood.

NOTE

Those who know the probable location of Drake's lost island (its exact whereabouts is still a matter for speculation) may possibly wonder at its having shifted north and west. Perhaps it was really a floating island, and was wafted there by the Southeast Trades.

October 24, 1578; Latitude 35°16′ South; Longitude 105°23′ West.

"... at lengthe they entered into the haven of an Islande and ankered above the lengthe of the shot of a great peece from the land at twenty fathome deepe where they stayed three or foure dayes and the wind coming southward they weyed anker ... having found fresh and very good water with herbes of singular virtue"

—Richard Hakluyt: *The famous Voyage of Sir Francis Drake into the South Sea, and therehence about the whole Globe of the Earth. London,* 1582.

1

THE Northeast Trades, following in the wake of the morning sun, paused over the magic city of Honolulu as though loath to spend themselves on the barren islets far to the west. They came whistling down from the jagged fortresses of the Pali, past deeply dissected ravines heavy with the early morning scent of azalea and frangipani. The sun peeped over the purple ridges and sent long shadows down into the streets of the fabulous city. The wind billowed the curtains in a hillside villa, and the sounds of a Hawaiian dawn stirred an errant woman to consciousness.

The name of the woman beneath the clinging sheet was Ruth Ryan. She had been born Ruth Bennett thirty-four years ago in the foothills of the Canadian Rockies. The man whose body had aroused her own and who now lay asleep beside her was not her husband. He was a Lieutenant Commander in the United States Navy and his name was Tom Griffith. He was a public relations officer. His own wife had recently divorced him, and was presently in San Francisco. But she would have recognized—and perhaps with more genuine affection than Ruth—the short curly hair which in sleep had dampened the pillow ever so slightly; the faint half smile that died along a cheek normally fat and roughened but now almost babylike in relaxed repose. But when he grunted and jerked in his sleep, the woman's body stiffened with distaste, and on her curving lips, as the wind from the Pacific brought her back from sleep, a smile tightened in prim disdain.

The sun climbed higher over Pali, shot through a cleft at twelve hundred feet and cast a shaft of vivid green on the sheer cliff from which King Kamehameha used to hurl his captured enemies. A heavy duty truck thundered up the blacktopped mountain highway leading from Honolulu across the island. Incredibly, a trolley bus squelched down the slopes of paradise bound for the pineapple canneries and the docks. Ruth Ryan stirred and slowly brought her eyes into focus. They strayed from the billowing curtains and the pandanus palm tapping insistently against the window, down and across to the heavily carved wood and moquette chesterfield. In its sober overstuffed presence the soap-bubble dream burst asunder and revealed a bed-sitting room as stale as the stuffy air against which the scent of azaleas strove in vain. On the chesterfield lay an untidy cascade of male clothes, stripped hurriedly inside out and cast down like the hastily drawn viscera of a gutted animal. Beyond the chesterfield a streaky mirror grasped in its frame tattered dance invitations and the stubs of movie tickets. Beneath it was a cheap vanity littered with expensive unguents and perfumes. A blackened cigarette stub had ended its life ingloriously in a jar of cold cream.

The smells of heavy sleep and of passion spent mingled with those of stale food.

Ruth Ryan shook out her chestnut hair on the pillow, raised herself on one elbow and groped on the bedtable for a cigarette. When she found onc she lit it with a match scratched on the frame of the bed, and inhaled voraciously. Then she turned and looked sidewise at the still sleeping man, propped the pillows up against the headboard and leaned back, surveying her lover with cool and disinterested contempt. A gust of wind came boisterously in at the open window and brought her the scent of mist on the grass. The part-Hawaiian newsboy pedaled by whistling, shot the *Aloha Times* expertly over the dew-laden locust hedge and rode on down the hill toward the big hospital. Beyond that lay the papaya trees and the cool lawns of Ala Moana Park; and curving beneath the rugged couchant lion of Diamond Head, a tiny strip of sand hemmed in by the fringing reef and crushed to insignificance by the rose pink mass of the Royal Oahu Hotel: Waikiki. On Diamond Head itself stood a member of the United States Coast defense. He had just come off duty at the reservation and had paused to watch the sun rise over the mountains. He stood at the extreme tip of the peak and looked down into the green water laving the reef at his feet. Then he looked upward to the southern horizon, blue and sharp. In his direct line of vision there lay between him and Antarctica, in almost eight thousand miles of heaving ocean, only a solitary atoll, a mile wide and less than thirty feet high.

Ruth finished her cigarette and watched the mottled shadows playing on the ceiling. A wisp of coffee smell drifted tantalizingly in from the next villa. She sat bolt upright and her eye caught the headlines on the front page of the paper thrown on the floor in the midst of last night's rapture:

ALL HOPE ABANDONED FOR MISSING B 77

She felt a hot surge of shame and as if to hide it jerked the sheet closer round her shoulders, pulled her knees up to her chin and clasped her hands round her shins. It was not the first time she had seen the headline or read the story. That was last night when Tom Griffith, swaying slightly at the open door of her room and brandishing the paper, had proclaimed: "Well, he's sunk. What're you going to do about it? He's sunk!" He was sunk now all right: her husband. He was probably lying in the lampless dark of four thousand fathoms, his once stalwart body subjected to the shattering pressures of the great deeps. "What're you going to do about it?" The memory of what she had done about it, she and Griffith, actually brought a flush to her cheek. She climbed out of bed, trying fiercely to recapture, if only for a moment, the first helpless, hopeless feeling that had overwhelmed her when she read the message which she had half expected ever since the great aircraft had been reported missing three weeks ago.

So Francis was dead. Dead, she repeated several times, staring at the crude black print; but her senses were numbed and she could not be sure whether she really cared or not. She put on a flared housecoat, dabbed lipstick expertly on her mouth and ran a comb through her hair. She still wanted to look like something when the man in the house woke up; but she prayed silently that he would stay asleep at least until she had finished reading the story again. She wanted to be alone with it for a little while and to savor, in the laconic script of the news agency, the epitaph of the man with whom she had spent ten years of her life. She picked up the paper and walked out through the French windows to the little balcony shaded by kona trees. She sat down in a rattan chair, gathered the housecoat across her thighs, smoothed open the paper and began to read:

PANGO PANGO, AMERICAN SAMOA, February 4 (AP). Naval officials at this South Pacific American base admitted today they had abandoned all hope of finding the giant B 77 bomber which disappeared somewhere between Easter Island and the Chilean-owned rocks of Sala-y-gomez three weeks ago today. The big aircraft, outfitted as a test and development weather laboratory, was on a long range flight from Hickam Field, Oahu, T.H., to the recently opened joint U.S.-British cold weather research station in the Falkland Islands. It carried a crew of five U.S. Navy Air Force officers, twelve enlisted men and eight civilian scientists. Names of the airmen will not be released until next of kin have been notified. It was learned however that the civilian scientists included five Americans: James Elmore of Grand Forks, N.D.; Lowell Whitman of Sacramento, Calif.; Morley Scott of Tuscaloosa, Ala.; Orville Freedman of New York City and John H. Holmquist of Chicago; and one Canadian, Dr. Francis Ryan, meteorologist from the University of Toronto on exchange duty with the U.S. Navy.

The big flying-lab, powered by six turbo-jets and four jet engines with a cruising speed of 550 m.p.h. and a range of 6000 miles was reported over Easter Island, lonely sentinel outpost of eastern Polynesia, famed for its grotesque statues, at about 2 P.M. on January 14 according to a message received in Santiago, Chile, by short wave radio from the island. It was flying low and its noise apparently caused consternation among the islanders who connected its appearance with their stone monuments. It is assumed the plane was regarded as some kind of evil spirit. The last message received from the plane was a standard bearing giving its position as lat. 28°S, long. 105°W. No further message was received.

The disappearance of the flying-lab touched off the widest and most exhaustive air-sea hunt in history. The Navy has methodically secured an ocean area of almost half a million square miles. Land based planes of the Chilean and French Ocean Establishments air forces have aided planes from U.S., British and French bases and carriers. But by February 2 the area of probability had been worked over from A to Z plus 2. Yesterday, February 3, navy planes had one last crack at Z plus 3. No trace of the aircraft was found. Naval officials here, while refusing to speak for attribution, said they held out no hope the mystery would be solved.

HONOLULU, T.H., February 5 (AP). Most of those on the plane were from the mainland, but one passenger, Francis Ryan, was well known in this city. Residing at 1211 Niihau Drive in the Nuuanu area, he had been working at Hickam Field since his arrival here from Canada six years ago. A quiet, reserved man of medium height, he was a prominent member of the local tennis club. He is survived by his widow, the former Ruth Bennett.

The former Ruth Bennett of Calgary, Alberta. A tramp; now a widow. She let the paper fall to the balcony floor. The rising sounds of morning traffic, smoothed by the heavy tropical foliage and muted from time to time by a playful gust from the trades, were slowly beginning to possess the awakening valley. Mingled with the eternal sounds—the whispering of the wind, the dry papery crackle of dusty palm fronds, the tinkling music of the waterfall on Nuuanu Creek far below—came the homely noises of the awakening city: the clack and clatter of milk bottles from the villa three doors up the hill, the sound of an automobile roaring off in low gear, some home carpenter hammering nails and whistling tunelessly *That Certain Party.*

As she listened to the morning's mingled sounds she sought in vain for help in achieving a contemplative mood. The marriage of Hawaiian luxury and Polynesian charm with Yankee drive and gadgetry had produced in Honolulu the strumpet of the Pacific. It beckoned to her with all the allure of the honky-tonk to which her own emotions had always responded so eagerly. She wished that she were looking out of a window in Papeete, Apia, Suva, anywhere rather than Honolulu. Then like called to like across the cascading expanse of purple and green bougainvillea that shrouded the portico below, and she saw not the jagged hilltops and the lush greenery but the Aloha Tower, the come-on billboards of the Chamber of Commerce, the skyscrapers at Waikiki, and the little factories where they made paper leis for the tourists. Saw them, sensed them and liked them: rejected the soft tropical sights and smells and sounds which might have given her solace in the misery which she wanted to feel but could not.

She frowned and shook her head in a conscious effort to think hard, to recollect: to recover something of the debris of her married life which now lay floating round the stale bedroom in ever fainter eddies. Soon it would disappear altogether unless she could catch it. Did she wish to remember? She could carry well enough the lighthearted widow's weeds which Honolulu would expect of her. Did anything else matter? Not unless she could recapture in memory something essential of her relationship with Francis. With Francis Ryan.

"Ruth, I'd like you to meet Francis Ryan."

The Hawaiian valley, complete with neon lighting, faded from her sight and she was back again in the raw crude glare of Alberta sunshine. Early spring in Calgary with a chinook off the Rockies turning the snow to slush in the streets. The sharp vertical thrust of skyscrapers, with wooden shacks, Bar-B-Qs, poolrooms and dine-and-dance joints huddled at their feet. Streets, devoid of all trace of greenery, were becoming gray canyons knit together with a tangle of overhead wires suspended from twisted cedar poles.

Young Ruth Bennett on the front steps of the Palliser Hotel, very fetching in a heavy camel-hair topcoat and fur bootees, with her windblown chestnut locks (earmuffs in the pocket of the topcoat just in case the chinook failed). Her nameless boyfriend of the period was introducing her to a dark-eyed young man, perhaps a little on the lean side, but with the same clean brown smile she had seen on so many of the young oil executives turned out by the assembly lines of American colleges for the jobs of minor satraps in the growing oil empire of the north. Almost without thinking she gave him the routine look from under the eyelashes, and with it the eager parting of the lips that reduced the recipient's knees to water. Instead he gave a solemn bow and removed his hat. His hair was an even ash gray though he was no more than thirty. She could not help staring. Her escort babbled on.

"Francis is from the East—Toronto. He's out here doing weather research."

"Oh, how very interesting"; and she was aware of how flat and uninteresting she had made it sound.

"Miss Bennett," was all he said, but he reached for her hand, which was perhaps unusual in Calgary, though no more unusual than that she could have been introduced to him, rather than he to her. He took her hand and looked straight at her. He had eyes of black smoke and they seemed to envelop her instantly and completely without either undue probing or false modesty. The rapid retort died on her lips and she was aware of a desire, already transmitted into a rising of the flesh, to be possessed by him.

That event duly took place. They were married three weeks later and there followed for both of them a process of slow, sad, sure disillusionment which lasted, growing progressively more gnarled and rutted, through four years in western Canada, and which did not survive transfer to Hawaii. Perhaps Ryan's sense of loss was the sharper, for he had created of her physical beauty a Galatea who did not exist; whereas she was merely disillusioned with herself. It came to him soon and sharply that the desires of her body were ubiquitous and uncontrolled. It came to her more slowly, and more bitterly in those early days still tinged with idealism, that her sense of personal surrender had for its focus no single pair of arms. With it came the acrid knowledge that what she had read into his eyes at their first meeting had been merely the reflection of her own desires.

Ruth Ryan flicked the stub of her cigarette over the edge

of the balcony. It landed in a small ornamental pool fringed with arum lilies and soon became a bloated soggy mass, adding to the fragrant garden the slatternly touch which had hitherto been confined to the apartment. Then she rose, smoothed the housecoat down over easy hips and passed behind a beaded curtain into the tiny kitchenette. The man on the bed stirred at the metallic rustle but did not wake. She was now truly preoccupied with her thoughts and began absently to prepare a meal without so much as a glance into the bedroom. She turned up the stove jet and the propane gas was ignited. She filled a percolator and put in six spoonfuls of coffee. She sidled gracefully to the refrigerator, took out a papaya and began to slice it on a breadboard. The succulent yellow flesh slid apart under her knife, displaying rows of winking black-eyed seeds; and the heavy overripe smell rose tangibly about her. Now the image of her husband stood before her with startling vividness. He was sitting across the breakfast table with his gray-white thatch of hair rising from his lean brown face. The empty plate, denuded of all save the papaya rind, was before him and he pushed it away with a gesture at once final and resigned.

"You're hopeless, Ruth," she heard his voice echoing sharply down the corridors of memory. "I've even lost count of the fellows. I can't even remember their faces. Can you?" They had both been past pretending and she simply shook her head. Then there had arisen in him a desire to goad her, to achieve in her private world at least the distinction of being noticed for his male qualities, to achieve some small triumph by arousing her anger.

"I don't suppose their faces matter any way. A pumpkin on a pair of legs would suit you just as well."

She thought: God, that's crude. But she essayed in return

only a sad enigmatic smile coupled with an ever so slight shrug of the shoulders. This infuriated him. He rose to his feet determined on making a scene.

"I guess I can hardly expect you to wait more than half an hour after the plane takes off before you phone Griffith. He'll be in this room before we're over Koko Head."

"He doesn't come off duty till late in the afternoon."

He looked at her with cold dislike, but her beautiful face, the asymmetrical oval ringed with the chestnut hair, was devoid of expression. She said: "I'd better do the dishes." He paused and they both seemed to look down for a moment from a great height on a heap of cold ashes from which rose a faint gossamer rope of bitter smoke. Then he took his brief case and walked out of the door, and as it now seemed, out of her life and out of the world.

"What's cooking?"

She started, the lock of her private thoughts burst open by Griffith's query, and turned to see him standing in the doorway. Distaste rose unaccountably in her throat. She was aware of the puffs beneath his eyes and the stubble on his cheeks. "You'd better come and help me get breakfast."

He yawned cavernously. She thought: his figure isn't bad for forty-two and the morning after. But she felt perverse and as if a nakedness more private than that of her body had been violated.

"I've been thinking about Francis."

"I know, tough business, but we went over all that last night."

"I saw the headline again when I got up this morning."

The possibility that she might be distressed slowly wormed its way into his mind.

"I'm sorry Ruth. I didn't mean . . ."

"It's all right."

"If I thought you really cared about him. . . ."

"It's all right, I said. Come and help me with the breakfast."

But he put his arms round her from behind, cupping her breasts in his hands.

"Oh to hell with breakfast."

He started to fumble with the housecoat and she tried to twist away. She said "Don't" mechanically, but physical release suddenly seemed enormously attractive not only for itself but as a drug for the unexpected pain of remembering. Her body relaxed while the memory of Francis Ryan reeled backward into oblivion.

· 2 ·

BATTERED by thunderous seas in its passage over the splintery coral reef, the body lay sprawled on the warm yellow sand. Far down inside it life flickered fitfully and, as the sun rose higher in the bright and brassy sky, ebbed and flowed like the fronds of an underwater plant caught in the eddies of a hidden shoal. Less than a quarter of a mile away the great combers came rolling in from the uttermost limits of the blue horizon, arched their silky necks and then crashed with tempestuous fury on the reef, sending up great clouds of spindrift. They shook the reef to its foundations and made the earth tremble. But the little insects had built well. They had been working for twenty thousand years on the crater of an extinct volcano now drowned beneath the ocean. On the landward side of the reef the lagoon was calm and torpid behind the dike they had built, ruffled only by an occasional breeze or by falling spray from the waves crashing beyond the natural breakwater.

Though the maelstrom raged outside, the waters of the still lagoon laved listlessly at the sand where the body lay. The lap of its minute and oily waves was a languorous beckoning to the half-drowned form to return to the water from which stubborn endeavour had so recently lifted it.

Down in the pink and white corridors of the reef, bright fish flashed and flickered: striped like tigers or barbed like porcupines; strange fish with huge voracious heads, eel-like bodies, re-curved teeth and finny spines. Deep in the secure interstices of the coral which shimmered in the green translucent water, tiny crabs scuttled and skittered, and sea anemones waved their delicate tentacles. In the lagoon fish leaped, and above, curve-beaked frigate birds swooped with deceptive ungainliness. Circling high over the bottle-green water, studded with innumerable coral heads and patches, scavenger gulls stared unwinkingly at the still form on the sand below, waiting for the shadows to creep toward it.

The sun moved behind a cleft in a towering peak of volcanic rock. Though the sand was now slipping into the warm shadows of the afternoon, a single ray shone through a crevice six thousand feet up the mountain and bathed the blood-stained limbs for a few moments longer. Then it slipped behind the rocky diadem, and a cool whisper of breeze twitched the forest edge beyond the beach and ruffled the hair of the unconscious half-clad figure.

Life, oozing slowly back into the mortal frame of Francis Ryan, flowed into his heart, and as it beat more hopefully, a shudder ran through him and the black veil lifted from his eyes. He became conscious of a gashed and lacerated left arm lying immediately in front of him on the sand. He did not at once identify it as his own. His eyes, blurred and wavering like those of a drunkard, took in a few square feet of sand

and a half-buried conch shell. With an immense effort he lifted first his eyes and then his head. He saw the sand grow more hummocky, and then rocks, a line of dark trees and beyond it mountains rising up so sheer and fantastic that he smiled, and thought he had uttered a cry of disbelief. Actually all he achieved was the horrible grimace of lips drawn momentarily back over broken teeth, and a curdled cackle that was barely human. The next instant pain returned to him in an agonizing thrust and great waves of nausea sent him back into the pit of the unconscious. The gulls circling above moved seaward and remained hovering over the lagoon, as the westering sun slowly turned the peaks of the mountain from green to gold.

Ryan lay on the sand until the sun sank far behind the purple headland to the west, hung poised over an infinite waste of waters, then plunged beneath the ocean as though it had fallen over the edge of the world. Darkness strode across the sea and enveloped the island. The stars rushed out into the velvet night and the breeze, sodden now with the warmth of the tropical rain forest, once again stirred Ryan's battered body. This time he woke more fully, and though the pain was still agonizing, he found that it was no longer all enveloping, but localized like burning daggers stuck in his flesh: his left arm, his back, his right leg. He tried to drag himself into a sitting position but he was still too weak, and earth and sky spun in his head as he started to move. He had no clear idea where he was. Great patches of mist swirled through his memory blotting out familiar objects. But through it all, and beyond the immediate threat of pain, there came in his mind the persistent roar of airplane engines.

As the pain became more localized and more intense, so the borderline between memory and hallucination, at first so fine and wavering, stiffened, hardened and finally became concrete. Now he knew that he was on land, that he was seriously hurt but alive and that the noise and terror that raced round in his mind were a memory, and were different from the roar and thunder of the reef beyond. Even the reef itself now became clear to his focusing senses as a long splash of white against the violet of the tropical night.

With an immense effort of will and moving very slowly, Ryan raised himself to his hands and knees. He placed his left hand on the sand and almost fainted from the pain. When he had recovered sweat was streaming down his forehead, but he hung on grimly and found that he could use his left elbow. His right leg dragging behind him like a wounded snake, he slowly crawled forward up the beach, a few inches at a time, using his left elbow and his knee as motive power. He had no clear idea where he was going, but an animal instinct drove him up the slight slope of beach away from the sea and towards the dark line where the forest fell back before the smothering assault of the sand.

It took him half an hour to crawl less than fifty feet, but when he reached the forest edge, blinded by his own sweat and moaning with mingled pain and exhaustion, it was at a small clear trickle of cold water pouring from a low rocky ledge into the sand. Lying on his belly he drank deeply and was at once violently sick. But he drank again, crawled painfully into the lee of a heap of sand tufted with marrin grass and was instantly asleep.

He awoke with a jerk and a shudder just before dawn. The air was warm and humid and though he was stiff and moved each limb and muscle with difficulty, the pain was deadened from the previous night. He was now convinced that he had no bones broken, though he was shocked to see that the top joints of the third and ring fingers of his left hand were shredded to a raw pulp. He stared at them for a moment in unbelief, not daring to touch them. He had no idea when they had been injured nor how long he had borne the pain. But they throbbed acutely and he wondered how much time he might have spent in salt water and with what beneficial effect.

He lifted his uninjured right hand to his face and found the stubble already growing silky. That would mean about ten days of growth. Where had he shaved last? At Honolulu, at Hiva-Oa, while refueling, on the plane? He could not recall. But as he awkwardly shifted his weight to gain relief he realized that the rest of his injuries, though painful, must be only superficial. While he moved he was aware of a subtle change in the light. It brought his head round sharply from the sea to the land and made him for the first time aware of his immediate surroundings. The sun bounced up suddenly over the eastern horizon, and the mysterious dove's wing darkness was instantly transformed to saffron. He forgot for a moment his pain and discomfort.

He lay at the top of a sloping sandy beach. Behind him a wall of dense luxuriant rain forest rose almost sheer to a rocky pinnacle about fifteen hundred feet high. As he watched, the sun's bright sword etched shadows on the cliff, and what had been in the pearly light of foreglow a scene painter's rock, suspended like a silhouette from the vault of the sky, now assumed substance and solidity. The sun struck sparklets from richly mineralized rocks far above his head, and in the shadows the cliff throbbed with a deep purple. To the left the lagoon receded inland past his line of sight, but about four miles to the east the land reappeared in a misty tumble of knife-edged hills, amethyst in the dawn and their tops hidden in a drift of lacy cloud. At his elbow the little stream sang cool and clear in its rocky cleft, emerging from a rich undergrowth of grasses and ferns above which rose the fleshy blooms of the familiar hibiscus, and the smooth leaves of the candlenut, its base festooned with liana creepers.

He felt hungry. He rose unsteadily and stiffly to his feet and surveyed his tattered clothes with a grin that now seemed human. As he did so a large landcrab scuttled sideways down the sand toward the lagoon. Its beady eyes on long prehensile stalks gave him a chill inhuman glare, and he saw with something of a shock that he must have shared his bed with the crippling crunch of its claws. He thought of sharing the island with landcrabs when he had nothing but shoes whose uppers gaped from the soles, tropical worsted trousers and a cotton shirt. It seemed less attractive. He must seek help. But from whom? Where was he? How far off the beaten track?

He walked jerkily down to the edge of the lagoon and looked across its turquoise waters to the jagged reef where the surf broke in white incessant cannonade. The lagoon here was not more than a hundred yards across, though it widened rapidly to left and to right, and the land receded toward the magic mountains of the interior, now gold and green in the morning light. The reef was almost close enough to be a fringing rather than a barrier reef and he was about to calculate the position of the island when the roar of surf beating upon his ears suddenly dredged up the memory of the disaster from which he had escaped. Was it three, seven, nine days ago? The realization that he was even alive smote him to his knees on the warm sand to pray to a God in whom he had often denied that he believed. After that he sat at the water's edge, remembering now with vivid clarity every significant moment of the last flight of the great B 77.

His mind flew over the vast imperceptible curve of the earth's surface and back through the blue skies of yesterday and the windswept caverns of the mind. He was at Hickam Field. The motors were growling in tensely governed spurts as the great plane champed at the bit. This monster of eighty-three tons would lift itself into the air from a speck of land barely protruding from the wastes of the Pacific. From the desiccated top of an old volcano rearing itself off the earth's floor through thousands of cubic miles of water, an engine of destruction would rise to scan the wrinkled face of those same waters.

The ramps whisked off; the door slammed to; the chocks jerked away at the bidding of strings held by unseen hands. The high-pitched whine degenerated into a sullen roar as the auxiliary jets cut into the main power plant and the plane lumbered grotesquely forward. The earth slipped by; bare cement began to streak horizontally beneath the wheels. Suddenly the green blur along the edge of the airport became the spindly spoked pattern of pineapples set in rows on their mulching paper. The jagged purple skyline of the Oahu hills slipped sideways and the dry grasslands of the Kona coast gave way to blue sea. They were airborne. All at once came a great peace, and the ten jet and turbo-prop engines seemed eagle's wings to bear them swiftly, silently and almost fluidly along far above the turmoil of the great globe beneath.

Twenty minutes in the air: alone in a smooth tubular world where the perspective was a row of heads seen from the back. In front the scurfy head of Holmquist, the meteorologist from Chicago; to the side across the aisle, Freedman of New York leaning forward slightly with his large prominent hawk nose in sharp outline against the window; beside him Whitman of Sacramento, the brilliant nuclear physicist, his thick lips pursed over a textbook. Conversation was impossible. He glimpsed, eight thousand feet below, the insignificant niche of Kealakekua Bay as they climbed past the shrouded shoulder of Mauna Loa. Then he was asleep as the jets droned soporifically on through the long lazy afternoon.

East-southeast almost three thousand miles in a timeless void of sea and sky, eating up the distance at over five hundred miles an hour. But high up above the woolly clouds in the blue-turned-black of the stratosphere where the sun burned with unwinking ferocity, he had no sensation of movement. A slight shifting of the shadow cast by the hatrack over the seat across the aisle; an occasional upward thrust as the great aircraft sank into a vast unseen pocket; outside, the wing extending far to the right in an unbroken sweep of burnished metal, swelling at intervals to admit the housing of the turbo-prop engines. Towards the tip of the wing, the double pod of the twin jet engines clung like a crouching parasite.

The dark leaped up at him. Through eyes heavy with fatigue he saw the blue and yellow flames from the engines slowly gain in intensity as daylight waned and the stars coursed over the heavens in a brilliant escadrille. Once, when a cloud of shooting stars burst out of the sector where the moon hung yellow and full as an overripe melon, he wanted to share his wonder with his neighbor. He even had a momentary twinge about his wife and was surprised to find dead embers stirring as he thought of her in Griffith's arms. But all words were swept from his lips by a cataract of sound, and Ryan fell asleep again.

Dawn found them over the Marquesas. They had covered 3071 miles of trackless watery desert in a little over six hours.

· 3 ·

TO Pedro Alvaraz de Mendaña and his Spanish crew in their caravels the Marquesas rose as sharp pinnacles from the terrifying expanse of the Pacific one May morning four hundred years ago. But to Ryan and his companions they appeared strung like spiky black beads in a great sweep of two hundred miles from north to south. Their frowning basalt cliffs lifted sheer from the water and their mountains rose up to four thousand feet. But from the withdrawn and Olympian heights at which the great aircraft cruised they were flattened into patches of olive and woolly verdure, linked by skeins of delicately drawn blue-green water, contrasting with the purple of immense Pacific depths.

Yet the very sight of land—any land—sent a flutter of excitement through the craft and necks craned against the ports. The island of Eiao slid beneath them and they could make out coconut plantations on its southern shore, with steep cliffs slipping vertically to white sand and the sea. Fifteen minutes later and drifting gently earthward, they passed over Nukuhiva, and saw its dense jungle part to reveal two crescentic cones, one cradled by the other like the old moon in the arms of the new. Where the vegetation thinned toward the knife-edged circular peaks, the island looked as lonely as a lunar volcano, as wizened as the head of a woman seen in an unguarded moment when carefully tended strands part to reveal the shockingly unexpected pink of the scalp.

The light on the wall behind the pilot's seat winked red, then green, then red again and the voice of the captain came stridently over the inter-com. "All personnel fasten safety belts; we are coming in for landing." Ryan grinned across the aisle at Freedman from New York and had, for an instant, the warm sense of kinship with a man to whom this was also a boyish adventure. The inter-com barked again. "We will land in ten minutes at Legouvé Field on the island of Hiva-Oa." Hyeva-Oa he called it. "There will be a refueling stop of two hours and minor running repairs will be made to one of the port engines. You will be on French soil and will therefore not repeat not be permitted to leave the airport. You are warned against contact with the natives at this airport. Many of them suffer from venereal disease and leprosy and the fruits which they sell may be conducive to bacillary dysentery. Over."

Ryan lay back in his seat contemplating, as the plane slid downward to the pinnacled island, the advance of civilization in the Pacific. In the year 1800 there had been fifty thousand tall honey-skinned Polynesians on the high volcanic islands to welcome the powdered and periwigged explorers: the emissaries both of Revolutionary and of Bourbon France. A century later when Gauguin, syphilitic and almost blind, painted his last great canvases living in filth with his fifteen-year-old Marquesan mistress, and fighting his last battle of morals with the local missionaries and their bishop, the number of native Marquesans had sunk to less than five thousand. They had been reduced in a single century to less than a tenth of their number. Venereal disease, tuberculosis, leprosy, alcohol and opium carried by Spanish conquistador, British sailor, French explorer, American whaler and Dutch privateer had almost brought them to destruction. Would any of them be at the airport? Were there any left?

The plane was falling rapidly now. The island lay ahead: a suddenly formidable barrier of peaked and jungle-covered rock. The aircraft banked steeply and in a moment it was below the mountains, which scudded by in a jagged comb of teeth. They came in low over the point enclosing Traitor's Bay. The landing gear slowly flexed its muscular grasshopper legs from the nose and belly of the great plane, and it touched down almost at the seaward edge of the runway which the French had diligently created on reclaimed land at the delta of the Taahuku river. The plane thundered to a standstill along the tarmac strip on its base of crushed coral, the doors flew open, and Ryan shuffled out, stiff-kneed, stiff-necked and sticky-eyed into the bright Polynesian sunlight.

The French had labored mightily since the conclusion of the Pacific Weather Treaty. All the Ocean Establishments were now included in a common defense plan: from New Caledonia to the Marquesas; from Rapa north and east to the remote and melancholy island of Clipperton, its castle of volcanic rock standing guard over a stinking weed-filled lagoon with a disused narrow gauge railway rusting in the sun seven hundred miles off the Mexican coast. French architectural skill, American machinery and Polynesian labor had smoothed the runways, filled the sea with rock and there beneath the rapier peaks and the razor-backed slopes, footed by coconut palms and breadfruit trees, the low, lean lines of the airport hangar hugged the ground, its sides adorned with the sign: "Buvez Coca-cola: ça vous ravigote!"

Ryan stepped down off the ramp as the yellow fuel tankers hurried to the plane's side. Wheeled ladders and work cages were neatly positioned; neatly built, intense French maintenance crew began to swarm over the aluminum nose of the aircraft like ants. It was Freedman, thick-lipped and quizzical. "Join me in the bar. A *fine à l'eau* should be as good here as in Paris."

Ryan felt pettish. "I doubt it." He wanted to be by himself to savor the Marquesas—even an airport—alone. With a wave and a shrug he sauntered toward the edge of the field. As he left the clamor of the airport and came closer to the palm trees fringing the taro plantation beyond, he was aware of a splash of color. Four women were kneeling in colored lava-lavas of bright red, orange and green, washing linen on the banks of a small creek. He moved closer and was aware of the stench of ordure. Against it the idyllic scene seemed to putrefy. Thus it must have been, he reflected, in Gauguin's cabin. He stopped and one of the women looked up. She had a broad clear brow, enquiring eyes and a slightly flattened nose with rich mulberry-colored septums. Her teeth flashed white in a smile and Ryan responded. She asked him something in a liquid sing-song Polynesian which sounded vaguely akin to that which he had learned in Hawaii. He shook his head.

"You want to see her?" said one of the women in English.

She pointed to another woman kneeling half turned away from him. Her loins were draped in a red and white lava-lava but she was naked from the waist up. Her coffee-colored breasts swelled and shook beneath her armpits as she scrubbed the dirty linen.

"You want to see her?" the girl repeated.

Ryan nodded. The kneeling woman suddenly turned, presenting him with a face hideously pocked by disease. As he recoiled, she in turn smiled. But though her eyes, shining from the ruin of her face, were gay and inviting, her mouth was toothless and deformed. Abruptly Ryan walked back to the waiting plane, pursued by the derisive shrieks of the women. He found himself trembling with chagrin and waiting: waiting for a real magic island, his own magic island, the coral island of his boyhood reading, unmarred by human vileness and the evidences of man's cruelty. It was a wish that was to be granted quite soon, though like all wishes, not under the precise circumstances which he would have preferred.

Later as the plane lumbered heavily into the humid sky, and Hiva-Oa slid below and astern, he found himself wishing not only for the coral island, but for the world's great morning, when adventurers like Mendaña had sailed into the setting sun, and the wild new dream of discovery came true with the sound of trumpets. The world would never again be so wonderful. Seated on his airfoam cushion riding at over five hundred miles an hour eighteen thousand feet above the ocean, in a machine of infinite complexity whose eighty-three tons glided on the wind like the albatross that followed Mendaña and de Quiros, he longed for the adventures of four hundred years before. He was aware of the scurvy and the dysentery that haunted those ships, rotted through by the teredo and trailing a foot of weed as they staggered, often broadside on, through limitless seas. He was aware too of the harsh discipline, the poor food and the inhuman savagery of the punishments. Just the same, he thought, as the plane droned on toward the far distant shores of South America, he would rather have his coral island.

Their great circle route from the Marquesas to the Falklands passed no land in its five-thousand-mile arc save the interposing tail of Patagonia, and until this land of Cain was reached there were only two insignificant dots which an aircraft might encounter. One was Easter Island, a triangular expanse of rolling grassland littered with huge stone statues of human form and ominous inscrutability. The other was Sala-y-gomez, a barren uninhabited volcanic rock.

Ryan did not see either of these two lonely islands; nor did any of his companions. At 3:35 that afternoon when the giant aircraft was approximately 573 miles E SE of Easter Island she began to lose altitude. The loss was not at first apparent to the passengers, asleep, daydreaming, or absorbed in book and magazine. Even when the nearness of the water did become noticeable, none of the scientists had enough aeronautical knowledge to exchange a meaning look with his neighbor: a look which, once intercepted, could start lay hearts and stomachs fluttering. It was only when the sea, so silken calm from the great height, began to look like skeins of blue wool spread over a troubled gray cloth that Ryan felt his belly contract and sweat erupt at his temples. Out of the corner of his eye he saw Freedman nonchalantly stub out a cigarette in the little tray on the back of the seat before him, and start donning his life preserver. Ryan felt himself gagging and he resolutely clenched his teeth as he adjusted the belt of his own life preserver. The plane was dropping like an elevator now. He wondered why there was no warning from the crew; but they were working frantically to keep altitude and to conjure life from a dead radio. The waves suddenly appeared horribly steep, and riding by at a tremendous speed. He flexed his muscles and swallowed, tense and ready as an athlete about to start a hundred-yard dash. Around him he could see white faces, and over the steady pulsing hum of the motors came an unaccustomed and unnerving whine: a high keening sound which grew ever fiercer in pitch.

The whole side of the plane leapt apart before his eyes. He felt an instant of pure white pain, and then blackness engulfed him. The booby birds, riding the tropical waves with the buoyant ease of fresh fallen autumn leaves, heard the roar of the thunderous explosion, saw aluminum and steel, flesh and fabric, gasoline and oil, shredded apart in the shattering impact. They saw the swath of pitiful debris undulating in an oil slick on the vast bosom of the Pacific: a sight utterly without meaning.

· 4 ·

THE moment of annihilation reeled backward in the velvet world of the closed eye. With a sigh of relief Ryan emerged from the corridors of memory and drank in the beauty of the island landscape about him. He felt like the sleeper awakened from the abyss of nightmare. He felt the indescribable relief of one who has been brushed by the cindery wing of death yet lives to taste a sweeter dawn. Despite his torn and aching fingers, he thrilled to the mere fact of his existence. It was wonderful to feel the blood streaming through his arteries, to feel his heart beat—at his chest, his wrist, his throat—and to inhale, however painfully, great lungfuls of the sweet warm air.

He rose and walked stiffly to the tip of the promontory and looked eastward across the lagoon to the main headlands of the island. The reef, running alternately dusty white and blood pink in the morning sun, showed here end on, traveling in a steady line till it disappeared round a point dropping steeply into the lagoon about four miles away. The clouds had lifted from the tall peaked mountain and it reared up above the morning fog in a diadem of rock. Its sheer beauty seemed to promise endless tomorrows of discovery. It was an airy crown, floating solid yet ethereal on the shrouding mists. As he looked, the sun pierced a cleft and it glowed mysteriously with an inner fire as of a live coal in the shimmering embers of a grate. Ryan narrowed his eyes in perplexity, but the sun shifted and the illusion perished. Only the plume of white smoke above the peak remained.

Now the pangs of hunger assailed him and he lost, in his animal appetite, the sense of wonder at the landscape. He retraced his steps to the little brook. His memory of how he had reached this island haven still remained breathless and confused. As he searched for fallen papayas beneath the smooth branchless bole of their parent tree, he tried to piece it all together. He had regained consciousness, he remembered, with the rush and heave, the furious assault of water. He was clinging, with a maniac's unreasoning force, to a piece of water-soaked rope. His body was wrenched to and fro by the buffetings of unseen waves, and to his bleary eyes, as he opened them, the landscape seemed all yellow. It was only after the salt water had deadened the shock that he realized he owed his life to his having inflated his life preserver. It was this, rather than the rope to which he clung, that supported him. The yellow bulging landscape before him was the rounded side of a rubberized canvas dinghy. With infinite labor, his limbs half numbed, and gulping great pailfuls of salt water, he clambered aboard to find himself on the flat bottom of a curved rubber raft about four feet by six. With only the thickness of the single sheet of canvas to protect him from the water, the rippling floor of the raft gave with every slightest motion of the sea, and beat his body till he ached all over from bruises. But he was alive: abominably sick, but alive.

He lay retching on the floor of the raft; pounded, banged and buffeted by the bottom and sides; lifted with nauseating speed onto the crests of great rollers only to plunge into the next trough. How long he lay there he did not know. When at last he awoke to some sort of coherent possession of his senses it was to find himself still on the floor of the raft, but with both hands stiff, blue and almost immovably clamped round the ropes on its curving inward side. But now the sun shone. His salt-caked clothes creaked at the movement of every straining muscle, but he managed to raise himself on one elbow and peer over the edge.

He saw a great desert of blue-green sea all round him. Close to, the water leaped with open jaws at the sides of the raft which sent a bubbling wake streaming athwart its axis. The sky was clear, the wind was fresh and the sun shone down like a brass coin on great parallel rollers which seemed, even from his lowly viewpoint, to have a relentless purpose. They looked as if they had already come several thousand miles. Sick as he was, gashed on the foot, burned from flaming gasoline, and his wounds already beginning to smell despite the sterilizing influence of wind, wave and water, his weatherman's eye nonetheless began to assert itself. Those great combers bearing him onward had indeed come a long way. They were driven by the southeast trades, roaring ceaselessly across the Pacific from Cape Horn to New Guinea. While half his mind watched the spectacle in fear and awe, the other half began trying to calculate where he was, in what direction he was going and what were his chances of survival. He still had not the faintest notion as to the nature of the disaster that had overtaken the airplane, though he surmised that it had been some kind of explosion either just before or upon contact with the water. He knew vaguely that they were past Easter Island and heading E SE but how far past he did not know.

The raft skimmed over the surface of the limitless ocean and each crest brought him a view of a succession of further crests extending to a horizon as sharp as a razor. He figured that these same waves would carry him north and east at about the rate of perhaps thirty miles a day. He knew enough of Pacific geography to realize that the chances of hitting an island at that rate were almost nonexistent. He was adrift in the largest area of landless water in the world. In the vast pie-shaped piece of ocean bounded on the north by the thirtieth parallel of south latitude, on the west by the International dateline, and on the east by the tail of South America and by Antarctica, there was not a single piece of land, not a rock, not a stone, not a sandspit. In an area more than four times the size of the United States, there was nothing at all but the lonely boiling of waters over the submerged crags of Maria Theresa Reef. If he lived long enough (if he lived) the trades might—just might—carry him to Pitcairn Island, provided he had started far enough north. But he did not know where his perilous journey had begun, and even had it started from the most auspicious point, his chances of hitting a mile-long island on a front of eight hundred to a thousand miles were, he knew, absolutely minimal.

As if to mock his misery, clouds began to appear in the southwest quarter; the sun shone coppery through a growing haze, then vanished. Over the water came a cross wind, whipping the tops of the rollers into a frothy foam, and with it came rain: great gusts of water that bounced off the raft like hailstones and drenched him to the skin. Clinging to the ropes he lay on his back with his mouth open, and as his frail raft whirled onward in erratic circles he drank the blessed rain, his first nourishment since the crash. He did not at first realize that the wind had sprung up in the southwest quarter and was driving him furiously, like a ping-pong ball along a polished table, at right angles to the course he had hoped to follow. But soon the wind began to cut across the swell of the sea and to create unpleasant choppy little maelstroms. The raft spun and tilted alarmingly. Once it stood shuddering and almost vertical against a jagged wall of cobalt water, and his nails, as he clung desperately to the ropes, gouged deep cuts in his palms.

The sky darkened to purple and then to black and he was alone in the nether pit. No moon nor stars lit the horizon and even the phosphorescent gleam of the sea was broken and faint in the storm. The engulfing darkness was shot through with the hiss of seething water. Ryan was terrified and exhausted. He clung to the ropes, alternately hoping for sleep to release him from the tense agony of fear, and longing to stay awake lest he be whisked off the frail craft while unconscious and consigned to eternity.

He lost all sense of the passage of time. He was aware only of the eternal rippling buffet of the floor of the raft, the constant feeling of nausea, the violent changes of direction—felt rather than seen in the penumbral gloom—and the everlasting roar of water all around him. He began to see phantasies in the night: strange protoplasmic shapes; noises that assumed the forms of horned animals. He seemed to see Ruth's face floating by in the darkness, mocking his inadequacy with her faint half smile. The image was bizarre, for her bedroom beauty had no place in the screaming blackness around him. He wondered if he were going crazy, then he remembered that illusion can be the product of an opposite. What was more natural for a man in a maelstrom than to dream of willowy scented charms, of eyes that were old when Troy was young, of lips that held unpossessible secrets?

Lightning split the sky. He crouched in the corner of the raft fearful of he knew not what. Was he still in love with that far-off creature? He must have slept briefly, for his next sensation was of the sky aquiver with gray light. It gave him the courage—Dutch courage, he thought with a dry grin as he clung to the rope—to think of life, of living and even of how he might control his own destiny. Cautiously, in the pearly light, he raised himself up and looked over the curving yellow edge of the raft. Between him and the horizon the waves boiled, rose and fell in knotted ridges of greenish blue. The storm had abated, but though the wind had died it had left a legacy of stupendous rollers. The sun jerked up out of the Pacific, the mist fell away and the top of each rugged heaving watery ridge was tipped with gold. Ryan drank it all in with relief.

As the waves receded they appeared to heave less violently, and in the distance one serrated wave was frozen like the arrested frame of a motion picture. When the raft dipped into a trough the distant wave was lost; but as the raft heaved up again onto a crest, the distant wave stood once again motionless in the growing sunlight. Ryan was fascinated and could not take his eyes off it. Presently it seemed to him as if it were the distant jagged wave rather than himself which spun and heaved—now in the abyss, now in the sky. Then the sun pulled completely clear of the mists, and invested the distant wave—now taller than its companions—with the deeply trenched impasto of light and shade. With a gasp of mingled joy and unbelief Ryan suddenly knew that what he saw was not a wave but a "high" island: the peaks of some long extinct volcano, probing up out of unimaginable depths into the morning light and the warm Pacific sky.

The memory of that other dawn warmed Ryan as he stood now at the edge of the lagoon. It mingled with the present vividness of what he had already come to regard as *his* island. Yet there remained his painfully throbbing wounds to remind him that the interval between the two dawns had nearly been the end of him, and that the earlier dawn which he had greeted from the raft might well have been his last. Once more Ryan flew backward in time to that last dawn on the raft. In an instant he could feel it heaving and rippling against his back and thighs. The magic castellated outline of the island was getting nearer.

His first wild hope had given place to the absolute certainty that the raft would sail straight to land. He was, he estimated, about ten miles off and as the wind blew him steadily toward it, he saw the island spread itself out in a long line of jagged hills rising to two peaks of about two thousand and six thousand feet. The island looked about five miles long; but when he thought of the reef his heart sank. In these latitudes, as he well knew, every island, whether of the low coral or the high volcanic type, was girdled by a reef. The only exception would be, as sometimes happened in the Marquesas, if the cliffs were so sheer that coral could not grow. In that case he would probably be smashed against the black basalt, unless he could find some cunning cleft. But in all other cases the island would have either a fringing reef, clinging to the shore like a band of giant barnacles, or a barrier reef separated from the main island by a lagoon. The lovely pink and green and white coral shimmering in the water, and the delicate tracery of the spongelike formations belied the cruel teeth which they bared to the rash voyager. Against their jagged spurs the seas hurled themselves with savage fury, and the unfortunate man whose body was borne down on them by the pressure of hundreds of tons of water would be pulped in split seconds. The very next moment the raft reared up on a wall of green water and for the first time he was both near and high enough to be able to see the tell-tale white line as the waves pounded the still hidden coral. Even in the cheerful morning light that line seemed to him heavy with menace, and he began once more to calculate his chances of survival.

The peaks of the island now stood out in separate contours, their flanks covered with a thick forest growth. As the raft rose and fell he could catch glimpses of a blue lagoon, of occasional sandy beaches, and behind them flat deltas of bottom lands between the ravines. Though he was utterly powerless to steer the raft he saw that it seemed to be making for a point at which the lagoon narrowed so that the reef and the island were only about two hundred yards apart. It would be a pity if he should survive the thunder of the surf only to be drowned in the lagoon. He hoped fervently that the raft would continue onward in the same direction. As it bounced forward under a coppery sun blazing high in a sky blue-gray with humidity, it kept on course as though directed by hand. Ryan now thought that he would reach the reef in less than an hour. The little raft was driving straight into it.

He decided to cling to the ropes and trust that his body, made one with the tiny feather-light craft, would catch an opportune breaker in the surf and be lifted clear of the reef which, he could only pray, would be narrow at this point. He had known reefs one hundred and fifty yards wide. If this was one of them he was doomed. Filled with the anguish of mortality, he lowered his eyes and, as the island sank once more behind the heaving sea, he lay on his back with his neck across the bulging thwart and looked at the sky. For a moment the undulating motion of the raft and the soft haze of the sky induced in him a sense of lazy contemplation almost as if he were swinging in a hammock on a summer afternoon.

He was aroused from his daydream by a low roaring sound, sullen and persistent, which seemed to turn the hazy sky a darker and more sinister blue. He raised his head. The island now filled almost half the horizon. The topmost crags were lost in a scarf of drifting mist; their purple shoulders were festooned with the vivid violent greens of a tropical high island; and at their feet, separated by a thin strip of blue water the surf boiled white along coral teeth. The furious cannonade jerked him sharply from his reverie. He tensed his body, thrust his toes through the stern sheets of the little raft and gripped with his hands the two loops immediately before his eyes. Now that he was near it, the great wall of water seemed to tower up like the fighting top of a battleship and he was borne irresistibly toward it. He prayed briefly but the prayer was wrenched away in a surging movement that set his stomach aflutter. The next instant light and consciousness were torn away in a thundering cataract of water which beat at him in a massive inhuman effort to crush out the last vestige of life.

He survived. But he himself was oblivious of the miracle until now: until this moment when he stood on the shore in his tattered garments looking out across the lagoon to the roaring surf two hundred yards away. There was no sign of the raft; that he might find later. But this feathery piece of resilient rubber must have been bounced clear of the first shattering impact and then tumbled before the next wave like leaves before a sudden freshet. He could see now that the reef at this point was narrow and that even as the next wave was smashing itself on the coral, its predecessor was swirling across the lagoon in the form of a current which might bear a fainting man onward until he felt the sand beneath his feet.

Ryan stretched his arms above his head and winced at the pain but he smiled at the warmth which flowed through his body in the morning sun. Slowly he limped across the few feet of sand between him and the water, searching for his unconscious landfall. It was not hard. His own trail, as of a wounded beast dragging its paralyzed haunches, lay clear in the sand for him to see. Where it disappeared into the water it was flanked with deeply gouged holes dug by his own desperate hands.

5

THE marks on the sand made Ryan conscious of his throbbing finger. It was bearable but still very painful and though the pain kept his other aches at bay, he knew he would have to treat it. Steeling himself for the effort he plunged his hand into the salt waters of the lagoon and, while he winced and sweated, gave it a thorough cleansing. He had a vague idea that seaweed contained iodine and that was good for cuts. Trailing at the edge of the water was a thin rubbery streamer of green-brown weed liberally sprinkled with boils and whelks and festooned with little stringy bags of seaborne beads. He broke a couple of the polyps and squirted the liquid onto his fingers. It did not hurt as much as the salt water. Using his teeth and his good hand he tore a strip off the tail of his shirt and managed to bind up the throbbing fingers.

Now his thoughts turned to rescue, and he remembered that he did not know where he was. He knew neither the latitude nor the longitude of the island nor if it was inhabited. He did not know whether it was near the great circle routes of either aircraft or ships. Common sense told him that his presence on the island would have been noticed by the islanders unless their villages were on the opposite side of the mountain. He had been on the island over forty-eight hours and had seen and heard nothing. Yet as he looked round at the purple and green hillsides, scarred here and there with patches of red volcanic earth, he had a distinct impression that the place, though silent, was aware.

If the island were inhabited he would surely receive some sign. He screened his eyes against the sun and looked upward at the cleft in the battlements where the plume of white vapor drifted lazily away to sea. Was it mist at the crown of the mountain, or was it smoke? His heart quickened but almost at once faltered and dragged. Islanders—Polynesians he supposed—would build fires near the shore or on level ground. They certainly would not choose the highest peak unless—and the thought intrigued him—there was some sacrificial or symbolic significance to the smoke. If it was smoke. He focused his eyes. There it rode, high in the humid heat, a thin pennon of white streaming to the trades, elusive, mysterious, free; but almost certainly not of human agency. He would have to go and see for himself, when he had the strength and the time. The time?

He stopped daydreaming and considered soberly that if the island were uninhabited, he was indeed likely to have all the time that anyone could ever need. Yet it seemed impossible to him that a place so fertile was not the abode of islanders. He knew that in Polynesia the only uninhabited places were either inaccessible pinnacles of rock, or raised limestone coral deserts where the water was brackish and the soil so arid it would support not even the Polynesian rat. If then, he were alone, his chances of being found would depend on two things: his distance from air or shipping routes, and his ability to draw the attention of any passing ship or aircraft. He knew that the Navy would of course start a search for the B 77. Even supposing, which might be possible, that he were the sole survivor, they would still want to find bits of wreckage. But the chances of his being found alive depended on his own ingenuity; for there was no knowing how long that might be. But of course, he consoled himself, it would not be very long.

Full of purpose now he rose painfully to his feet. He must place a distress sign of some sort in a prominent place. He must take an inventory of his personal belongings, and his immediate environment, to see if an existence on the island—only until he was found, of course—could be possible; could be supportable. He ruffled his matted hair and passed his hand over his silky beard. He wished he could remember the exact number of days since last he shaved; since he left Honolulu in fact. He wished he had a mirror.

The image of a mirror conjured up again the image of his wife. It was ludicrous that her memory should have any place in his newfound lonely man's world. Yet simply because of this he felt feminine chimeras crowding to his senses, beating at his mind's eye with soft wings. As he walked painfully back to the sand dune where he had spent the night, he found himself thinking of Ruth, and through her of all the familiar sights and scents and sounds of the life which he had so violently left behind. They were so vivid that as he reached the shelter of the dune and felt the warm air rising from the bleached friendly sand, and heard the trickle of the little stream among the broad-leaved pandanus palms, he had to force himself hard to think of immediate necessities. Even as he stripped to examine in the most minute detail everything he possessed and on which his life might depend for the next few days, or weeks or even years, he had to brush aside, like cobwebs before his eyes, sharp memories of his life in Honolulu and even of his life in Canada.

He saw his assistant bending over a wet bulb thermometer, notebook in hand, and remembered the little crop of pimples on the back of his neck, like tiny sulphurous islands in a pink Pacific. He heard the soft fall of feet in the galleries of the Bishop Museum; and then the strident incongruous honking of cars down Kapiolani Boulevard amid the scents of frangipani and the bold bright colors of the bougainvillea. He remembered a dance at Hickam Field, the officers resplendent in white duck and the women, perfumed and padded, gossiping on the terrace. And behind that he saw a vision of a young couple wonderfully in love—was it so very long ago?—striding hand in hand over the bare shoulders of the Alberta foothills with the foaming curve of the Bow River below them careering out of the Rockies like a freight train.

He stripped off his underwear and stood naked in the sun grinning at the memory. Then he stepped back and looked at the little bundle lying forlorn and shoddy on the fine white sand. It did not amount to much. For clothes he had a single pair of trousers of tropical worsted, badly torn and shredded at the cuffs, a pair of underpants in fairly good condition, a thin singlet of cellular weave, a shirt of good quality with the tail torn where he had ripped off the bandage for his finger, a pair of light woollen socks and the remains of a pair of brown oxfords. They were scuffed, salt-stained and gaping between the seam and the welt, but they would protect his feet against the clambering and tramping he would have to do if he spent any time at all on the island. His heavy clothing had gone down with the plane along with his briefcase with all his papers, and his watch which had been hanging on the hook beside his seat. His tie he had discarded to use as a belt.

There remained three objects that might be classed as useful, in fact as real treasure trove. Round his neck he carried his identification disc on a plastic string. This he now began to see as a possible line for fishing. In the battered hip pocket of his trousers there were, besides some at present quite useless dollar bills to the value of seven dollars, a small single-bladed jack-knife and a cigarette lighter. Both were now badly corroded and he supposed that the fluid in the lighter would long since have evaporated. But he might be able to use the flint and steel to make a fire. He laid the lighter, the knife and the disc and string to dry on his singlet in the sun's heavy-lidded heat. Then he turned his back on the green rain forest rising behind him, and looked out across the pounding reef to the tantalizing blue distances beyond.

Now that he was alive and ravenously hungry, there came to him, along with the return of hope and desire and pain, the languorous call of a whole host of metropolitan appetites which made the island seem more and more unattractive. To memories suddenly less blurred were now added visions of nourishing meals and stimulating books. The smell of gasoline exhaust on hot tarmac seemed sweeter far than the enervating air about him. He thought of the fat weed that rots in ease by Lethe wharf: it must have been born here. Naked, he walked down to the beach and stared out to sea. The horizon was boundless: yet as sharply bounded as the edge of a sphere. He felt like a fly caught under a glass tumbler. As he listened to the deafening thunder of the surf he knew that he would never hear the sound of an airplane. He would have to rely on his eyes—and theirs—to find him: if they ever came to look. He would need a sign: wave a shirt or wiggle a piece of metal in the sun? That would be like dissolving a drop of blood in a swimming pool. The island on which he stood, though perhaps five miles in diameter, was no more than a grain of dust on the face of the ocean. A man waving a shirt on a grain of dust.

His eye traversed the beach once more and he noticed that it differed sharply in color from its surroundings. It was a yellowish-white crescent half a mile long and perhaps a hundred yards wide. Anyone coming to the island would see this crescent of gleaming gold against the deep blue of the sea, the turquoise of the lagoon and the heavy purple-green impasto of the hills. It was here that he must make a sign. Eyeing the long level stretch of hardpacked sand he concluded that if he scraped a sign a foot deep, and twenty-five feet by a hundred and fifty feet in area it could be seen from perhaps—he narrowed his eyes and calculated—two thousand feet up and two miles off. A long chance, but worth the taking.

He knew that to do this would take strength, and he doubted that he possessed it as yet. He went down on his knees in the sand and began to scrape it aside with long sweeping movements of his right arm. Though the sand came away easily he found that about half a minute reduced him to the point of exhaustion. Sweat poured freely from his forehead, his breath became forced and shallow; he felt his heart beat furrily at the back of his throat shaking him as a galloping furnace shakes an old frame house. He lay for a moment on the cool damp sand which he had scraped out while his breath became slower and deeper and his heart stopped racing. Then he walked unsteadily back to the sand dune where he had left his things.

All his wondrous dreams of civilized appetites had now withered away to be replaced by one overwhelming desire for food—any food. He had not eaten since dawn and he judged by the sun—now an aggressive copper-colored sphere drifting behind wet wisps of overcast—that it must be early afternoon. He felt faint as he reached the cool rocky ledge where the stream fell down. He was sharply sunburned, and the world oozed and reeled before his eyes as he fell on the cool sphagnum moss beside the stream. He lay on his belly and drank the water. It struck the pit of his stomach like a block of ice; and then he fainted from sheer fatigue.

When he awoke the sun had westered over the low hills across the inlet to his left. He lay for a moment trying to get his bearings. As he lost consciousness he had been aware of a rushing noise. Was it "noises in a swound," or surf, or was it simply the memory of the nightmare ride in the crashed plane? He staggered down to the water's edge, taking with him the plastic fishing lure. Hunger assailed him now with renewed force and he was ferociously determined to catch a fish—any fish, eat it raw since he had no fire, adding it to his diet of papaya and water. But when he reached the lagoon he found that the shallow trench which he had dug earlier in the day was now under two feet of salt water. The shoreline had receded perhaps twelve feet up the sloping sand. He stood still, his brows knit in thought.

Though he had not placed the true bearing of the island, he knew enough of Pacific tides to be pretty sure that an open unprotected beach, subject to the direct force of the ocean's sweep would not vary by as much as a couple of feet between ebb and flood. But this rise bore all the marks of permanency. There had been, earlier in the day, no scurfed line of driftwood, seaweed and old shells to mark a higher shoreline. What was more, tufted grass which had earlier stood on bone-dry foreshore now waved fitfully from the expanse of salt water. But if not a tide, a subsidence? His weatherman's mind rebelled at the idea. Subsidence involved seismic or volcanic activity. There would have been a shuddering of the earth to awake him from his coma.

But suppose, far out at sea, the ocean floor had gently slid or risen and, thousands of feet above, the displaced water had flowed silently inward to drown the skirts of the island. What then? It would mean that the island lay in a belt of volcanic disturbance. Well, that was nothing unusual in the Pacific. Great clashing edges of trough and ridge ringed the ocean from the Aleutians round to Japan and then south and west to New Guinea and the Solomons. They stretched long fingers out to the Hawaiian islands and lay in a deep trench, starred with volcanoes, geysers and mud solfataras, north from New Zealand clear up to Samoa. Almost all the "high" islands of the Pacific were of volcanic origin.

He bent down and laved his hand in the water. It was unexpectedly chilly, as if it had come up from a very great depth. Then he noticed that the thunder of the waves on the reef was of a different pitch and intensity, that the wave pattern had been modified. No longer did the great combers arch their green-blue necks and crash thunderously, throwing spray scores of feet into the air. Though they now smashed down with equal force, they seemed to flatten and bulge as on a deeper cushion of water over the reef. Beyond the reef and cutting at a sharp angle to the shore, he could see in the water the line where the blue marched with the green, as if the cold were moving slowly and deliberately through a gap in the warm and keeping it at arm's length as it did so.

It was clear that while he slept some vast movement of great masses had taken place deep in the body of the earth and that this was one of the results. Yet if his calculations were even remotely right he was in an area of the Pacific where volcanic action belonged only to history. Easter Island was grounded, like a blanket over three balls, on volcanoes: but they had been extinct for centuries. As he searched among the rock pools for whelks and tiny crabs with which to bait his line he was in a pensive mood. More than once he glanced to the right where the towering diadem of rock rose above the remote mountain fastness of the island. From its mysterious cleft the wisp of white vapor trailed into the torpid air.

· 6 ·

HIS first attempts at fishing were not very successful. Trailing his plastic lure baited with crushed crab, he dangled it over the limpid rock pools that lay at the edge of the promontory. Gaily colored fish whose names he did not know flashed back and forth in the sub-aqueous forest like brilliant parakeets. There were long thin fish shaped like swords and awls; short fat fish with faces like finned suns and cherubim; grotesquely shaped fish with beaks, with whiskers, with heads larger than their bodies. They darted blindly through the watery grottoes or cruised leisurely with their noses an inch or two from the lure. After an hour of frustration and growing hunger he was prepared to give up when he noticed one of the giant landcrabs crouched on the sand in the cool shade of a rock. It looked like a miniature of some grotesque armored monster of the age of the dinosaurs. Its shell, a foot wide, came down over an ungainly mass of jointed arms, legs and claws. Its beady black eyes surveyed the island from their long stalks with an inhuman stare.

Ryan felt a tingling along his spine which he was man enough to recognize as a mixture of revulsion and fear. The animal—if it was an animal—was watching him with its buttony stalk eyes. He got the impression that though its legs were folded neatly beneath its carapace, it was ready on the instant to leap forth at him and bury its two thick powerful claws—large as a monkey wrench—in his leg.

He stood still and watched, weighing in his mind the chances of moving to a nearby rock without being detected, then of throwing the rock, hitting the crab and maiming it. Man and crustacean eyed each other with the tense watchfulness of two Western badmen in a barroom. Ryan's overwhelming need was for food to assuage his hunger and to build up his strength. Only when his strength had returned could he dig his warning symbol in the sand. Until that was done his chances of attracting a passing plane were close to zero. The thought decided him; for the desire to return to his own world was far stronger than the desire to turn his new island world into a fit dwelling place. He simply refused to contemplate the possibility of being left here until the end of his days—and in refusing, recognized its possibility. But the thought gave him the combination of strength and stealth which he required. Keeping his eye on the crab he moved slowly and warily to the right until his hand grasped the sand-roughened end of a loose rock. As he moved his feet slowly, one at a time, to get them into the line with his body, the crab waved a claw and settled its hairy limbs more firmly beneath its shell. Its eyes wavered on their stalks and he wondered if the beast were short-sighted or whether its eye was already fixed on some smaller prey invisible to him. He had an impulse to shout and see what might happen. But if the crab should charge him or run away, either movement would spell failure.

He grasped the rock more firmly. The crab stared unblinkingly, shuffling its grotesque fingers beneath its carapace. Slowly he raised the rock above his head with both hands, then with a sudden movement hurled it straight at the crustacean's cave. The crab decided to move while the rock was in mid-air, but it was too late. Though the fall of the stone was broken by the edge of the rock, it caught the animal, crushed one of its claws against the rock and buried its smashed carapace in the sand. In an instant Ryan was on it. Scarcely troubling to disengage smashed shell from fleshy pulp, and flesh itself from yellow viscera, he scooped what pulp and ooze he could from the saucerlike shell and ate avidly what two weeks ago would have made him retch. It was still not pleasant but it was filling, and when he had finished he washed it down with water from the stream and felt refreshed. He went down to the beach, took the remains of the crab, washed them carefully in salt water, wrapped them in sphagnum moss and put them on a rock high above the edge of the sea in the naive belief that this would preserve them.

Now he returned to his task of digging. Though it loomed immense, it did not seem so hopeless as before. He lay down on his belly and scraped the sand away with his fingers. He had decided that the most logical symbol for him to use would be the dollar sign. It was universally known, easily distinguishable and simple to create. In about an hour and a half he had done the vertical bar. It was twenty-five feet long, two and a half feet wide and its trench was about a foot deep. As he progressed he became more expert and was able to make great scoops with the curve of his left arm. By the time he had the sign completed, the sun was dropping behind the bay to his left, and he felt once again weak from overwork and lack of food. But the crabflesh, when he uncovered it, had rotted in the heat: it was purple and inedible. He longed for something tender and succulent and well cooked. His mind roamed aimlessly in the conventional but soul-satisfying world of roast beef, steaks, fried eggs and beer, steaming cups of coffee, and even glasses of canned juice and prepared breakfast foods.

He went over to the sand dune and examined the lighter which had been drying all day in its hot airless oven. It seemed to him that the verdigris had receded a little and he wondered if he might get it to strike fire. He took the jackknife and cleaned away the remaining corrosion. It was a British style lighter operated by turning a small wheel with the thumb. He could not move the wheel. Dusk was falling fast and darkness leaped like a great panther out of the east. As he sat in the encircling arms of the sand dune listening to the thunder on the reef, he felt more lonely than at any time since he had come to the island. The velvet sky, so welcome after days at sea bouncing in the yellow rubber raft, now seemed deep with hidden menace. The friendly roar on the reef sounded like the cataract of approaching dissolution. He was conscious of the vast emptiness which surrounded him and aware for the first time of how very long the odds were against his ever being found.

He was filled with a profound melancholy, and as he gazed out at the darkling reef his earlier desire for activity faded under the continual dew of self-pity. He began to consider less how he might survive than how he might make himself comfortable. He began to brood on how cruel fate had been to cast him up on an uninhabited island hundreds of miles from the nearest shipping lanes or airways.

He gazed sightlessly out to sea and he tortured himself with masochistic images of the city: the twitch and flicker of neon signs; the close, sweaty, satisfyingly pungent smell of human flesh crowded into a rush-hour streetcar; the smooth sure touch of handrails and baggage, sheets and crockery, newspapers and cigarettes. Instinctively his hand, which had sought the lighter lying among his poverty-stricken collection of valuables, began to fumble with the little rowelled wheel. To his amazement it produced a spark. For perhaps thirty seconds he sat looking fixedly into the dark where the spark had been, watching the little negative after-image of vivid green bob and fade into the night. Then he tightened his thumb on the wheel and, half fearful lest he should be the victim of an illusion, gave it a sharp twist. Again the spark spurted across the blackness. He tore off a piece of his shirt and shredded a couple of square inches into fluff. The lighter, lying all day in the hot dry air of the sheltered sand dune, had dried itself out. The verdigris and salt had been cleared away and Ryan was now in a position to emulate Prometheus.

He placed the tiny ball of fluffed-out cotton in a cup of sand. He tore up other pieces of his shirt and piled them in readiness. Then he stumbled about the beach in the damask night, picking up pieces of driftwood: from small sticks no bigger than a pencil to large twigs, and smooth weathered roots shaped like antlers. He forgot his fatigue and his wounds and worked until he had a large pile of driftwood stacked in consecutive sizes. Then he prepared to banish the night and to announce the primacy of man over nature. But as he pulled the lighter out of his pocket, it caught on the frayed lining and fell into the sand.

He searched for it, at first cat-like and methodical, prodding and brushing specific areas of sand with his fingers and palms; then faster and more aimless, making larger sweeps with his forearm, cursing beneath his breath and finally cursing out loud. Then he stopped and looked up at the night. The sky was moonless and strewn with winking stars which looked like myriad points of light from some blazing region that lay above and beyond the dusky sky. The air was motionless. There was no moon, but there would be no rain. While the lighter would not betray itself by a glint, yet it would remain dry. He knew that unless he stopped searching he might crush or trample the lighter into the sand and never see it again; so he composed himself unwillingly for sleep, curled once more in the dune and thought—fairly happily—of fires as well as of rescue.

He awoke at first light with a start. The cigarette lighter winked at him, set slantwise in the sand less than a yard from his elbow. But what brought him to his feet and sent him racing madly down to the edge of the water was not the lighter, though he had the presence of mind to pick it up as he ran. Flooding in with the morning light and beating on his tautened ears was the long-lost, hauntingly familiar sound of an aircraft. It droned insistently on the frail air presaging the dawn; it beat on the thin gray waters of the lagoon and seeped into his consciousness like snow through the chinks of a closed window in a blizzard. He stood on the edge of the lagoon in the nacreous half light, his legs apart, his fists clenched, straining every nerve to locate the direction and movement of the sound. It was all-pervasive, yet at the same time as elusive as an autumn ground mist. It seemed to ebb and flow, to advance and recede, to go in circles, to become muffled and then suddenly sharp and acute. If he turned his head the noise seemed to shift in perspective. He held rigidly still and waited, his spirits mounting.

Suddenly the sun rose from the oily sea in a blaze of glory. The whole world leaped into light and life, and at the same moment he saw the aircraft. It was flying at about three thousand feet, and as closely as he could judge, about five miles away, coming in from the east-southeast.

What craft would be patrolling these forgotten waters at first light, two thousand miles from the nearest landing strip? He was seeing it edge on and it exposed to him the whole length of its fuselage. It droned placidly on through the still morning sky, the beat of its engines throaty and satisfying.

It was obviously a search plane, it must be: an arrow of scintillating aluminum cleaving the morning blue. To Ryan it seemed to fly with maddening slowness. It cut a broad lazy arc across the sky and with each moment he expected it to bank in a steep and delectable curve toward the island. But it kept straight on: a silver fish in a bowl of blue, heading inexorably west nor'west, and away from the island.

Ryan was incredulous, then angry; then for a few dreadful moments almost hysterical. He cursed and roared at the retreating plane, waved his arms and stamped up and down on the beach. Then as the craft dwindled from a sliver of silver to an indistinguishable dot and finally to what it had been at first light—a mere sound in the aching void—his hysteria gave way again to slow, bitter anger. He stood there like the last man on the edge of the putrid sea at the end of time when the world has grown cool and the sun has slowed down, while the sound of the airplane ebbed away out of the sky like water draining silently from a pool. When it was completely gone and he was alone with the sea and the sand and the sky, he sat down by the water's edge and burst into great racking sobs.

· 7 ·

TOM GRIFFITH turned off the car radio and eased the Chevrolet to the curbside. Though it was still light the lamp on top of the Aloha Tower blinked busily across the sad square shapes of office buildings and warehouses. The southern sky was laced with the jib cranes and gantries along the waterfront. Beyond the oil storage tanks opposite the flat desolation of Sand Island, a big freighter sat high and dry at a refit in Kapalauna Basin. He sniffed the sea breeze coming in off the ocean and jounced the palms of his hands on the steering wheel.

"Well, what about it? Do we go?"

The woman at his side did not reply at once. She was hunched into the far corner of the brown leather seat staring absently out of the car at a big blinking neon sign over the sidewalk. FANGAHIVA'S FINE FOODS. The flashing letters turned her face alternately red and green; but the finely drawn features with the slightly petulant lips remained the same in outline. He stole a glance at her. The white shark-skin shirt, open at the throat, was stretched tight over the swell of her breasts. He swallowed and scratched the stubble on his left cheek. The sea breeze sent the tattered fronds of a cabbage palm scraping together in brittle chatter. The big tree stood right beside a street light—a lamp standard crowned with an imitation bronze and plastic flambeau—and seemed the poorer for its company. Griffith pushed his naval cap back off his head, feeling the sweatband stick and the air cool where it had been. He spoke again, with a trace of annoyance.

"Well, are we going out or not?"

"It was your idea." Ruth shrugged, and the chill dissatisfied phrase dropped into the evening air, adding a shade of green to the saffron of the sunset.

"I like that! He was your husband, wasn't he?"

"Don't say 'was.' "

"The search is called off."

She said without moving or looking at him: "We'll go if you like."

"It isn't if I like, it's if you like. I've seen Hickam Field and Pearl City a thousand times. There's nothing in it for me. Or do you want to eat?"

His voice trailed upward like campfire smoke; but she looked at the neon sign for a moment and then said: "No. We'll go to Pearl Harbor first."

He grumbled: "After all, the Navy asked for the interview with you. I'm just offering you a lift and maybe I'm a bit conspicuous at that."

Earlier that morning a naval petty officer in a blue jeep had called at Ruth's apartment to tell her that the Rear Admiral wanted to see her. The petty officer was a tall impassive

Swede with blond hair and eyebrows almost as fair as his skin so that his pale blue eyes carried an expression of perpetual astonishment. When she asked him why the Admiral wished to see her, he shook his head slowly, and his almost non-existent eyebrows seemed to express involuntary astonishment that she should ask such a question or expect him to answer it. All he could muster was: "Sorry, ma'am; Admiral's orders. Do you care to come in the jeep or can we send a car for you?"

"Thank you, but I'd prefer to drive myself."

"Yes ma'am. Please halt at the barrier on the Pearl Harbor Road."

He saluted and was gone, impassive and astonished, and Ruth felt slightly hot and uncomfortable lest he should have thought her rude or abrupt. She automatically patted her hair into place and smoothed her skirt over her hips to give his departing back proof of the womanly charm which her nervous anxiety had denied to his impassive face.

Her first thought when the petty officer had gone and her annoyance with herself had subsided was to telephone Griffith and seek his help. She had already started to dial his number when it occurred to her that the Admiral might have some news about her husband. She replaced the instrument quietly, realizing that almost any news about him now was bound to be unpleasant. For she had been told that he was "missing, presumed dead" and in her own mind he was already indeed quite dead; dead beyond the possibility of producing even the faintest whisper in her animal dust. Any news about him would mean that he was not dead, or was presumed to be not dead. Unless, of course, it was nothing to do with Ryan at all but was merely to say perhaps that the search had been ultimately and finally abandoned; or that a funeral service was to be held which she would be asked to attend. As these possibilities opened to her fancy, she sighed and felt relieved and was slightly annoyed that she should feel relief. And in the end she did call Griffith, just to have someone to lean on. Then she put on the white sharkskin shirt and a fetching hat that crawled down over one eye. She tripped downstairs whistling to Griffith's car.

Now she looked out of the window with unseeing eyes and as the car swept past the pineapple canneries, out by the Bishop Museum and past Kalihi along the storied and terrible road that leads to Pearl Harbor, she was still sweeping the dusty passages of memory for an image that could make her feel her husband's loss. She wavered momentarily between resentment and self-pity; then a tear, offspring of the latter, oozed out of her eye. She smeared it away. She knew dimly that she could not make herself have feelings that were not natural to her; but the fact that she could not conjure up warm images of Ryan made her feel that her life was a dusty answer to the passion flowers lying at her feet.

Griffith rode morosely beside her, pulling the car hard on the curves. He was beginning to feel that he was getting unnecessarily involved in Ruth's affairs. The long rows of pineapples ripped by like the spokes of a turning wheel, and when they saw the gleam of water on Pearl Harbor with the forest of fighting tops rising from the still unseen hulls of great warships, the honky-tonk strip of Pearl City was doing battle with the orange of the sun as it sank behind the rugged toothcomb of the Waiahae Range. Griffith swung the car off the highway onto the blacktop road. Rounding a slight curve the black and yellow barrier flew upward as the rating on duty caught sight of the license plate and also heard the driver lean on the horn. They skirted a flat-topped administration building, the lowest common denominator of all islands which have played host to the airplane. Lights sprang up on towers, on W/T antennae, on planes and on ships. Griffith backed the car to a standstill at the edge of the tarmac.

As he opened the door for Ruth to get out he saw that she was dabbing her eyes and he thought, half with sympathy, half with resentment: "My God, she still loves the guy." She climbed out of the car and stood erect, giving him a look of mingled affection and contempt which he was at a loss to fathom. Then she called: "Good evening, lieutenant" to a figure in white duck emerging from the naval building. The "Evening, madam" with which the young Lieutenant JG greeted her indicated that others were susceptible to her charms.

"The Admiral will see you now, Mrs. Ryan," and he added, "I guess you're anxious to know . . . er . . . what there is to know."

She smiled radiantly but with sweet resignation. "Why, yes; thank you. Wait for me, Griff?"

The young man could hardly bring himself to say, "Follow me," for fear of breaking the spell of her smile; but discipline and good manners prevailed and he said it. Griffith grunted assent and settled back behind the wheel of his car.

They negotiated a long cement path covered by a breezeway, went up six concrete steps and then along a corridor smelling of floor polish, printers' ink and stale sweat. Opposite a ground glass door the Lieutenant JG stopped, summoned his courage, knocked and opened.

"Mrs. Ryan, sir." He saluted smartly and stepped aside.

Across a pool of red carpet a plain desk stood foursquare, and from behind it rose a lean and wiry man with great neck strings leading from his jaw to his collarbone, and a high domed forehead. Rear Admiral Niles Fleming, grizzled veteran of many a naval skirmish, extended his hand with a grin that gave nothing away.

"Mrs. Ryan? Won't you sit down? I know how you must feel—about Dr. Ryan."

Ruth sat on a cane-bottomed chair facing the admiral. He was framed by the striated lines of a plastic venetian blind which cast raking bars of sunset red down one side of his face. Through the slits she could see the ragged mountains to the north. She glumly contemplated a roller map of the Pacific, held in simple awe by its vast expanses of open water and the way all the islands clustered in the southwest corner. Then she heard her own burry contralto.

"There's no chance that he'll be found?"

"I don't say he won't be found." The admiral glanced over at the map. "There might be a chance. He might conceivably have reached an island; but it's extremely unlikely." He swiveled round in his chair and made a vague gesture in the direction of the Society Islands. "As you can see, there aren't many islands thereabouts; and even if there were they'd be so far apart that his chances of being washed onto them are practically zero."

"Is that the only chance?"

Her golden voice dropped the innocent appealing words into the silence like sorrowful amber beads; yet as they fell they glowed with the secret hope that the answer they seemed to seek would be denied. For if she could conjure up no tender vision of the dead, then dead they should remain.

"Well, what alternatives are there?"

The Admiral turned his chair around and spread his hands out palm downward on the table.

"He might—just might—have been picked up by a small

native vessel and landed at an outlying island with no communications. But even in these outer islands—some of the atolls in the Tuamotu group, for instance—the natives have ways and means of getting the news to Tahiti or some other main island. Now if that happened I agree we might not hear from him for several weeks possibly. But it's a very slim chance. That's the reason I asked you to come here."

He leaned back in his swivel chair and put his hands behind his head. Ruth was suddenly hunched up and withdrawn, her brown eyes turned inward on her own dark thoughts. In the battle now joined in the deep recesses of her mind she was as certain that she did not want Ryan alive as she was shamed by her conscience at entertaining the wish. But in answer to her unspoken thoughts, the Admiral's words came startlingly clear.

"But . . . I *may* have some news for you." He waited for her to reply, but she gave a faint smile and remained silent.

"Mrs. Ryan, I don't want you to take what I'm going to say as giving the slightest indication of hope to anyone. . . ." He paused.

Her heart sank, not because of the prospect of hope unfulfilled but because of its mere mention, bringing with it the possibility of a renewed Ryan.

"Of course not, I understand."

"Not the faintest indication," he repeated a trifle sententiously. "At the same time I have to tell you that one of our aircraft—not one of mine, you understand, but an operational aircraft from another sector of the Pacific which is under the command of my colleague Admiral Gonzalez—this aircraft has sighted what is apparently an uncharted island."

He paused impressively. She listened, the picture of detached and slightly uncomprehending enquiry.

"Yes? And . . .?" she permitted herself. The Admiral laughed in a gently superior male manner.

"Of course, Mrs. Ryan, I can quite see that this doesn't mean very much to you and it certainly doesn't tell you why I called you in here. But wait!"

She waited again. He rose, walked over to the window, then returned to the desk and faced her, leaning on it with his arms at his sides.

"The reason the island was uncharted we don't yet know. But we do know that the plane that sighted it was way off course. I'd like you to look at this map here."

He pulled down a wall roll map of the Southeast Pacific and pointed a gristly finger at the area near Easter Island.

"This plane was on a routine flight from Juan Fernandez—that's here—to Easter Island, which we use as a refueling base by arrangement with the Government of Chile. All these islands are part of a chain of weather stations which all of us operate in this area. The plane was off course—far off. This was partly deliberate to avoid very rough weather in the area of Podesta Reef—here, and partly that the craft got slapped about by the tail end of that weather. I needn't worry you with the details, need I?"

He looked sideways at her from under thatched brows, and she nodded.

"Okay. Here's what we think happened. This plane is cruising along here, trying to regain westing, you understand. Fortunately these craft have auxiliary tanks so that fuel's not a major obstacle. Now down here—roughly latitude 35° South, longitude 105° West—a good five hundred miles off the course your husband's plane was on, as you can easily see, they ran almost slap into a high mountainous island."

He paused and added slowly: "In an area where no island has ever been reported since before the days of Captain Cook. But also an area where ships and planes almost never go: the loneliest stretch of water on the face of the earth." He walked round the desk and sat down.

"But why do you tell me this? Surely you don't expect my husband to be on this island, and to be alive? And suppose you did, wouldn't you explore a bit first before contacting me and holding out any hopes? Wouldn't you?"

"I can answer those questions in a moment, Mrs. Ryan; but will you first let me finish my statement?" She inclined her head.

"The U.S. Navy, along with the other associated navies of the free world, is fundamentally interested in that island. The fellows who spotted it were unable to stop and investigate. They couldn't assume the presence of a landing field or any refueling facilities, and they couldn't afford to spend any time horsing around wasting fuel. They had to make Easter Island or go in the drink. But they took bearings; they gave a very precise location of this supposed island; they gave a very full account of how it looked and one of the fellows made a sketch of it."

He emphasized this point with his finger and his steely eyes peered out at her. But she was only confused, thinking: why is he telling me all this? The Admiral resumed his staccato delivery.

"We're going to send out a search party to locate and explore that island. We think it entirely possible that it may have been overlooked since the days of the whalers, maybe over a hundred years ago. Possibly, though this is unlikely, it's never been spotted at all. Things like that can happen even in this day and age." His eyes crinkled. "Why, I can remember when I was an ensign on the old *Seattle* in the First World War, we found an island off the coast of Sicily . . . but I see I'm boring you."

"No; indeed you're not."

"Anyway, to answer your questions, which is the real reason I asked you in here. Those fellows flew near enough to that island that they think—only think mind you—they saw something on the beach."

"Something? What?"

"They're not prepared to swear to it. You'll appreciate that at three thousand feet and a couple of miles off you're apt to make mistakes. . . ." He paused.

His intense manner was irritating her, yet it was also stirring her sluggish interest. She leaned forward with a carefully modulated "Yes?"

"Yes, indeed. I'll tell you. They *think* they saw a large dollar sign cut into the sand. Now, you couldn't invent a thing like that."

"Then why didn't they fly around a bit and take a look?"

"I've been trying to tell you. They were way off course and short of fuel. They just couldn't take a chance. It meant not only their own lives, but valuable U.S. Navy property."

This seemed unanswerable.

"I see."

"Okay, now this dollar sign on an uncharted island can only mean one thing. An American, or someone who knows America, or someone who thinks American planes might possibly fly in that area, has landed on this island and wants to get off it. Is that a fair inference?"

"I suppose so; well . . . yes."

"Well, now, I ask you, if he weren't an American or someone who knows America he wouldn't have made a dollar sign. And if he was happy on the island and didn't want to get off, why, he wouldn't have written any sign at all. And if he was dead, the same thing would apply."

"Then it seems as if whoever it is may be alive?"

"*Was* alive when those airmen saw that sign, Mrs. Ryan. At least, it's a very strong presumption. Now we got this report day before yesterday by radio. That's about a month after we formally abandoned the search. I've examined the report thoroughly and I myself have talked to one of the men who was flown in here from Easter Island, specially for the interview. Now what I want to ask you is this; and I may tell you that I'm asking all next of kin the same question: From your knowledge of your husband, and supposing him somehow to have been landed on that island—a very long 'if,' I'll grant you—is that the kind of thing he would have done?"

"Written a dollar sign in the sand?" she said dully.

"Yes. But remember it's more than just doing it with your fingers. For a sign like that to be seen from the air it would need to be very large indeed, and it might take several hours or maybe even days to finish it."

She started to heave and shake with laughter. The Admiral looked very serious. She took out a piece of tissue and dabbed her eyes.

"I'm sorry, Admiral, it's—it's so fantastic. I'm sorry. You see—well—dollar signs, of all things. Besides, I rather thought my husband was dead so that it's a bit hard to adjust to . . ."

The Admiral looked relieved. It had crossed his mind that she might have hysterics in his office and he wondered briefly whom he should summon that he could trust not to make capital of the incident afterwards in the mess.

"Quite so, quite so," he said soothingly. "But do you think he might have done it? It's ingenious, you know. It's the one sign that an American would be bound to notice. What do you think?"

"Well, my husband was certainly ingenious. He might have done it but, well, anyone might have done it. Honestly, Admiral, I really don't see why you asked me to come here."

She rose as if to leave, but the Admiral held her with an unexpected change of voice.

"Just this, Mrs. Ryan. The Navy will investigate that island no matter who's on it, or even if nobody's on it, simply for a routine examination of its strategic resources and potential. But . . . if your husband or one of the other scientists were on it, if there were even a chance of their being on it, we should do two other things: we should give the most urgent priority to the operation and we should take with us experts in meteorology to gather any information they might be able to impart orally, though not in written form, they mightn't be up to it."

"Well, I certainly appreciate your solicitude; your interest. . . ."

"It's not an unselfish one. Don't forget that your husband, or one of his colleagues, if they are alive on the island, could also give us information about the plane crash: the B 77. Besides which, if it did happen to be Dr. Ryan, we wouldn't want to lose the chance of talking to him about the weather data he may have secured on the trip."

She straightened her shirt and said with the wry self-pity of one who gets slapped, "So that you're really only interested in the information he can give you, not in rescuing him."

The Admiral shrugged his shoulders.

"That's begging the question, Mrs. Ryan. Don't let's examine motives. We can't get the information without him, or his colleagues, so to that extent we're interested in them and in him. Now before you go, can you give me a more specific answer to my question about the dollar sign?"

"I really don't think I can, Admiral." Ruth was genuinely puzzled and at a loss. "It *is* the kind of thing he might have thought of; but perhaps it's the kind of thing anyone in his position might have thought of. I do know that his gadgets and crazy ideas are usually concerned with the saving of his own effort."

The Admiral held out his hand and escorted her to the door.

"I think we can take a chance on that kind of reply, Mrs. Ryan. And now, goodbye until we have further news for you. Please remember that the information I've given you is classified."

"In other words, don't blab. You needn't worry, I won't."

"Fine. You'll be the first to be informed when we hear anything. The Navy will get in touch with you officially. Goodbye."

As she walked down the cement corridor, her mind was curiously dead. The Admiral's story, fantastic though it was, she accepted; but it no longer seemed to concern her or her husband directly. It was just something that had happened to someone in a story. Then she realized that her lack of interest was due to her subconscious wish that the story should not concern her husband, or else that it should be untrue.

Male laughter, only slightly raucous, seeped through the glass door. Anger rose like a violet stain within her. She wanted to rush out and smash her clenched fist into Griffith's face, and simultaneously to be possessed by him in fierce disregard of her own pain. She swung through the door and jauntily down the six cement steps toward a group of gossiping officers which parted as she came.

"So sorry to be late. Oh! Where's Commander Griffith?"

Two lieutenants, their faces hid in shadows deep as wet sand falling from a bucket, murmured together: "Gone to see the Admiral."

"Gone to see the—?" She laughed; she was piqued. "But I've just come from seeing him. I don't understand."

"Maybe you went by a different corridor," said the other lieutenant. "Maybe it's a different admiral," said the younger seriously. "There are two, you know. There's Rear Admiral Fleming and there's Rear Admiral Molyneux."

"One's ops."

"And the other's Admin."

"Leatherface . . ."

"And Chairborne."

Ruth smiled but was secretly annoyed that the Admiral should have called for Griffith without telling her. She thanked the two young lieutenants, went over to Griffith's car and sat there in the dusk waiting. He was out in a few minutes and as he climbed in beside her seemed pleased with himself.

"Well?"

"Well, what?"

"What did he want you for?"

"Military secret."

"Oh Griff, don't be tiresome."

He laughed and swung his lights in a broad arc as he turned onto the main highway back to Honolulu. The city glinted like a swarm of fireflies beneath the burnished shoulders of Nuuana Pali, caught in the silver net of the rising moon.

Griffith had in fact been told substantially what Ruth had been told, but with a slightly different emphasis, and in considerably more detail from the security standpoint. There was, however, one significant omission: the presumed identity of the man on the island. The Admiral had his own reasons for this. Griffith he knew as a good public relations man. He wanted him to build up his story about the island in an atmosphere free from preconceived notions. He therefore gave Griffith a great deal of detail regarding the island, but did not connect it in any way with the crash or with Ryan. He had another reason for doing this. Until the existence of the island had been proved beyond a doubt, its resources at least cursorily examined, and sovereignty proclaimed, he did not want to impart any additional information to unfriendly countries. If anything leaked to the press, this might happen, and the Admiral correctly judged that if Griffith's contacts with the press were to be lubricated by the venom of personal animus, the press might come to know more than they ought to.

The result of all this was that Griffith emerged from the Admiral's office with a fine conceit of himself and with the secret knowledge that in a few weeks he would be airborne on his way to an advance base in the Tuamotu Archipelago to take part in a search for a mysterious new island.

From the silence of the onrushing night Ruth caught something of Griffith's self-satisfaction, but as the lights on Kapiolana Boulevard leaped up at them, her mood softened. Her pique gave way to the curious almost sensual excitement that Honolulu—sleazy but magical child of Yankee drive and Polynesian languor—always aroused in her. Griffith sensed her mood and an answering excitement mounted within him. He cleared his throat.

"Where to?"

She slid across the seat toward him and drove her leg hard up against him.

"Why, honey!"

An army truck threw a curse out of the dark as it swerved to avoid them and roared on into the night.

· 8 ·

WITH the passing of the airplane, Ryan lost all sense of time but not of shame. Long after the last trickle of sound had ebbed from the sky, he began to pick up the remnants of his pride and with them his self-assurance. He walked back to the dune and carefully examined his preparations for fire making. Then he took the lighter from his pocket and with vague memories of boy scout days opened the back with his knife and took out the remains of the wick. It smelled of the merest trace of gasoline, but it was enough to raise his hopes. He bedded it down with the shredded cotton and turning the rowelled wheel with his thumb he shot a spark into the little ball of fibers. Each time the spark ignited he blew, lying face downward on the sand. At the seventh attempt his patience was rewarded. The fibers caught, smoldered, caught again and finally burst into tiny flames. Quickly he plied the burning fibers with pieces of shirt, then added twigs of driftwood. In a few minutes he had a roaring blaze and it made him feel astonishingly cheerful.

He drank from the stream, bit deep into a papaya, monarch now of all he surveyed, and his spirits as ridiculously high as they had been, an hour ago, lamentably low. He went over to his store of tainted crabmeat. He argued that boiling would cure any phosphorous poison, and hunger drove him to the experiment. He roasted pieces of crabmeat on the end of a long pointed stick of driftwood. It tasted ambrosial. Twenty minutes after eating it he was violently sick; but he broiled some more and ate it, this time with no ill effects.

Ryan was now beginning to feel pleased with himself. He flexed his muscles, bared his chest, struck attitudes on the sand and called out to imaginary friends and foes. With the creation of fire he had conquered both cold and darkness. With the success of his meal he had proved that he could feed himself, at least for the time being. For the first time he felt in command of the situation and was rather proud that a mid-twentieth century city dweller should have been able to adapt himself to the primitive life. His experience might be useful for the atomic age. He would write a textbook on the subject upon his return to civilization and retire on the proceeds.

This thought gave him pause and he ceased his posturing. It occurred to him that he was still basing his conduct on his eventual return to civilization. He now forced himself to face the fact that he might never return: that he might have to eke out the rest of his life on this island alone. It was a bleak possibility; but he could now admit it, for his stomach was full. In the meantime he decided to make his little camp shipshape and explore as much of the island as he could conveniently cover in a day. He banked down the fire with damp driftwood and a revetment of sand, and went to the edge of the point to look back over the island.

He could see that it was divided into two unequal parts joined by a low sandy isthmus. From his nodding acquaintance with Pacific high islands he assumed that each section was the remains of a volcanic crater, and that the wooded hills to the west, being lower, represented the older crater. So far he knew he must be roughly in latitude 37°S, but this was the merest surmise. He might be almost anywhere within an area of half a million square miles. He might be on an uninhabited island in the Gambier Group. Or he might be on a quite well known island whose inhabitants lived on the other side of the hills. He glanced up again at the taller mountain to the east.

Beyond the isthmus and about two miles across a deep bay the tropical foliage clambered breathlessly to beat in waves at the feet of the rocky battlements soaring six thousand feet into the sky. Their fantastic shape reminded him of Orohena and La Diadème on Tahiti, which he had once seen on a cruise he had taken from Hawaii with Ruth. They were indented, austere and remote; quite unlike the razor-sharp but friendly ranges of Oahu. The mist which usually shrouded them was hazy now. He wondered if the tall remote crags enclosed a quiescent volcano. But reluctantly he turned his back and decided to explore the lower and nearer part of the island first.

He began by walking east along the beach past the little headland where he had been cast up. Half an hour's walk, mostly on sand but sometimes on raised coral shelves which tore his shoes badly, brought him to a little sandspit. He looked out across a narrow channel of gleaming water scarcely a hundred yards wide. Beyond the channel the water opened up and revealed an almost completely landlocked harbor which bit deep into the hills behind. This must be the crater of the older and extinct volcano, breached by the sea and drowned. He looked out northward across the lagoon to the reef: the wall of white spray was broken by a gap of perhaps fifty feet of smooth water and silence. The reef was breached too. He wondered whether, to save himself the long painful trek round the head of the little harbor, he had the nerve to dare the sharks and swim the channel.

There was a rustling in the forest behind him and he turned to see the tall marrin grass in violent commotion. A moment later an animal burst from the bushes and ran straight towards him. In evident fear of its life it raced across the sand and in its blind career almost brained itself on Ryan's shins. It was a small pig. Ryan grabbed it by the leg, but in an instant found himself wrestling with a slippery torpedo of squirming flesh that filled the air with squalling. Ryan plunged himself and his unwilling charge into the lagoon and exerting all his strength, he held the animal under water. Several times he was almost jerked off his feet by its violent convulsions. But eventually these subsided and with visions of a good supper before him, though still holding grimly to the piglet's legs to make sure of his prey, Ryan raised his eyes to the shore. At a distance of about nine feet, returning his stare with unwinking savagery, crouched an enormous cat.

It was about half as large again as the biggest domestic cat he had ever seen. But he knew at once that it was not a small puma, ocelot or other member of the feline family. It was definitely a domestic cat; but more ruggedly built, more gnarled and grizzled than the oldest and fiercest of alley tomcats. As he returned the crouching animal's fierce stare, saw its bared teeth and extended claws, its heavily muscled body and leonine head cut and scarred by many battles, Ryan was certain that he looked on an animal whose ancestors had once—how long ago he did not know—been tamed. Grasping the dead pig with his left hand he waded to the shore. The cat stood its ground but flexed its limbs as if ready to leap. On an impulse Ryan picked up a handful of wet sand and threw it in the animal's face. The cat dodged the sand; then with an angry hiss and an eldritch growl turned tail and in two quick bounds reached the thick tangle of grass and disappeared.

For a long time Ryan stood looking after it, the dead pig at his feet. The thought that feline eyes might still be watching him from the undergrowth of the rain forest troubled him not a whit. For the presence of an animal was at least evidence that the island had once been inhabited. Perhaps the ancestor of the cat had been brought to the island by Cook or Wallis or Carteret; perhaps it was a Spanish cat that had sailed with Torres or de Quiros. On the other hand it might be no more than a mascot left on the island by allied soldiers during the Second World War, and simply grown old and fierce alone.

Ryan gave up wondering. He buried the pig deep in the cool wet sand and piled rocks round it to keep out cats. Then, making a quick decision, he plunged into the water. The lagoon was warm green and crystal clear; only in the middle of the narrow channel did he strike the cold current marking the ebb and flow of the tide from the drowned volcano crater. Then he was shaking himself dry on the hard shingle of the farther bank, with nothing more to boast of than a brush with a leatherjacket which had grazed one shin. Sharks, if there were any, had not paid him a visit. At a rough guess from the position of the sun the morning was now well on, but he decided to push forward and do a tour of the smaller part of the island by sundown.

At first the going was easy. He walked along a series of curving beaches broken by flat beds of reddish rock and occasional patches of roughened coral shelf, deeply pocked like half-soaked lumps of dirty sugar. The steeply wooded hills he kept on his left. By about mid-afternoon, he was walking southeast when the hills flattened out into a long sandy peninsula of undulating dunes splotched with rough grass and cacti, and extending a finger about half a mile out to sea. He was now getting round to the back of the island, and the great fortress of the taller mountain assumed a different aspect from this side. It rose more gradually and suggested a sizable river valley meandering down to a small coastal plain. But if the slope was more gradual its ending was more dramatic: sheer cliff which, viewed from this distance, appeared to be about two thousand feet high and to offer no more foothold than the wall of a skyscraper. At the top of the precipice the tangle of battlements rearranged itself, and the cleft with its shaft of light was no longer visible. But the plume of vapor still streamed from the summit.

He looked in vain for any sign of life: for the smoke of a fire, for the outrigger of a canoe, even for a coconut that might show the cut of a knife. On the whole of the vast and romantic landscape nothing stirred; and there was no sound but the distant beat of the surf and the harsh whisper of the wind through dried grasses on the dunes. Ryan looked along the back shore of the island to the isthmus joining the two hourglasses. He judged the distance to be less than two miles and figured he could reach it and cross it to his camping ground by sundown, provided he could get through the jungle. During the morning he had once or twice tried to quicken his pace by taking short cuts across small headlands. But though he could negotiate the mangrove roots with their clutched gristly fingers and the marrin grass beyond, he found the steep hills too heavily covered with a tangle of underbrush and a thatch of heavy liana creepers with leaves like hairy hands.

If he had a stout piece of driftwood to use as a stick he might break a trail and smash aside the noisome tendrils of the rain forest. He clambered over the dunes looking for such a stick. On a lee slope, its base buried in rank grass, stood a large candlenut tree. It had been choked to death by the sand and now stood, a perfect replica of its once living self, but stripped of leaves and bark and with its wood a whitish gray like the ashes of a long-dead fire. It raised supplicating arms to the sky as if in mute witness to the passage of the years. Ryan had seen such trees on cattle ranches in southern Alberta where ranchers had ringbarked the trunks and they stood frozen in silent entreaty till they rotted at the base and fell. Walking round the tree, his eyes open for a piece of spiky driftwood, Ryan noticed near the base of the trunk, a pattern of cracks looking vaguely like the outline of a human skull.

The wind sent a dry asthmatic rattle through the long grass. Ryan moved nearer to the tree, his feet dragging in the heavy sand. The marks, as a skull, dissolved, but were replaced by those of a six-pointed shield carved into the trunk and surmounted by some four-legged heraldic animal. Part of this had been broken away by a falling limb so that only the hind legs were decipherable. Ryan could hear his breath quicken. He leaned closer and cleared away some more sand with his fingers. Beneath the crude shield he made out the following inscription:

—H— —A S K— —L— —R E—

—y s b— —e s

— —7 8

The inscription raised within him a tumult of surmise. He made no attempt to decipher further, but turned the legend back into his memory and, as he plodded on to his camping ground, pondered over its meaning. This much was clear: the letters had been cut into a living tree in memory of some long-dead sailor or explorer, and that man had been English. The cryptic "—ys b— —es" was unmistakably the time-honored "his bones." The use of the "y" instead of the "i" placed it, he felt pretty sure, at least as far back as the eighteenth century, though had the carver been unlettered, it could have been the early nineteenth. But the strange, awkward, stylized script suggested that the carving might have been made even earlier. Only the choking sand had preserved the tree which must otherwise have rotted and fallen long since. When the inscription was carved, the sand dunes were as yet unborn, he guessed, and the letters would have been about on a level with a man's eye.

What sailor, he wondered, had put in here to water or revictual, bound on some adventure of exploration or piracy; and then fallen victim to an island disease and been buried by his fellows? Or was he some rough tar who had run foul of his captain and suffered the hideous fate of the maroon? Or was he—more likely—the captain himself, the victim of mutineers who, while they were desperate enough to seize a vessel, hesitated to take a life? How many centuries ago had it been? How many thousand suns had risen and fallen on this strange hieroglyph slowly rotting away with the years? Perhaps the sailor had not been alone. He might have had companions: had they lived and been rescued, or had they died? Or had they lived on unrescued and if so, for how long?

His plodding feet reached the isthmus almost before he knew that the two miles of dragging shingle had been covered. He found the jungle no more than breast high, and he crawled across the isthmus to his camp, fed the hot ashes of his fire with fresh driftwood, and fell asleep in the warm sand almost where he stood.

· 9 ·

RYAN HAD now adapted his physical skill and his emotional outlook to life on the island. But after the first few days he realized that two of the most demoralizing aspects of this life would be his inability to mark the passage of time, and hallucinations induced by loneliness. To counter the first was fairly simple. Each morning when he rose from the sandy pit in the dunes he went to the large pandanus palm that overhung the stream behind his sleeping place and cut a small notch with his knife. He found it an enormously satisfying thing to do. It appealed to the same deep instinct which had made him as a boy construct a vast calendar lasting for the whole school year, and cross off each day that led to the paradise of the long vacation. Each new notch was another day snatched from time; another small miracle to repeat his first day on the island when he had come to consciousness and pain after his tempestuous crossing of the reef. His calculation was, he knew, subject to initial error; for he could never be sure how many days he had been semiconscious. But from the state of his wounds, which he assumed had been inflicted in his passage across the reef, he calculated that he had lost two days in semi-coma, and that the first notch on the tree represented his third day. On this basis he had now spent a little over a month on the island. As his wounds healed, stiffened and healed again, and as the diet of fish, pig, papaya and fresh water gradually became suited to his system, the attacks of dysentery wore off and he began to feel strong and well. No aircraft returned. In all that vast changing yet changeless horizon there was not so much as a whisper.

Yet he had so far only managed to explore the smaller bowl of the island's hourglass shape. This was due partly to physical weakness and partly to his fear lest he might be absent when a rescue plane came. Many days passed before he finally abandoned this hope. The thought that a plane might come while he was scrambling somewhere off in the remote jungle filled him with alarm. But as the days slid by into the stream of time he found himself becoming a fatalist; and he comforted himself with the thought that if a plane did come and see his enormous dollar sign on the beach, it would radio its position and a search party would be sent to the island. Keeping the sign neat and legible was not an onerous task. It was deeply scooped out of firm damp sand and the only hazard was the odd squall which whipped the dry sand from the dunes across the beach like a blizzard and choked or obliterated the curves and corners of the sign. Occasionally, too, an upwelling of brackish water made the edges cave in. Each day Ryan climbed a steep scree of slippery rock and from this height made his inspection of the sign. Mostly he was satisfied, but once or twice a week he would spend perhaps the best part of an hour patting, scooping and grading. He wore the nails of his left hand down to the quick and scraped most of the hair off his left forearm.

Having made up his mind about the effect of this sign on any stray plane, he determined to make a major expedition and to try for the top of the cleft peak through which the mysterious shaft of light shone at sundown. With its plume of streaming vapor, it dominated the whole island, and held, he vaguely felt, the key to its mystery.

Though he had accepted his life on this speck of volcanic rock, he was far from accepting all its implications. There were too many question marks. What was the steam that came from the summit of the mountain? Was it a dormant volcano or were there hot springs in its sheer battlemented sides? Perhaps there was a cup or punchbowl at the summit; if so, what did it hide? Could the smoke conceivably come from any human agency? Then there was the enigma of the spring tide, or tidal wave: he was not sure which. It had raised the level of the water in the lagoon by several feet. There was the baffling fact of the seas being warm enough to produce coral in a latitude which he was almost certain was too far south. The riddle of the sand-choked tree, wan and ashen as a winter dawn, still haunted him. Who was —H— — AS K— —L— —RE—, and why had he visited the island? Who had carved an inscription over his bones?

On top of this there was something enigmatic—something faintly menacing—about the landscape which alternately intrigued and frustrated him. He had an unaccountable feeling that unseen eyes were watching him; that somewhere, hidden perhaps in the rain forest of the tropic hills, behind the mountain parapets, perhaps even in the lagoon itself, beings of some kind were examining his movements and waiting to see what he would do. Ryan was sufficiently well aware of the dangers of solitude to know that these feelings might be due merely to a heightened sense of loneliness. Tautened nerves and controlled hysteria might invest nature with a faintly sinister cloak. But knowing all this, he still could not dismiss the feeling of being haunted.

He had puzzled over these illusions as he fished in the lagoon with his plastic lure, explored the immediate hinterland, and did his best to turn his sandy lair into some kind of shelter against the rains which he knew from experience must one day fall in torrents. But though he at length began to feel that his little camp was home, he never let his precious fire go out. It was to him the only link with the world which he had forsaken. It gave him warmth, comfort, a kitchen and a sense that, if he was not yet equal to the landscape, he was at least holding it at bay.

Twice indeed was he supremely convinced that the island had its own eyes and ears. He woke suddenly from sleep one night completely certain that some human agency was near. Though he waited, straining every nerve, he saw and heard nothing. But there shone from the cleft in the castle rock a bright bluish light which flashed on and off in a jerky but patterned rhythm. Though the moon soon rose from behind the cleft Ryan was convinced that its passage could never have produced this effect. On another occasion he forded a small stream at noonday, and saw in the wet sand, between the various runnels of its tiny delta, slowly contracting stains of dampness as though feet had trod the sand just before his own. Though the imprints were too vague and amorphous to suggest anything human, they did suggest something alive and something quite close.

When this had reached the point where Ryan, to calm his

nerves, found himself singing snatches of song, he decided that a long day's exploring was the only cure. It would make him physically tired, in itself a good thing; it might also yield some positive results. Accordingly one azure-winged morning about six weeks after his arrival, he wrapped cooked fish, wild pig cutlets and papaya in liana vine leaves, stuffed them inside his battered shirt and started off along the shore towards the foot of the northern face of the great mountain. He took with him a stout gnarled piece of driftwood which the sea had cast up some days before. By heating it in the fire, burnishing it in the sand and scraping it on a rock, he had made it into a formidable weapon: part-sword, part-club, part-spear. It was his only form of protection against he knew not what. For water he would rely on springs and mountain torrents.

His way lay at first along familiar ground to the low isthmus connecting the two halves of the uneven hourglass. He had walked this section many times in his search for driftwood, medicinal seaweeds and shellfish. He was beginning to delight in the familiarity of the scene and even in a welcome sense of proprietorship. At the end of a brisk mile he reached the little reed-choked flat of brackish water which protected the north side of the isthmus, and he paused, facing seawards, between the two craters of the island. The wooded hills of the small crater lay now on his left, breached by the sea to make the little landlocked harbor. Almost he thought of it now as home. It held familiar things: his camp and his precious fire; plants he knew and whose fruit he could eat; animals he had fought with and killed; sand on which he had gasped and bled; the big dollar sign on which he had spent so much labor. He turned sharply and faced due east.

Before him rose the formidable mass of the larger cone,

unknown and perhaps unfriendly. It reared its craggy head six thousand feet, thrusting through the dense jungle like a clenched fist. It was at once beautiful and stark; brutal, and yet, as its battlements towered to heaven, almost ethereal. It rose above the olive green of the tropical rain forest, spattered here and there with bursts of color from red earth, with flowering bushes and filtered sunlight striking a green stream through the dense trees. The rock was blue, red, azure, pink or purple by turns as the light took it. It was malachite, lapis lazuli, marble, garnet, mother of pearl: a richly varied tapestry of sumptuous color. Though bathed in the searching light of noon and swept clean by the southeast trades, it remained austere and aloof. From its topmost cleft the plume of vapor was borne upward, then trailed north and west at the trades' bidding.

Ryan ran a calculating eye over the western approaches to this grim bastion. The approach to the summit from the isthmus looked safe but tedious. Once past an initial steep climb through the forest—perhaps a thousand feet in half a mile—he would be high enough to survey the whole island and perhaps see a shorter way to the summit. He ate some of his papaya and cold pig, washing it down with water that oozed from a rocky ledge; then he cached his food among the reedbeds and plunged into the damp matted growth of tree-ferns, candlenut, dwarf casuarina and pandanus palm, fringed with great natural trellises of liana creepers, and began the steep ascent.

It was not as bad as he thought. His chief difficulty lay in keeping a foothold on the damp slippery slope. Several times, feeling himself on a greasy incline he grasped lianas only to have them strain and snap, dumping him in the muddy humus. Soon he was beslimed from head to foot and there was one particular vine with tentacles as colorless and clinging as those of a squid that gashed his hand as he grasped it, leaving long parallel cuts that were to smart for many a day. Three times he had to retrieve his mangrove stick which was more of a hindrance than a help. It was like climbing under water. His limbs dragged beneath the clinging vines and slid on the wet soil. The light was green and sepulchral. The sky lay far above and the sunlight, filtering through layers of hairy leaves, pressed down on him with the moist enervating heat of the greenhouse. But he learned how to balance himself on the slippery hillside, how to grasp the lianas close to the ground, how to pull himself up by roots.

He was glad that he had left his food behind for by the time the green cathedral of undersea light began to retreat before the blue of the sky, his shirt was shredded and his trousers strips of cloth dangling from his waist. At length he stood, then squatted, then finally sat panting on the brow of the hill in a small clearing of marrin grass. When he had caught his breath he looked round, but the view was at first disappointing, being obscured by trees. A few yards further on the vegetation thinned and died along the outer edges of a steep slope that was continually buffeted by the trades, and here the prospect was more rewarding.

Just below him to the south the green tangle of the island fell away to the white fringing reef and beyond it the water shaded steeply from palest amber-green through cerulean blue to indigo. Only a light surf broke on the reef which from this height hid its fangs as in a skein of raw silk washed by the sea. To the west the smaller part of the hourglass stood in perfect relief: the jagged crater peaks surrounding the snug landlocked harbor and beyond, the long spit of sand dunes where he had found the buried tree with its strange legend. He looked for his dollar sign but it was hidden by a shoulder of low hills that cut him off from the reef and the place where he had first landed.

All this, though exhilarating, was to some extent known or foreseen. But to the east the great bulk of the mountain fortress now loomed sharp and clear, blocking out half the horizon. The towering rocks seemed to form part of a complete circle and to frown down from an impregnable redoubt. He turned his back on them and at once the sense of oppression was replaced by one of freedom. As he looked at the smaller half of the hourglass, girdled on three sides by the ocean, he felt like a captain gazing down from the forepeak on some craft which was almost a personal possession. But if the freedom was gained in this view, the sense of challenge was lost. Irresistibly he was drawn back to the great rock bastion and its frowning crags.

Up here on the windswept heights the undergrowth was almost entirely absent and the trees grew much less thickly. The slope he had scaled stopped at the far end of a long razorback ridge which led to the base of the rock fortress. Gauging the distance with his eye it appeared to be about a mile and a half to the foot of the crags. He judged by the sun that it must be about two in the afternoon and decided to try it. He set off gingerly along the razorback using his driftwood stick as a balance. This became increasingly necessary, for the ridge was in places barely five feet wide and its volcanic tuff, partially denuded of trees on the seaward side, sometimes crumbled as he passed. At other times the ridge broadened out to fifty yards in width, and he would walk for a time in forest.

He was passing through the third or fourth of such wider spaces when it struck him that the path he was following along the knife edge was not a natural one but had been made by some animal or human agency. To make certain of this he went back to the last widening, examined carefully the pathway through it and compared it with the one he had just left behind. In both cases he could see that the path bent to avoid certain trees and that branches had actually been broken though the breaks were old and gray. It was less a footpath than a series of tangible and definite impressions such as might be left by a long line of soldiers sleeping overnight on damp leaves. Ryan's pace, as well as his heart, quickened a little.

The last quarter mile was horribly difficult going. The path got ever narrower and was pitted with unexpected potholes hidden by matted grass and a species of thistle whose spines stuck in his hands and made them red and swollen. Then both ridge and path melted away against a wall of rock rising sheer and smooth as if from the ocean bed. He leaned against the hard face of the stone quite exhausted by his effort and looked back at the path which he had traversed. Seen in retrospect it was awesome and he was considerably surprised that he had managed to negotiate it.

From the base of the rock bastion it looked like a bridge of vines thrown across some jungle ravine. Even as he watched, it seemed, like a bridge of vines, to sway slightly. The next moment, with a soft rumbling sigh, about three hundred feet of the ridge dissolved and sank into an abyss which yawned for it about half a mile away. Moments later there was a shattering roar, great clouds of red dust boiled upward blotting out the landscape and filling the air with a pungent ocherous vapor that tore at his throat and nostrils. Ryan staggered back against the basalt cliff and shielded his face with his hands.

The roaring subsided and a tremor ran through the ground as if the whole island were shuddering in response to some ponderous shift far below the ocean bed. Ryan opened his eyes. The pall of dust was subsiding. The wall of rock behind him remained solid, and above him the mysterious cloud of vapor still trailed idly into the sky. But immediately in front all was destruction. A gaping hole perhaps four hundred feet square had been torn in the razorback ridge, and the mass of rubble from which dust still issued like steam from a dying fire now lay at the bottom of a hole a hundred and fifty feet deep. Ryan was shaken and surprised. The dust in his mouth tasted ashen and bitter; he had difficulty in swallowing and he shook with coughing for several minutes. But otherwise he was unharmed and as he collected his wits, standing at the base of the great cliff, he saw that no matter what other results the disturbance might have had, he was, at least for the present, cut off from a retreat to his little camp.

This strengthened his determination to attack the mountain at his back. He turned and examined its cryptic face. It rose straight up at an angle of eighty degrees with about enough foot and handholds for a fly. But the faintly impressed path forked at the cliff base and crept around it both to left and to right, clinging precariously like a rope thrown round the middle of a globe. He walked a few steps in either direction to test the firmness of the ground and see what progress was possible. To the south the path led by gentle and easy grades gradually forward; as it went, it became more definite and positive in character. To the north the path very quickly became almost impassable and strewn with great boulders cracked off from the mountain by terrific force or by violent alterations of heat and cold. The rocks were suspended on the edge of a steep slope that led down to the rain forest and would need, Ryan thought, to be negotiated with the greatest care. Beyond the rocks the path narrowed until it gave room for no more than single footholds: but it led upward.

Ryan glanced again at the sun. At a rough estimate it was about four in the afternoon. Night would overtake him within three hours, but he decided, after resting awhile, to tackle the upward path. He sank to the ground with his back to the rock worn smooth by time and warmed by the sun. In this sheltered corner, as his breathing eased and his heart slowed down, he became aware of the silence around him. The monotonous boom of the surf was here reduced to the whisper of a cowrie shell held to the ear. Among the bare rocks there were no trees, bushes or grasses to murmur at the bidding of the trades. The sun beat down out of a bronze sky. The heat and the stillness became oppressive. Ryan longed for a sound made by some creature other than himself to break the compact of streaming sun, warm rock and silence. Yet when a small stone clattered down from the screes beside him, he started violently. The stone lay at his feet and he stared at it as if asking it to reveal that it had come there by human means. But when he picked it up and matched its one raw edge with a tiny fissure a little above his left shoulder, he was forced to smile and, such was the relief from tension, eventually to laugh out loud.

It was not a pleasant sound. But compared with what followed it was music itself. For after a brief interval of quite deadly silence, the laugh was returned to him by a distant battlement in the form of a ghoulish guffaw, followed in quick succession by others—loud and soft, high and low—chasing each other in growing cacophony round the castellated rocks until the volume of sound burst earthly bounds and cascaded across the brassy sky in a cataract of insane giggling. Then it vanished into the blinding sun as if whipped into outer space by the trades.

Ryan stood his ground but was badly scared. In vain he kept reassuring himself that it was only an echo; for it seemed, among the silence, the rocks and the sky, to possess a life of its own, to perpetuate itself and in repetition to become more sinister with each increasing gale of idiotic noise. Yet he wished, at the risk of exposing his nerves to further strain, to calm his own unreason and to turn the deadly silence into something he was capable of controlling. He opened his mouth.

"Ahoy!"

Ryan stood with his mouth still hanging open, his own words unuttered. Amazement and unbelief fought against each other and against a sound that had come from outside himself: from far off, for it had in it the undulating quality of a voice borne on a wind from a distance. But he did not answer, for he feared it might be a hallucination created by the silence and the heat.

The minutes crawled by on leaden feet, each moment crashing against the warm hard rock as time trickled on. No second cry came. Ryan waited until he had counted to fifty, then in his turn he shouted at the top of his voice.

"Ahoy!"

There was the same interval of deadly silence; and then, as with his laugh, the sound was thrown back at him, grotesquely multiplied and hideously distorted, till it spent itself against the dome of the sky. Silence reigned again; and then, cool and clear and undulant on the sea-borne breeze there came from far off once more a single cry.

"Ahoy!"

Seconds later Ryan was clambering rapidly up the northward path.

· 10 ·

THE ASCENT, once begun, held few terrors beyond its first two hundred yards, though these were awesome enough. The path was never unmistakably present but showed itself as a rough stone ladder. Now it followed a series of broken fissures in the face of the rock with convenient foot and handholds few and far between; now it emerged onto a small plateau or landing stage, rimmed with boulders among which grew brief and stunted rhinus bushes, their white pods rattling in the wind. Ryan, panting, sweating and covered with grime, estimated that during those first two hundred yards the vertical climb was nearly four hundred feet. But he kept close to the rock to quell the nausea in his stomach; and in his ears, mingled with the pumping throb of his heart, was the memory of the strange cry borne inward on the wind, ebbing and flowing on a current of air.

Abruptly the steep ascent stopped, the rocks vanished and he climbed over the lip of the precipice onto a grassy upland sloping steeply toward the final redoubt. Alone and resplendent in this sea of waving grass it reared up like the wisdom tooth of some long dead dinosaur, sculptured along baroque lines by time and the wind and the rain. It was about a mile long and he did not know how thick. The full force of the trades howled along the edge of the plain, beating the coarse kunai grass flat in its passage, and leaving a fluid and changing wake in the ruffled herbage.

Ryan toiled up the slope, bending his head against the wind which seemed, in its ferocity, to be blown straight out of some interplanetary funnel whose orifice was the sun. The plateau-like slope was utterly deserted save for the howling wind, but Ryan had not really believed that he would see the author of the shout which he had heard. The sound still rang in his ears. A month ago he might have mistaken it for some exclamation in a Polynesian dialect, perhaps even for the cry of an animal. But his ears had been sharpened and attuned by weeks in the wilderness, and he felt certain that the challenge shouted across the wastes had been made in English: and his Canadian ear told him that it had been made by an Englishman. But to whom it had been made he did not know. In answer to his laughter? As a warning to someone else? As a greeting to a friend?

Viewed close up the castle was not nearly as formidable as the lower barrier; but it was certainly more strange and rococo in appearance. The nearest thing to it that Ryan had ever seen were photographs of the Giant's Causeway in Northern Ireland. It was a rocky escarpment perhaps a mile long and four hundred feet high made up of thousands of fluted vertical columns of shining black basalt. Ryan stood off and examined its face for a clue. Almost at once he found it: a series of rising columns, as of notes in a stave of music, making a giant ladder clear up the face of the escarpment to the top. The graded steps were enormous, each riser being about four feet; but they were at least as susceptible of climbing as the stone blocks of the Pyramids. Whether the ladder had been made by man or nature Ryan did not know; but he doubted whether any human agency could have carved and graded the immense fluted columns, each of which was a hexagon twenty feet across. Ryan pushed through the last of the kunai grass and reached the lowest of the columns. Grasping its topmost edge he pulled himself up onto its rough but level surface. From the little table thus formed he reached upward and repeated the process. It was slow work but each step found him about four feet higher. He counted ninety-eight steps before he breasted the last column and reached the top of the escarpment. Almost involuntarily he drew back. Less than fifty yards away, the ground fell from his feet into an enormous crater. He might have been looking at some blackened landscape of the moon.

The floor of the crater was of ashen-gray pumice and harsh yellow tuff. There boiled up from it like poisonous eruptions on the skin of a dinosaur, scores of cinder cones, darkened and distorted by the force of their creation. Within the crater itself, its lip almost on a level with where he stood, was a perfectly formed *caldera* or secondary crater. It rose in a shapely cone like a tiny Fujiyama, a gentle sweep from base to summit, from blackened desolation to blue sky. Its lip was faintly edged and smeared with a rich vivid green: probably, Ryan guessed, chemical deposits from the fire within. Across the entire circle of the main crater, a distance of perhaps half a mile, the pumice and congealed lava froze in writhing contortion: blacks, bilious yellows, the grays of dead skin, the white of lime pits—a desert of destruction.

But the mystery of the plume of steam was far from being solved, for the floor of the crater was cold and congealed. That it had been active in recent geologic time—perhaps even human time—Ryan had no doubt: the evidence of the titanic struggle between the elements lay before his eyes. But there was now no sign at all of movement or activity. The volcano might not be extinct, but was certainly dormant. The plume of vapor he found did not belong to this dead crater, but came from the smaller *caldera* across the fire-blackened waste. He determined to test the surface of the crater bottom and, if he could, to walk across it to the *caldera* and probe its secret. Though the sun was now westering fast, he decided to make the attempt. The crater had broken sloping sides and was not more than two hundred feet deep. Ryan climbed gingerly down, now and then dislodging small stones and boulders which clattered onto the gray and black crater floor. The descent, though tedious, was not hard, and within fifteen minutes he had reached the bottom and was feeling tentatively with his feet for the strength and consistency of the floor, with his hands for its temperature. It proved to be as solid as a concrete pavement and no warmer than he would have expected it to be after a day's exposure to the sun.

He started across. It was like walking on a heap of boulders set in congealed toffee. On the way he passed several cinder cones emerging like fire-gutted chimneys from the crater floor. They varied in height from four feet to about twenty. He peered into one or two of the smaller ones. From Stygian depths came a pungent and sulphurous smell that caught at his nostrils and made his eyes smart. But the smell was also stale, cold and dead. There was in it no hint of life or activity of any kind.

When he was a little more than halfway across he wondered if he were taking his life in his hands. The volcano might at any moment erupt violently. But he contented himself with the cool solid feel of the crater floor beneath his feet. Less than ten minutes brought him to the *caldera.* It was about two hundred feet high and perhaps a thousand yards across, with sides sloping smoothly upward at an angle of forty degrees. He started up the slope which in composition was almost the same as that of the main crater. He slipped and stumbled a good deal on his way up and again sent little avalanches of stones and gravel down to the blackened floor behind. As he approached the summit he was surprised to find green vegetation peeping over the *caldera's* rim. He wondered how it could have survived in the midst of this blackened holocaust. The small branches of unknown bushes peered down at him like ladies from a box at the opera. He reached up with his left hand, grasped a small bough, and with a final heave jerked himself up so that he looked down over the crater's edge into the *caldera* itself.

For some time he stood silent drinking in the strange and unexpected beauty while heady scents filled his nostrils. If he had stumbled on the Garden of Eden he could not have been more surprised. The gentle inward slopes of the *caldera* were filled to bursting with a profusion of trees and shrubs, some spangled with brilliant blooms. Their feet were swathed in a sloping carpet of green and yellow grasses from which shone a vivid tapestry of wildflowers ranging from deepest red and flaming orange to pale pink and blue, and among them a wonderful white double-bloomed orchid. The whole of the amphitheater was covered from the lips of the *caldera* down the symmetrical slopes with this many-textured carpet of color. And as the color assaulted the eyes, so the singing and chirping of many birds possessed the ears, while scents both powerful and delicate were wafted through the air. Outside was the bleak fire-scorched world of the great crater; but here in this secret paradise all was damp and green and warm.

To complete a picture already perfect to Ryan's tired eyes, the bottom of the rich green amphitheater was filled by a little lake of the most wondrous deep pewter gray. It was as if the Pacific had reflected its waters upward into the sky where they were caught by the sun and reflected back to earth again to be held in this exquisite sheet of water almost perfectly circular and about a hundred yards across. Almost perfectly circular, but not quite: for at the shore on Ryan's right it became slightly pear-shaped and dropped a few feet into a small funnel in which water of a different color, a greenish pink, bubbled and boiled and threw off a great cloud of steamy vapor. It rose upward and then was snatched by the trades and trailed off to the northwest across the island and out to sea.

Ryan drank in the scene forgetful of time, while the sun slowly dropped and the wind softly sank to a whisper. The birds sang their evensong. The scents, it seemed to him, of roses and lilies and even of pear blossom, crept in his nostrils and filled him with a sense of exhilaration. Then, half hidden in a clump of flowering bushes on the far side of the lake, he saw the outline of a small rowboat. From the stern flew a little pennant: it was the flag of Saint George.

· 11 ·

RYAN'S first impulse was to shout, his second to retreat silently and discreetly over the lip of the *caldera* and await developments. He was now certain that the sense of having been watched, the feeling of awareness in the landscape no less than the mysterious light and the shout drifting in with trade winds, all centered in the flag which he had seen hanging from the stern of the little boat. The possibility that the island might be inhabited had been present in his mind ever since he had seen the dead tree upright in the sand. That possibility was now certainty; but he had no idea whether the inhabitants, whoever they might be, were friendly, and he thought it well to proceed with caution.

As he waited, he realized that if they had been unfriendly they could, of course, have done him harm long before this. It also occurred to him that they would know the island far better than he did, and might even now be watching him, perhaps from behind. On an impulse, he wheeled round but the harsh blackened pit of the crater remained ferocious and utterly silent. He pulled himself up cautiously over the edge by the green trellis of flowing vines and looked down once more into the little punchbowl paradise. Not a breeze ruffled the pewter-green surface of the little lake, and from beneath the clump of flowering bushes, the stern of the boat still protruded with the flag of Saint George hanging limp from the staff.

Slowly Ryan rose to his feet and took a couple of steps down the softly carpeted slope. Then he cupped his hands to his mouth and shouted:

"Hullo there!"

There was no echo, the voice went dead as if it had been thrown into the cellotex walls of a radio studio. But the birds stilled their chatter and a tiny breeze sent a feather of water rustling over the lake with a touch as light as the fall of a snowflake. Ryan looked westward over his shoulder. The sun was less than an hour from the horizon of the sea, straight as a ruler for three hundred degrees all round him. Whatever happened he would certainly not be able to make the six miles back to his camp by nightfall, especially now that he would have to take the long way round. This gave him an added reason for finding out if anyone was at home in the little inlet where the boat lay. Before going down the slope he called out once more.

"Hullo there!"

The incongruous words buried themselves in the toneless depths of the thick green foliage. Without hesitating more than a few seconds he started off down the softly carpeted slope. The turf was springy under foot, and as he brushed against soft tall grasses, their scent clung to him, and he seemed to go forward in waves of changing perfume. Once he had dropped below the summit of the *caldera* peace descended. The horizon contracted to a vista of flowering trees, and the trade winds, caught by the crater lip, eddied slightly, and then dropped in the softest of breezes to waft the perfumes among the full-throated rookeries of birds in the trees. A few hundred paces brought him to the edge of the lake which was fringed with a curtain of small yellow and white orchids. The water was as still as glass and the little flowers were reflected in its surface which here hung in a transparent sheet about eight feet above a bottom of golden-green sand.

There was no path round the lake to the boat save through this carpet of orchids. Reluctantly Ryan resigned himself to crushing scores of them at each step, and started clockwise around the little lake, keeping a foot or so from the shore. As he approached the boat, the foliage hid it, and he paused. Nothing stirred and there was no sound. But the unmistakable scent of apple blossom came to him fragrantly across the still air. He looked around and almost at once he saw on his left two old moss-covered apple trees. They stood on the edge of a little cleared plot of ground surrounded by a windbreak of pandanus palms. The plot which had been hidden from him by thick bushes surrounding it was no more than twenty feet square, but in it he saw tomatoes, cabbage, onions and carrots.

He examined the apple trees more carefully. They were of an incredible age; gnarled, twisted and pollarded many times, but with fresh shoots still coming out of the old clenched fists of boughs which remained.

He had no idea how long apple trees lived, but he could not believe that these trees were much less than fifty or sixty years old. He turned back into the path of his own making and walked on along the shore until he came to a clump of thick mangroves. Among the exposed roots were a couple of very stringy weeping willows. He climbed up on the mangrove roots, picked his way among them like a tight-rope walker and, finding a firm place where he could plant both feet, cautiously pulled aside the curtain of greenery and peered forth. The boat lay below and in front of him, its bows up on a tiny sand beach, and its painter tied to a stout mangrove root. The flag still hung from its stern, but when Ryan looked shoreward his heart quickened. Beyond the mooring post was a small hut made of boughs laced with stout vines. As its center was a rough door closed by a thong of twine, and above it was a design in small boughs which reminded him very strongly of the china penny bank he had possessed as a child, and which had been cast as a replica of Shakespeare's birthplace at Stratford-on-Avon.

Ryan was now thoroughly mystified and, as the light began to fail, anxious. He called out once again, not shouting this time, but in a friendly and what he hoped was nevertheless an authoritative voice. Again there was no answer: absolute stillness, broken by his own breathing which he realized was beginning to be a trifle heavy. The thought of spending the night here alone in the silence made the more biting by his own clumsy movements filled him with a vague unease. But when he considered the distance and what lay between him and his friendly little camp in the sand dunes, he had no choice. The thought of his camp brought with it the thought of food. He had not eaten since morning, and the salivary juices rushed to the base of his tongue in anticipation of a meal he was now pretty sure he would have to do without.

Climbing down from the mangrove roots, he crossed a small weed-filled expanse of spongy moss, and reached the little beach. He went over to the boat and peered into it. Apparently he was not to go hungry. Lying in the bow on a couple of large glossy leaves were three bright silver fish, each about ten inches long. They looked like very small brook trout. He leaned over and smelled them; they were perfectly fresh. What fisherman had been abroad on the lake and how recently? Had he been disturbed by Ryan's coming and was he still lurking in the bushes? Ryan felt pricking between his shoulders.

Then he put his hand into the lake, scooped up some water and dipped it to his lips. It was clear and fresh and wonderfully cool. He lay down on his belly on the sand and drank his fill. Then he turned to examine the boat. It was the most curious craft he had ever seen, for it was made of what looked like large, leathery leaves, stitched together with the tendrils of a climbing plant and cemented with resin. The leaves were stretched on a frame of boughs braced by two or three stout thwarts that looked as if they might originally have come from a professionally built boat, though they were now gray with age and soft and scuffed in their surfaces.

The little craft was perhaps five feet long and was probably propelled by a paddle, though of this he could see no evidence. In the gathering darkness he examined the flag. It was, as he had thought, the cross of Saint George, or as it would now be called, the White Ensign: a red upright cross on a white background. The cloth was fine and extremely strong, it looked like unbleached linen, and the red cross was not dyed, but was made of a separate piece of red cloth sewn tightly to both sides of the white linen. He crumpled the flag in his hands. It did not rapidly regain its original shape but remained creased and crushed. He put the cloth to his nose. It smelled faintly but perceptibly of tallow.

The birds had now ceased and the sun, though he could not see it, must be dipping into the sea; but the air in the amphitheater remained warm, scented and fresh. He turned and faced the little hut which looked out at him from a distance of about twenty feet in the luminous dusk. The strange "half timbering"—for that was how he thought of it—seemed to form, together with the little door beneath it, a smile of welcome, yet he felt an unaccountable hesitation, or was it fear?

The sun settled the matter for him, suddenly sinking far behind the rims of two craters and an ocean and leaving the tropical moon to bathe the lake and the beach in a cool silvery light. Picking up the fish, he followed the well-defined pathway from the beach up to the house and stood before the door. Once again he called out in a firm but friendly voice.

"Good evening. Is anyone there?"

Silence.

He advanced two steps, loosened the thong and opened the door to find himself looking at the business ends of a pair of pistols protruding from the velvet darkness of the hut, their muzzles two rings of silver in the moonlight. Ryan stopped dead. The two silver rings moved slightly. He swallowed hard.

"Come no further."

It was the voice of a woman.

· 12 ·

IN THE suddenly electrified darkness Ryan held his breath and waited for the voice to repeat itself. As he waited he attempted to analyze its quality and timbre. The voice was high-pitched—possibly she was afraid—and with a curious slurring of the "rs" such as he usually associated with Middle Westerners, but which could conceivably be West of England. He would have described it as musical save for the peremptory tone. It was undeniably female.

After a few moments of complete silence, Ryan felt a strong urge to relieve the strain. He could see the gun barrels trembling slightly in the moonlight that was now streaming into the little glade, and he wondered if the woman behind the gun were as nervous as himself. He thought hard of something simple and unequivocal to say which would relieve her anxiety—if she was anxious—and at the same time have the ring of simplicity and truth. Finally he said in as kindly a tone as he could manage:

"Believe me, I mean you no harm. I am lost."

That seemed to him to sum up the situation pretty well, but all it produced from the woman was a cold: "Stay where you are." Ryan waited for a moment and then spoke.

"My name is Francis Ryan. I am sorry to intrude. I mean no harm. I was wrecked on this island a month ago and I have been searching . . ."

She interrupted him: "I know you are shipwrecked."

"If you know that, then you also know that I have done no harm since I came."

"You speak truly. Wait."

Still covering him with her pistol, the woman moved slowly out of the pitch blackness of the hut into the now silvery gloom of the glade. In the half light Ryan could see her face and flesh pale against the dark forest. She seemed to be clad from the waist to the knees in a kirtle of skins. But her legs were bare and so was her body above the waist. Her face, to Ryan, was a blur in the moonlight, but the deep shadows which the moon threw from her bosom to her small neat waist told of a figure fit for the gods. Now she stood her ground and pointing the guns at him once more said peremptorily:

"Sit on my boat and tell me your story. Do not presume on my mishandling of these pistols, for I warn you I am as a Spaniard in their use." She laughed. Her laughter consumed Ryan with unreasoning desire, for it told of strength, constancy of purpose, tenderness and passion. But she also sounded as if she could and would use the guns to some purpose if necessary. He retired to the little boat and sat down on its edge. It was sharp and uncomfortable. The woman flourished one of the pistols.

"Begin your story."

"Well, perhaps I had better start by saying that I am a meteorologist."

"What is that?"

"A man who knows about the weather."

"Then you are wise indeed. Go on."

She sat down on a smoothed stump, keeping him covered with the pistols. Ryan strove to keep his story simple.

"I was with a group of other men of science, and we were flying across the Pacific Ocean."

"From whom?"

"I don't mean fly in the sense of trying to escape. We were just flying in the air."

"You fly?" she asked incredulously.

"Yes—madam."

"You lie!"

"On my honor, no. We do not use wings as a bird does; we travel in great airships which are borne through the skies by engines."

"Engines? Engines of war?"

"Well, sometimes, yes. But do you not know of these things?"

She shifted her position and flourished one of the pistols again.

"Do not scan what I know or do not know. Finish your story."

"Certainly, but may I sit on the ground? This boat is very uncomfortable."

She gave a short, defiant laugh.

"Stay where you are, sir."

Ryan sighed. "Well then, as I said, we were flying across the Pacific Ocean when this airship—airplane as we call them—fell out of the skies and crashed into the sea."

"Where was this?"

"I don't know; but it was some distance from here, because I was saved—I think I was the only one. I had a small raft and on this raft I was carried for many days and nights until I came to this island."

"And then?"

"I was thrown across the reef and wounded. I lost part of this finger, and had other wounds. But I survived, and I made a camp near the entrance to the little harbor in the lower part of the island."

"You mean Drake's harbor."

"Whose?"

"Captain-General Sir Francis Drake, dead these many years but still captain of this island, and the harbor called by his name."

She said this proudly but mechanically, as if reciting a well-learned lesson. It dawned on Ryan that he was about to ask her a stupendous question; but before doing so, he had to ask a very obvious one. He felt ridiculous as he asked it, like a schoolboy talking to one of the illustrated pages of his school history book.

"Do you mean Sir Francis Drake who sailed round the world in the *Pelican* and . . ."

"Aye, and the *Golden Hind*."

"And who played bowls on Plymouth Hoe when the Spanish Armada hove in sight?"

"Of that I know not, nor is it to me a seemly story."

"But it is the same Sir Francis Drake?"

"Assuredly."

Ryan drew a deep breath.

"May I ask, madam, if you are a descendant of his? Is he your ancestor?"

In reply she moved slowly in the darkness from her sitting position, and pointing the two pistols directly at his heart said with much venom, "Do not question me on the subject of my ancestry. Hold your peace."

"I'm very sorry," said Ryan lamely, "I ask your pardon."

"It is well," said the woman putting up the pistols, "and now I will tell you what has happened since your landing on this island."

She began, in her strange musical voice, with echoes and overtones that reminded him wildly and vividly of other voices, to give him a highly circumstantial account of all his doings since he had first been wrecked on the island. She left out many details regarding his actual search for food and his attempts at self-medication, and at finding clothing. But she told of his having lit a fire, of his swimming the little passage leading to the harbor, of his visit to the dunes where he found the sand-choked tree with the carving on it, and of his long struggle to reach the crater ending with his arrival at the hut.

"Thus," she concluded, "I have known of your coming."

"But how do you know all this?"

"Enough questions now," she said, not ungraciously. "Later you shall hear. In the boat is fish, and for its cooking, you may place it in a hot spring I shall show you, wherewith it shall become marvelous soft and good to the taste. Wait."

Still keeping him covered, she backed into the hut. From inside came a faint illumination, and she came out with a horn in which burned a small white flame. She held it in front of her so that he could not see her face, but the light cut shadows of an exquisite beauty on the curve of her bosom and on the clear cool line of her legs as she moved towards him. He noticed that she had only one pistol, and remarked on it.

"A single weapon may be used with equal effect," she said. "Now, go before me, where I show you."

She flung out her free arm with a lovely wild gesture. Picking up the fish from the boat he stumbled down a path in the mingled light of the moon and the torch. The way led from the beach past the hut to a small clearing where a miniature version of the great spring at the far end of the lake bubbled and hissed, and a cloud of steam floated up into the velvet night. The woman beckoned him over to the edge of the pool and set the torch on a rocky ledge. Then, still covering him, she backed down the path.

"I leave you now; do not follow me."

Ryan shook his head.

"I leave you my light."

"Thank you, madam."

"Then, goodnight, and do not stir in the morning before I give you leave, or it may go ill."

Ryan bowed gravely and agreed; and then as the woman turned to go, he sought the answer to at least one of the many unanswered questions which had been singing in his mind ever since they had met.

"Before you leave me, may I ask one question?"

She paused on the path in the moonlit darkness, a superb figure with a regal poise, her head thrown back on her supple shoulders. "Ask it then."

"What year do you reckon this is?"

"I do not know how you reckon the years, but by my calendar this is the three hundred and seventy-sixth year of our life on this island. And now, goodnight."

"Goodnight, madam," cried Ryan, strangely moved.

She walked away down the patch and melted into the gloom behind the oleander bushes. After a few moments he heard the rustic door close in the distance and silence descended save for the hissing and bubbling of the little geyser at his feet.

For some time he sat beside the pool in the shadows cast by the flickering light, his mind stirred to its depths. Like a ground bass to his emotions ran the vague and disquieting presence, less than fifty feet from where he sat, of a woman of surpassing beauty. The mysteries of her origin, of her presence on the island, of how she had known of his doings, were as nothing compared to the stirrings within him of desires which he deluded himself into believing might become a holy passion. And yet as he thought about the strangeness that lay like a veil over the entire island, he found his pulses quickened also by his sense of history as he ran back over the strange discoveries of the day.

Although the historical landscape which he now saw was imperfectly pieced together, and floated in his senses as a mountainous island, seen from far out at sea, its peaks shrouded in mist, he had enough of its essential outlines to fill him with excitement. In an unknown latitude and longitude, but presumably far to the south of the beaten tracks of boats and aircraft, was an island surrounded by warm water and clothed in verdure of tropical exuberance. On this island lived a woman, and perhaps other women and men, who spoke of Sir Francis Drake as if he were a vivid, present personality; who counted time from the day when the island had been seen or discovered; and whose little boat, now in the cove behind him, carried the flag of Saint George.

Sitting there at the edge of the bubbling hot springs, Ryan tried to dredge up what little history he remembered from his schoolbooks. It seemed to him that Drake had circumnavigated the globe about 1578 or 1580: it was at any rate before the Spanish Armada and the death of Queen Elizabeth, which would make the date about right. But he knew the Southeast Pacific well, and there was no island like this anywhere in its vast expanse. If it had existed, it must surely have been charted by one of the great English sailors and cartographers of the eighteenth century: by Byron, Wallis, Carteret, by the great Cook himself as he criss-crossed the Southern Ocean disposing of the vast bogus continent, Terra Australis Incognita, invented by his contemporary Alexander Dalrymple. It was surely incredible that such an island should survive without being detected. He would have to find out from the woman.

Yet on the other hand, he remembered that this section of the ocean in which he presumed the island to lie was the most desolate lonely sea in the world: a vast triangle, its base running from Mangareva to Cape Horn and its apex stretching southward into the dead heart of Antarctica. The island might have survived unseen over the centuries since its discovery. The year 376 the woman had said. That would mean Drake had discovered it on his voyage round the world, and had presumably stayed there, long enough at any rate to leave someone behind to start peopling the island. But surely women did not travel on ships in Elizabethan times? Even the glorious and remorseless Gloriana would not have wished that. Yet here was a woman speaking in what he was now certain must be west country accents, dating the island's existence from a time that corresponded with the voyage of the *Golden Hind*, flying the flag of Saint George. There *must* have been a woman. A Polynesian perhaps? Or had the island been inhabited when Drake found it—if he did find it?

Ryan sighed and gave up. He would have to ask the woman in the morning, if morning came, if the whole thing were not some trick designed to lull his senses while her friends polished him off with poison or a knife. He had to admit that his position, while pleasant in a physical sense, was remarkably insecure. He was alone, unarmed, in an unknown fastness on an unknown island. The woman and her accomplices, if they existed, held him completely at their mercy. Even the fish might be poisoned. And yet his position had been precarious ever since his arrival. If they had wanted to kill or capture him, they could have done so at any time since he came, bruised and unconscious, to the sands of this magic island. They had not done so, therefore he was safe. Besides, the woman, though brusque and authoritative, had not been unpleasant. He began to dream dreams again, and a great peace descended on his mind bringing it into harmony with the scented peace that pervaded the little glen where he sat, close to the lake at the bottom of the green and mysterious crater.

He lowered the fish on a shred of vine into the boiling spring, and as the gossamer steam ebbed and flowed in the ghostly light from the torch, he sat cooking his strange supper. The fish, when done, tasted not unlike a fresh water turbot. He ate heartily, blew out the light and, as he had done for the past month, curled himself up on the ground. But tonight, though the same moon shone warm and yellow out of the musky sky, his bed, instead of sand, was springy turf, carpeted with tiny blossoms, their faces closed for the night.

As he lay still, he heard against the silence that enfolded the crater, the faintest of whispers coming from the surf crashing on the reef, thousands of feet below. Then he slept, and the yellow moon slid slowly earthward through the scented night.

· 13 ·

LIKE everything else in the crater, dawn came in its own special form. When the sun, boiling up in a gold-red glow from below the horizon, bathed the island in saffron light, the outer lip of the crater was touched; but the lovely green slopes and the little lake within remained enveloped in a nebulous gray. This changed to blue as the sky grew paler and eventually about half an hour later, the sun peeped over the trellis of vines and bushes at the crater's edge and shot a shaft of light across the limpid waters of the lake.

This daily miracle Ryan saw for the first time as he rose from the springy turf and smelled the scent of the flowers which he had crushed in his sleep. He wanted to rush down to the edge of the lake and plunge into it: then he remembered the woman's warning and decided that he had best observe it, less because he feared a reprisal, than because of good manners. Though their position was anomalous, he presumed that he was her guest, and not her prisoner. So he washed himself in the run-off from the hot springs and, such is male vanity, regretted his beard and longed for a comb or a mirror. After that he sat and waited for her to come.

At the end of about half an hour of waiting, he made so bold as to call out, "Madam! Oh, Madam!" in a loud clear voice. Nothing happened; the call sounded ludicrous. Since he was hungry, he decided to walk slowly up the path to the hut with his hands clasped on top of his head to show his good faith. From a hole in the roof of the hut smoke drifted into the sky. On the fresh flowered turf at the edge of the water lay, neatly folded, a kirtle of soft fur, a robe of grass, and a pistol: an ancient flintlock with an intricately carved handle and richly chased barrel. The pistol was cocked. Cleaving the pewter waters of the lake less than a hundred feet from shore was a head of golden tresses and two lithe white arms.

Ryan thought of stealing the pistol, or of leaving a note saying that he could have taken the weapon, or even of hiding the clothes. His maturity triumphed, however, and he contented himself with simply uncocking the pistol. Then he retired to the warm springs till she should summon him. When she came, it was in a frowning mood and he heard her voice before he saw her. It came loud, but not strident across the morning air.

"What means this moving without my word, and tampering with my pistol? I should give you the palm of my hand to teach you a lesson."

As she came into view, Ryan was struck speechless by her beauty.

"Well, have you no answer?"

Ryan had no answer. Lovely though she had appeared to

him in the darkness the night before, he was utterly unprepared for the beauty of her face which was chiselled from a block of vibrant rosewood, and flushed with color from her morning swim. Above the finely cut nose curved two brows of golden brown, and though her lips lacked something of the bright color he was accustomed to, they were full and exquisitely formed, while her arching forehead was crowned with a mass of red-gold hair which she had wound roughly into a knot. Her eyes were a deep and wonderful gray, like lakes beneath a clouded sky. In contrast to the previous night her bosom was covered, whether out of regard for his presence or because this was her normal daytime dress, he neither knew nor cared. For at that moment he knew that he was head over heels in love; he knew that the only reality the island, the world or his life could ever have for him would be in possessing this woman. Instinctively he lowered his eyes and gave a deep bow.

Something in his manner or perhaps in his silence told the woman of his contrition for the schoolboy escapade with the pistol, and of the intensity of his feeling, for she said more gently:

"Well, if you will not answer, let us see what food will do. Follow me."

She evidently trusted him enough to turn her back. Ryan's heart went out to her and he followed submissively enough, though at a distance, until they reached the little hut. Here, spread out on a scrubbed wooden table on the green sward outside the door, and flanked by two chairs, was a meal full of strange delight. Fruits, fish, little biscuits, a dark meat and what he judged was unleavened bread. Some of the fruits he knew and recognized, the papaya, the apple, the pear: others were unknown to him. To see fruits of the temperate zone on a tropical table did not surprise him; he had in fact expected it. But he was delighted to find that he was to wash down this meal not with water, but with a pale straw-colored wine, of great lightness and delicacy, subtly flavored with the scent of many fruits.

When they had begun the meal, seated opposite to one another, Ryan so drunk with the woman's beauty that he scarcely knew what he was eating, she laid aside her pistol, and spoke.

"I place my pistol at arm's length as warranty of my trust. Do you trust in me?"

"I shall, believe me."

"First I wish to hear from your own lips a true account, more to the point than you were able to give me last night," she smiled very slightly, "a true account of who you are, whence you came and the particulars of your estate and up-bringing. Afterwards, if you will, you may hear what I have to tell."

"Madam, I shall tell you truly all I can, and I cannot think of a greater pleasure than that you should be the object of the telling." She inclined her head gravely.

Ryan then gave her a brief and, inspired by her presence, a dramatic account of his previous life. But he telescoped his biography, up to the time when he had set out in the airplane, to a few brief details; and he dwelt with relish on the account of his life since the airplane crash and his wreck on the island. He was not normally a gifted speaker, but such was her influence, as she sat across the table from him, that he found himself a vivid storyteller, and was indeed astonished at the way in which he held her interest. Her gray eyes remained fixed on his, and when he dealt with the disastrous crash of the B 77 and with his perilous journey on the raft, her lips parted and she held her breath, sighing with relief when the raft finally landed him, torn and tattered, on the sand of the island beach. When his tale was told, Ryan sat silent, hoping against hope that perhaps a part of her interest had been aroused by his ardor rather than by his story. She too sat silent while the sun climbed up above the crater lip and warmed the air, sending perfumed breezes in soft eddies about them, starting the birds to sing again, and probing with long fingers down through the green waters of the lake. Her gray eyes looked at him abstractedly and again he had that curious sensation of being engulfed into a cloudy pool; it was the only thing about her strange beauty that frightened him a little. Then unexpectedly she spoke.

"You have a wife?"

He did not dispute it.

"Why did you not say so in your story?"

"Because I did not want you to know."

She sat silent for a moment, while Ryan watched her; but though her eyes never left his face, her right hand stole out, clasped the pistol and slowly brought it round until it pointed directly at him. When she spoke her voice trembled slightly, though the hand that held the weapon was perfectly steady.

"You are most foolhardy."

"If I am foolhardy, it is you who have made me so. Why did you ask me if I had a wife?"

"Because I wished to know."

"And why did you wish to know?"

She put down the gun and turned abruptly away.

"Do not press me. It is unmannerly in a guest."

Ryan felt a stab of disappointment, for her reply, utterly free from maidenly blushes or indeed maidenly signs of any kind, seemed to hint at a reason that did not concern him.

He held his peace, hoping that enlightenment would come, but it did not that morning. For suddenly she smiled and her gray eyes engaged him for the third time with their cloudy fascination.

"Come," she said, "let us drink, and I shall tell you something of this island."

They drank and Ryan drained his glass.

"First, I must address you and I shall call you Francis, for it is a strange omen that you should bear the name of our great Captain-General. Shall I call you Francis?"

"Please do."

"You may call me Margaret, for that is my name."

"Thank you—Margaret."

As the sun, never too hot in this blessed climate, covered the glade with its dappled shade, she began a strange tale.

"Know then, Francis, that I am directly descended from George Eckford, an ordinary seaman, though a well-lettered man, who sailed with Drake in the *Pelican* in the twenty-first year of the reign of our Sovereign Queen Elizabeth, and of Maria Aspinall. You may ask how it came that a woman should reach this island, and of that you shall hear more later, for to understand it something of the great voyage must first be told."

As she told her tale, Ryan felt that he was present at the unfolding of history, and he dared to wonder if he were the first human being, other than the islanders—if there were other islanders—to hear it. Her voice cast a spell about him and he seemed to glide away from the present, magical though it was, and to slip backward in the stream of time until he stood on the threshold of that most wonderful era in Anglo-Saxon history and saw the great sun rise in all its splendor.

The intrepid men of the Renaissance, mingling in their small, neatly built frames strange contradictions of exquisite lyricism and ferocious savagery, generous romance and finely spun metaphysical subtleties, flamboyant gallantry and a flesh leeched with the filth of mediaeval midden heaps, streamed forth in their thousands from the ports of Europe. They searched for Atlantis, for Eldorado and Taprobane, for Lyonesse and Zipangu and Terra Australis Incognita. They found, in most cases, disease, death and destruction. But never since that time had the world been such a wonderful place; for beyond the blue edge of the western seas lay, for those generations, all the answers to their hopes and dreams.

The trend was westward. Outside the safe barriers of the Pillars of Hercules, far past the western isles of Scotland, beyond the tip of Ushant and Finisterre, out where the uttermost rocks of the Azores strung their magic pearls—Terceira, Fayal, Pico, Flores: there lay discovery, romance, adventure and perhaps gold. There lay the great Western Ocean into whose bosom the sun was received each night.

From Corunna and Ferrol, from Cadiz and Lisbon, from Nantes and St. Malo, from Bristol and Plymouth and St. Ives they sailed out to unknown seas; over the rim of the world into the vast outer deep. They went in frail coracles of wood, exquisitely carved and fitted, but pitifully weak to breast the gray and wrinkled face of the cruelest of oceans. They tossed and bounced in their little ships of no more than fifty to sixty tons burthen. They sank beneath the towering waves and brutal, spume-flecked swells of the ocean which a malignant fate had placed between the old and the new homes of the western world. In summer a cold and sullen blue, in winter slate-gray and hoary as the beard of Thor himself, the great

Western Sea met their frail cockle shells with an inhuman fury. Yet they conquered and prevailed.

In their tiny ships, stinking and unsanitary, ill-provisioned, crews rotting with scurvy or trembling on the verge of mutiny, they laid the great webwork of their thin white wakes all over the Atlantic and then the Pacific: the Venetian, Cabot; the Genoese, Columbus; the Spaniards, Cortez, Pizarro, Mendaña and de Quiros; the Englishmen, Drake, Hawkins, Raleigh and Gilbert; the Dutchmen, Schouten, Lemaire and Roggeveen; the Frenchmen Cartier, Champlain, d'Entrecasteaux and Bougainville.

Their tale of adventure was shot through with the crimson streaks of blood and violence, with mutinies, piracy, flogging and keel-hauling, marooning and murder, blasphemy and piety, wooden legs, hooked arms and black-patched eyes. Their exploits were those of rough and cruel men who ruled their crews with the harshest discipline, prescribing for the most petty offense either flogging with the cat o'nine tails and salt rubbed in the gaping wound, or impalement through the hand to the foremast with a cutlass. Yet these men could at the same time compose a sonnet, or an exquisitely balanced essay about the strange beauties which they saw.

But the portrait of these extraordinary men, thought Ryan, was still fragmentary. It lacked depth. Up till now they had seemed to him to move as lay figures across the vivid and violent tapestry of their days, because he could not completely grasp their motives. Drake, for instance: Captain-General, later Admiral Sir Francis Drake; that small dark intense man of Devon who was the first to sail round the world and live to tell the tale. What sent him forth? Was it plunder, the desire for glory, the sense of adventure, commercial shrewdness, natural curiosity, or the wish to please the immortal Gloriana, Elizabeth of England? What spurred onward the expedition which stood out of Plymouth roads one gusty November day in the year 1577? As Margaret spoke, its purpose slowly became clear.

The fleet of five vessels was led by the *Pelican*, a carrack of 120 tons burthen, and carried one hundred and sixty-four "gentlemen and sailors," the latter hardy ruffians from the seaports nearby: those little clefts in the rock and red earth so dear to the hearts of Englishmen. They sailed south and west across the heaving bosom of the Atlantic to the sandy, desolate lands lying on the eastern shore of the great spine of rock that protrudes, like some huge pointed baffleboard, far to the south of any other continent: the dwindling crocodile's tail of South America culminating in Cape Horn. Here in Deseado Bay, Drake landed, careened, scraped the barnacles and grass off his ship's bottom, and then entered the strait, named after his illustrious predecessor, winding past the hideously jagged coast of Tierra del Fuego. For two weeks he beat to westward through the Strait of Magellan, and on September 6, 1578, stood out into the Pacific with a fair wind from the southwest.

Far behind and below him lay that other strait that was later to bear his name. Through Drake Strait, which separates South America from Antarctica, roll the largest and mightiest seas in the world. Nourished by wind, tide, deep upwelling currents and by the very rotation of the earth upon its axis, they travel endlessly round the bottom of the globe with not so much as a speck of land to stop them in 18,000 miles of travel. But when forced into the narrow neck of Drake Strait, they set to eastward with a current of three knots; and in the Antarctic winter, these huge, unchecked seas carry on their breasts icebergs seven miles long and five thousand feet thick.

The *Pelican*, encountering these enormous rollers, born of the moon and the sun, and of cosmic forces far out in interstellar space, wallowed and pitched, lasked and clawed and at last raced onward under bare poles, bending to the fury of the onslaught. For twelve days the *Pelican* ran before the blast; and then the trades, born in the dreary wastes of Kerguelen, caught the little cockle shell and hurled it right about, far from its laboring companions, *Elizabeth, Swan, Christopher* and *Marigold*. Battered and buffeted, her seams starting, her masts shattered, her furled shrouds rent and her sheets tangled, the tiny ship bore on. Her crew was scurvy, seasick, starving and mutinous. Her captain, tossing and pitching in his stinking little cabin aft, knit his black brows and calmly weighed alike the chances both of failure and death.

And then the clouds lifted, the winds fell, leaving the ship wallowing in the heavy swell; and there on the port quarter, sitting fair under the blue sky, rose a green and mountainous island. Never was land more welcome. The *Pelican* close-hauled; the leadsman sounded and found twenty fathoms and a clean sandy bottom. Then they sailed down a narrow gut between wooded cliffs into a little harbor, a haven of seclusion and rest. The *Pelican* dropped anchor and Drake, with the chaplain Fletcher and a hand-picked crew, went ashore, knelt on the golden strand and gave thanks to God. "In this island," said the grateful Chaplain Fletcher, "were growing wonderful plenty of the small berry which we name currant, or as the common sort call them, small raisins, and herbes of grete virtue." They stayed in the haven, which the Captain named Port Sir Francis Drake, for five days, careening and taking on water. Before they left, on a voyage round the world that was to bring them sailing into Plymouth harbor two years later with Spanish treasure worth over three hundred thousand pounds, Drake took possession of the island in the name of her Sovereign Majesty Queen Elizabeth. His ship's name he changed from the sturdy *Pelican* to the romantic *Golden Hind.* His new-found haven he named to the glory of Gloriana "Queen Elizabeth Island."

When Margaret's voice finally ceased, it echoed in Ryan's ears with the hollow boom of an insistent questioning. How had this island been "lost"? How had it remained for all these centuries undiscovered? If it were as close to Cape Horn as Margaret said it was, how could it possibly nourish living coral and tropical plants? Might the Elizabethan sailors have been mistaken in their navigation, and have placed the island too far south and east of its real position? Or was it possible that the hot springs were merely the outward sign of one vast volcanic ferment which warmed the surrounding seas? He dismissed the final notion as fantastic. It would require so much energy even to raise the sea by a few degrees that the island would have to be made of continually renewed molten lava. And yet . . . He was far from satisfied.

Another and less pleasant thought strayed into his mind, poking damp busy little fingers into the dream world which he was beginning to create for himself. Had the island been in truth already discovered and was he the victim of some elaborate hoax? Would he waken—as from a dream—to find the air hoarse with the laughter of GIs or Seabees, come by some easy mountain path from their camp where they were building an airstrip on the far side of the island?

A bar of sunlight crept slowly across the rustic table, bringing with it an agreeable feeling of lassitude. The twitter of birds and insects mazily murmuring mingled in his mind and he wondered idly what mysterious fruit or grain had given such potency to the thin cool wine. But the greatest mystery was the woman herself. Was her story true? He shook his head and looked at her again.

He received a shock. Her cloudy gray eyes were wide open, fixed and staring, her fists were clenched, and her lips were parted in an expectant smile.

"Why, madam. . . ."

But he said no more, for his lips remained working in the empty air and no sound came, while his own cry was wafted to him as from far away and through a mass of absorbent cotton. He realized that the wine or the food had contained some poison that clouded the will and numbed the faculties, and he had an instant of sheer panic. At the same moment he seemed to see, through the now tensely drawn lines of the woman's face, a hint of years so crushing in their weight as to be far beyond any computation of age, to have become in fact agelessness itself. And he wondered, as the lassitude engulfed him further, whether the woman herself was as old as the island, and if she had discovered some elixir of youth.

As he slid off into the timeless pool of the unconscious Ryan was dimly aware of a bearded face floating beside but apart from the woman. It swam above him, pulsating back and forth as if striving to remain in focus. The eyes, though gray like the woman's, were small, penetrating and cruel. They were rimmed with a choleric red, so that even the gray seemed to smolder. Yet Ryan's consciousness, before it slipped from nerveless fingers, told him one thing: though he had longed passionately to be rescued from the island, he now longed with equal passion to be left to spend the rest of his days there. How strange and far-off seemed the time when he had wished to leave.

· 14 ·

TOM GRIFFITH was in his element. He was engaged in the favorite pursuit of all public relations officers: the manufacture of a mimeographed handout which, while inflating outrageously the importance of the subject, would leave the press in comparative darkness as to its precise details and its inner significance. As usual, such an exercise involved the creation of a heavy smokescreen of abstract nouns and generalizations. He worked at it diligently, for he knew that the twenty-seven pressmen, radio men and photographers who were presently killing time by drinking rye and bourbon in the nearby community hut, would descend upon him in less than an hour for the daily press conference.

His present surroundings—apart from a desk, a chair and a typewriter—were quite different from those in his office back in Oahu and a good deal more to his liking. The desk and chair stood in a small neatly whitewashed room with a floor of crushed coral, and almost the whole of one wall was open to a patio sheltered by a corrugated iron roof. Beyond the patio two steps led down into a courtyard full of patches of rough tufty grass, bordered at its far end by a thickset row of lofty coconut palms. Between their roughened gray trunks he could see a slit of bright yellow sand. Beyond it lay a lagoon about three miles across, its further edge marked by another low line of feathery tufted palm trees.

This was H.Q. Expedition Treasure Trove—as the Navy had decided to call it—and it was situated on Rotifanga atoll in the Tuamotu Archipelago, 4200 miles southeast of Hawaii. The islands, which were owned by the French, had been made available to the U.S. and British Navies under the terms of the Quadripartite Pacific Pact. In immediate tangible form this had provided him with a half-caste Tahitian stenographer and girl Friday named Aimée. She was petite and honey-colored and had two enormous brown eyes, which she rolled in great oval saucers of white. Her little figure, though rather abruptly contoured for Griffith's taste, was sufficient to keep his mind off his work for minutes at a stretch.

With a sigh, Griffith returned to the typewriter from his contemplation of south sea island romance, and with the skill born of long years as a newspaperman raced away again, on his old hunt-and-peck system at a steady thirty-two words to the minute. Outside the room and beyond the palm trees, the lagoon shimmered in the sun. There was no somber chiaroscuro, no changing moods of light and shade and shifting shadow as on the "high" islands. These coral atolls were rarely more than seven to ten feet above the roll of the Pacific swell and their apparent height was often only the height of the feather-fronded coconut palms with which generations of French settlers had sown them. From the cloudless skies the sun's rays pelted down ten months of the year on yellow sand, gleaming white coral, and a blue green lagoon; and each evening at six o'clock the sea breeze came sailing in to take the edge of the day's bright heat.

This particular island stood some way to the south and eastward of the main Archipelago, strung over a sea as large as half Europe, but with its total land area considerably less than half of Rhode Island. Rotifanga, on the map of the southeast Pacific, was an obvious staging point in the great network of bases and weather stations now being constructed, under the terms of the Pacific Pact, all the way from Hawaii to Tierra del Fuego. Conscious of this, the busy French had worked with American tools and British technicians and Canadian weathermen to grind one end of the island to a powder and fill up a pocket of the lagoon to make an airstrip. Then, when the administrative buildings were completed, they had with true Gallic taste planted a screen of palms and flowering bushes just beyond the take-off points at either end of the giant triangular runway. The work was still going on and the faint hum of bulldozers and power shovels came to Griffith as he twisted the roller of his machine, twitched out the draft release and began to look over it again, blue pencil in hand.

Griffith read the release with some satisfaction, making a few corrections as he went. It was not a long one—about three hundred words—and he doubted whether the press, which had been invited to come on the expedition at the express wish of the Admiral, would greet it with more than Bronx cheers and horse laughs. But it was the best he could do. It was almost a week now since the air convoy had left Oahu, and in the press plane and at each touch-down point, the newsmen had been put off with such vague phrases as "an expedition whose discoveries may change the whole weather set-up in this area of the Pacific"; "a search for latter-day treasure trove"; "Yankee conquistadores seeking new horizons" and so forth. As a result the newsmen were cynical and restive, and some of them openly annoyed and threatening to resign or to "go see the Admiral." But it was the Admiral who was responsible. Like all true service brass, his classic play was to titillate the press with the promise of a big story, thus getting his name in big print, and then, with an access of service cold feet, to shut up like a clam leaving the newsmen frustrated and annoyed, and putting Navy public relations at a new low. But today they would at least get something. Griffith had goaded the Admiral until he gave in; and though the press release was still pitifully generalized, it would be meat to men who for days had had to feed on air. He decided it would be better, before having it mimeographed, to read it aloud, and he pressed the bell to summon Aimée. She came with a lilt to her hips and a flash of her brown eyes and stood expectantly before his desk. He eased himself back in his swivel seat, hitched his belt up, and waved her to a chair.

"Hiya keed. Get a load of this."

"It is your release at last?" she asked as she perched herself neatly on the edge of the chair and crossed her legs. Griffith's eyes popped.

"Whaddya mean, at last? This is the real McCoy. Shut up a minute and listen."

She shrugged her shoulders and fluttered her eyelashes.

Griffith said, "Attagirl," cleared his throat and began to read:

"TREASURE TROVE EXPEDITION, ADVANCE BASE, TUAMOTU ARCHIPELAGO—dateline, agency colophon, blah, blah, blah.

" 'When we leave here tomorrow we shall be setting out on the greatest adventure undertaken by men since the journey of the Kon-Tiki,' said Rear Admiral Edgar Bolton at a press conference today to the twenty-seven newspapermen, radio men and photographers who are following Operation Treasure Trove in its thrilling journey from Oahu, T.H., to the South Seas. Making a dramatic announcement the Admiral added: 'We have every confidence that we shall add a new island, possibly a very large island to the map of the world.'

" 'We cannot at this stage,' said Admiral Bolton, 'say precisely where this island lies, for such information might give aid and comfort to certain nations which are anxious to convict the U.S. of imperialistic ambitions. But its precise latitude and longitude are known to the Navy and in collaboration with our British and French friends we have every confidence that the island will be dealt with in accordance with the principles of the U.N. Charter.'

" 'A hundred questions naturally come to the mind equally of the trained observer and of the layman,' said the Admiral. 'Is the island inhabited? Has it any strategic significance? Does it contain any critical metals or minerals? Above all, why has it remained undiscovered for so long? Is it an island of recent volcanic growth? Was it discovered sometime in the mists of antiquity, and since been lost? Is there, on some yellowed manuscript gathering dust in one of Europe's museums, the paean of joy that some early navigator felt when the lookout cried "Land Ho!"?'

" 'We cannot say,' said the Admiral, 'at this stage. But one thing we can say. In two days' time we shall be able to reveal details concerning this new island which—subject of course to security regulations—will astound the world, and will add new luster to the annals of the American nation and to the exploits of the U.S. Navy.' "

Griffith waved the press release in the air. "Thirty."

Aimée descended from the desk and stood before him with one hand on her hip and the other fingering the coral necklet that circled the honey-colored triangle revealed by her deep-cut blouse.

"Is fine, but too many Admirals."

"Whaddya mean? There's only one Admiral. Oh, I get you. Too many mentions of the one Admiral, eh? Well, maybe you're right. I'll take a look at it and cut a couple of them out. But otherwise, okay eh?"

"Sure, okay."

Griffith stretched out a hand. "Come here, honey. You don't even need to talk. There's other things you do better."

"Please, Commander Griffith." But she came.

After a while he said: "Come on, baby, I hate to do it, but we've got to get this press release out."

She descended and stood awaiting instructions while he scanned the paper again. There was a sudden clatter on the tin roof followed by a scrabbling sound. A frigate bird, having alighted on the corrugated iron, found itself unable to keep its feet on the slithery slope, and skidded down to the eavestrough before taking to the air again with a slow lolloping flight. Both of them looked up startled at first, then Griffith laughed, gave the girl a kiss, patted her behind, handed her the paper and said: "There, I've cut out two Admirals. Get it mimeographed, sweetheart, and have it by my desk in the briefing room at eleven-fifty-five sharp. The wolves will be ravening at midday. Now git."

Aimée grabbed the paper, squealed daintily and tripped out of the room and down the corridor to the duplicator. Griffith let out a guffaw, hitched his pants and walked across the dusty coral yard to the row of palms. He circumnavigated their rough gray boles, furred at the feet with fetlocks of coir, and crunched down the yielding shingle to the edge of the beach. He lit a cigarette and stared out across the lagoon at the airport a mile away to his left. The foreground was a grotesque forest of cranes, jibs, excavating machinery and power shovels, of gasoline and oil drums, bags of cement and stacks of galvanized iron sheets. Immediately in front of the forest the elephantine bulk of two flying boats squatted at anchor. Beyond the forest he could discern the outline of three huge B 77s, and to the left an aircraft carrier, its flight deck crammed with craft, their folded wings an echelon of praying mantises against the opalescent sky. To the left again a couple of destroyers lay like porpoises surfaced on the water's edge. The clatter of pneumatic drills and the surging roar of bulldozers and earth loaders oozed out across the lagoon; and over it all rose a fine cloud of pulverized coral dust which drifted slowly over the water like a heated shroud.

Griffith looked at his watch, then sat down on the sand and took a drag at his cigarette. He had twenty minutes before the press conference and he wanted to spend them in contemplation of the mechanical might and ingenuity assembled before him; of the object of his journey; of the part which he might play in it and to what advantage it might lead. Recollection induced a frown. His mind whirled back over the uneventful air journey of the last few days to the six crowded hours before his departure, and he saw himself, with a good dinner beneath his belt, leaning on the bell-push at Ruth's apartment and growing more restive because no one came to answer its insistent summons. Then the mulish determination to wait her out, and the long semi-comatose vigil on the doorstep, broken only by the squelching on the road below of a suburban bus, leaving in its wake a curious mixture of crushed eucalyptus leaves and gasoline.

When she finally came she surprised him asleep and he underwent the indignity of being stirred to sulky wakefulness by the prod of her toe. By then he did not know, apart from the normal male reason, why he had come. Was there any other reason? He blinked in the light of the street lamps and rose unsteadily to his feet, his head feeling as though it were full of broken glass. She spoke with weary resignation.

"Griff, what are you doing here?"

"Dunno really. Came to see you, I guess; leaving tomorrow."

"Leaving? Where for?"

"Military secret—naval secret rather."

She pushed past him with her latchkey. "Oh, don't be tiresome."

"Well it is."

She turned with her back to the door and her hands behind her, and her hazel eyes looked directly at him, black in the musky night.

"I'm not going to let you come in, Griff."

"Jeeze, I don't *want* to come in; I just came to say goodbye, that's all."

He spoke with a tone of deep injury; but she was sufficiently aware of the ways of men to know that a tone of injury was often a prelude to further demands. She said evenly: "Well then, where *are* you going?"

He felt a desire to smash through her complacency. "I'm going to have a look for that husband of yours."

But her response disappointed him.

"If you're going to look for that island, I know all about it because the Admiral told me. It's no use. You may find it, but you won't find him. He's dead; I know. And on top of that now you've given away a military secret."

She paused in the cool flow of speech and looked at him again without emotion. In spite of himself he laughed.

"Gee, Ruthy, you're a card. What the hell? I came round here sore, and wanting you; and now I'm not sore and . . ."

"You don't want me?"

Momentous decisions and potential conflicts stirred deep in the caverns of his inarticulate soul; but all that seeped slowly to the surface, cleaving the viscid emotional processes with a few feeble bubbles of clear thought, was: "I just don't know."

He did not know. He had sensed her growing reserve and now he wasn't sure whether he wished to smash it down with male directness and brutality, for he was dimly aware that this would gain him nothing but ashes in the mouth. "I just don't know," he repeated.

She gave a thin smile, as bitter as the rasp of the palm fronds in the night breezes on the street below.

"Then we're friends. We understand each other."

Griffith nodded: "I'm leaving in the morning," he said matter of factly. "Flying down to Canton, then Hiva-Oa, then the Tuamotu Group. After that, I guess, they'll clamp the lid on."

"Well," she said with a small sigh, "good luck. If you find

him—but you won't—remember I'm dead to him. I've withered up inside, Griff, and there's nothing can make me feel any more."

She held out her hand and he shook it with no more and no less warmth than he might have shaken the hand of a fellow officer whom he knew well, but not intimately.

She turned, opened the door and walked in, shutting it behind her. Griffith shambled off down the path to the front gate, past the azalea bushes, clambered into his car and slid off down the street. The wheels hummed on the pavement and the cool night air whistled in through the vents. But as he drove back to his mess, he felt, in some extraordinary way, as if he had been robbed of his manhood.

The lagoon shimmered back to life, as his abstracted eye came once again into focus. He ground out his cigarette in the sand and rose to his feet, stretching and yawning hugely in the midday sun.

His manhood? The thought of Aimée could send that flooding back in next to no time. He sauntered slowly up the shingle, his feet slipping backward a little at each step, like mushing in deep snow back home. When he got to his office he looked at his watch. Five to twelve. The wolves would be ready in the briefing room—all twenty-seven of them. Well, he could deal with them; he and the Admiral between them. Maybe he wasn't so hot as a Public Relations Officer, but here the Navy called the tune and he was superior to any A.P., U.P., Time-Life or I.N.S. man who ever lived. Manhood. That was manhood too. And after giving the wolves their food, maybe he could get a few hours with Aimée. He tightened his belt, straightened his collar and his cap and strode off to meet the Press.

· 15 ·

RYAN CAME simultaneously to consciousness and to the sensation of pain. He tried to move but could not, and since all was black, imagined himself in a cave deep in the marrow of the earth. As he stirred and strove vainly to penetrate the gloom, rough hands tore at the back of his head and a bandage removed from his eyes let in the blinding light of noon. His head ached abominably and his eyes blinked with stabs of pain as he strove to bring his thoughts into focus and to find out where he was. He closed his eyes again and tried to move his limbs. This time he was more successful, flexing his arms and legs and finally opening his eyes again and raising himself on one elbow to find that he was lying on a rush bed just inside the door of the hut, with the hot sun streaming in.

Slowly the pain began to subside and was succeeded by a strange feeling of lightness, a sense of strength combined with a curious irresponsibility. As he lay there on his bed of rushes and tried to accustom his eyes to the hot gray gloom inside the hut, he was reminded of his days as an undergraduate in Canada when life seemed to stretch endlessly ahead, and with a group of fellows returning from a football game on a crisp darkling October afternoon, he would suddenly leap up and clutch the bough of an overhanging tree in sheer exuberance of spirit. The red and gold maple leaves lay in vivid piles of color at the gutter's edge, stirred now and then into a dervish dance by a gust of wind from a passing automobile. On the damp sidewalks those leaves which had fallen earlier had left delicate skeletonic patterns, in quinquefoil, like the exquisite shadowgraph on an X-ray plate. The air held the electric promise of a winter season ahead in a big city. Tingling with good spirits, the boys would run, leap, walk with ludicrous swiftness and as suddenly stop, vibrant with controlled energy and warm with the feeling that they could do anything successfully and that they cared for nobody. The fact that nobody cared for them was not evident to boys of twenty; it would become evident only about five years later. They needed no girls to giggle or applaud; they were their own best audience.

Something of this tense strength and controlled careless joy began now to surge into Ryan's arteries, and as it did so, the pain ebbed away and left him with a sense of immense well-being. He began now to look at his surroundings and to take note of the inside of the hut. He was in a room perhaps fifteen feet by ten; a roof of palm leaves and the fronds of creepers which penetrated the interstices of the roof with living flowers so that he had the feeling of being in an arbor. The floor was of beaten earth, covered in the middle with a small drugget of woven rushes. On a neatly carved wooden table were six worn and polished pewter tankards and a large gourd full of the amber fluid.

Hanging from one end of the room and almost covering the palinged stakes was a faded arras showing a dim and dusty battle scene. It was surrounded by a Latin inscription which at this distance was barely decipherable. Ryan rose from the couch to get a better view. There was an as yet unexplained and unexpected spring in his step. As he approached he could make out the phrase: "Here the Third Richard was overcome by the Illustrious Henry Tudor, founder of our line."

It was the final skirmish at Bosworth Field in 1485 when the White Rose of York, in the person of the much-maligned Richard the Hunchback, finally yielded to the Red Rose of Lancaster and set firmly on the throne the steely-mouthed, level-headed grandfather of Gloriana. He it was who sent the Cabots westering over the hoary Atlantic waves in search of Ryan's homeland. And now Ryan stood lost in thought before this ancient arras, wrought in Flanders for some wealthy Tudor earl enriched by the sequestration of the monasteries, while the heady scent of strange flowers filled the air and the blood surged in his arteries.

A hoarse and rough-edged male voice broke in on the silence:

"It is a true representation, Master, do you like it?"

Ryan turned to see, standing now in the doorway, the apparition of his dream. The face was bearded and hairy and the eyes were of a curious occluded gray, rather like the woman's eyes; but they were covered with a webwork of wrinkles such as a man might get from staring long at the horizon. The mouth had the pursed corners of someone much used to hardship. He stood before Ryan, a fellow with long matted hair, a striped jersey of fieldcloth and a kirtle of skins; a fellow of about medium height, tough, rough-skinned and alert, with sailor written all over him. He gave a crooked grin at Ryan and lurched forward with an easy roll.

"Hold your wits about you, Master," again the curious cracked voice, "you look upon honest George Eckford, servant to Mistress Margaret, and as good a man as ever shipped sail with Drake."

He stood there, his kirtle dangling before him, and bending on a crooked stick held under one arm. His attitude suggested shrewdness, caution and yet a willingness to make friends. Ryan hesitated a moment and then shot out his hand.

"Glad to meet you, George Eckford. My name is . . ."

"I know your name well. It is Francis Ryan. Many a time unknown to you, I've watched you scramble up our cliffs; and well done too, I'll not deny, even when the hill foundered under your feet." His tone held a grudging admiration.

"Ah, you saw that?"

"Did not see exactly, but knew of it. Mistress Margaret was afraid for you," he added.

"Why afraid?"

"Why, Master, that you might be killed."

"Did you not perhaps wish me to be killed? How could you tell I might not be bent on some mischief?"

The sailor gave him a curious look; half friendly, half suspicious. Ryan was reminded of some small fierce animal peering uneasily from its burrow at something it did not understand.

"How indeed?" the sailor echoed. "But for that we wait until you're come to our home here. If you're not to our liking, why, either Mistress Margaret or myself . . ." He drew his hand significantly across his throat. Ryan nodded, bent on being friendly.

"I want to hear more about you, Eckford. And where is Mistress Margaret, and what happened to me? Was I drugged or something like that? And tell me what you mean by saying you shipped with Drake?"

Eckford slapped his thigh and roared with laughter until tears rolled down his leathery cheeks and into the tangled forest of his beard. Ryan thought the demonstration a trifle exaggerated and watched him narrowly, wondering if the solitary life had made the man a little crazy. When he could finally speak, the sailor turned his gray eyes to Ryan.

"What do you wish to know?"

"Well, first, where is Mistress Margaret?"

"She's gone from here to her temple at the other end of the lake where she studies the winds."

"The winds? Then she and I have much in common."

Eckford looked quizzically at him. "So I think."

Ryan was annoyed to feel himself reddening.

"I mean that we are both interested in weather."

"Just so."

Ryan decided to try another tack.

"May I see this temple?"

"If Mistress Margaret is willing, for it is her writ that runs in this island. I am but her servant." He spat on the pounded earth floor of the hut, and ground the spittle thoughtfully underfoot.

"Have you been long in the post?"

Eckford turned his deep-set gray eyes direct on Ryan's face: the same strange gray that, when turned on him by Margaret, had given him the sense of falling into a clouded pool. Then he asked Ryan the same question that Ryan had asked Margaret the night before.

"What year is this?"

"By my reckoning it is the year 1954."

"The Year of our Lord?"

"Yes."

"To us it is the three hundred and ninety-sixth year of the reign of our glorious and sovereign Queen Elizabeth."

"Three hundred and ninety-sixth? Nonsense, man. No woman—no human being—could live so long as that."

"Say you so? Well, now, the Holy Writ according to the Established Church of England tells us that Methuselah lived for more than nine hundred years in the days of his life." The strange old salt seemed to be thawing out, and showing a talent for disputation. "How old am I, do you think?"

Ryan floundered. "Well, I've no idea. I should say, or I *should* have said before I came to this strange island, that you were about sixty odd."

"And right you are, Master," said Eckford, drawing up a rush-bottomed chair. "So I am. So I am indeed: sixty-four to be sure. But for all that," he added slyly, "I was born in the thirty-eighth year of the reign of bluff King Hal, that is to say in the year of our Lord 1544; and shipped with Drake in the *Pelican* in 1578."

"I simply don't understand. You are asking me to believe the impossible."

Eckford gave a secretive grin and held up his forefinger.

"You wish to hear? Listen then, and I will tell you. You have heard from Mistress Margaret how the *Pelican* came to Elizabeth Island? Then lend an ear."

While the *Pelican* was being careened in the small land-locked harbor at the western end of Elizabeth Island, the sailors were sent by Drake in groups of three to fetch water and to gather any fresh edible fruits. Eckford, who had risen from able seaman to the rank of bosun's mate, was chosen to lead a party of three consisting of himself, Thomas Killigrew and James Bassett. Killigrew was a dark intense combative little man with a foul temper, while Bassett, who was a lissome lad, but very young and apt to suffer from fainting spells, continually fell behind. He was savagely cursed by Killigrew, while Eckford tried to keep the peace.

As they wandered westward along the coast of the island towards the long narrow promontory, they were an ill-assorted trio, staggering along in deep sand, the broiling sun casting their shadows like grotesque marionettes on the ridged furrows of the beach. They gathered a few plantains, Killigrew cursing the heat and the work, young Bassett growing more morose and silent, and Eckford, naturally a cheerful soul, trying to keep up their spirits. At high noon they paused beside a small stream to rest and refresh themselves in its clear waters. Eckford and Killigrew stripped to the waist and lay panting on the cool mossy bank; but the lad, Bassett, sat moodily beneath a tree with his legs drawn up to his chin and his hands clasped round his shins. Killigrew, ever anxious to improve the shining hour by creating discord, began to tease the lad, riling him about keeping himself covered in the heat. Bassett stood it for a while in white-lipped silence, but eventually Killigrew's raillery got the better of him and he responded with a bitter taunt. Killigrew leaped to his feet with an oath and threw himself at the lad. With Eckford straining at his hose to hold him back, Killigrew tore at the lad's shirt, crying: "I'll have thee naked yet, for a mother's milksop!"

Bassett fought like a wildcat, kicking, punching, scratching Killigrew's face with his nails, pulling out great tufts of his beard and even biting his ear till it bled, and Killigrew howled with enraged fury. But his superior strength told and in a couple of minutes he had torn the boy's shirt clean off his back. Having done that both he and Eckford stood motionless and astounded; for the bosom he had incontinently bared was that of a woman.

But Killigrew was a man of lust and action, long denied the sight of the female body; and it took him less than a few seconds to recover from his astonishment. With a cry of "By God, 'tis a lass," and entirely oblivious to Eckford's presence, he threw himself upon the woman intending to take her by force. The terrified girl kicked and screamed afresh. But Eckford's passions had also been aroused and, whether his intent was honorable or not, he drew his dagger and in the ensuing three-way brawl, though he suffered severe thrusts from Killigrew's poniard, he emerged the victor. When the dust cleared, the woman was crouching terrified, her back against the tree; Eckford, reeling unsteadily, was wiping the blood from his dagger; and Thomas Killigrew, late able seaman on Drake's *Pelican,* lay face downward in the trampled moss, dead in a pool of his own blood.

Eckford's first thought was to reassure the woman, but she shook her head and gave him a frightened stare. His next—and it came with a shock—was to look at the sun. When the brief glance of his trained seaman's eye told him how much time they had wasted in dallying and arguing and fighting, he forgot the woman, and raced like one possessed for the nearest headland. He mounted its bare rocks, breathless and panting to see what he had hoped against hope he might not see: Drake's carrack well off shore, standing out to sea in a cloud of white sail. He watched it with a sinking heart till it neared the northern horizon and his eyes ached from straining to catch a last glimpse of its gossamer beauty. Then he was alone with the sea and the sky, and like another man three and a half centuries later, he kneeled on the ground and wept and then prayed.

When he rose again the woman was standing a little apart from him, watching him thoughtfully. Holding her head aloft she said: "Seek not to know the manner of my coming on this voyage, but take me as I am; for we shall be long together." Then she led him back to the scene of the quarrel, where she had lit a fire with the aid of Killigrew's spyglass and was preparing a meal of plantain and wild duck. Looking at Maria Aspinall, both as a woman and as a cook, Eckford felt that the enforced companionship of the next few years could be worse provisioned.

First they were married, and then they buried Killigrew. Both ceremonies, though simple and sparse, were attended with the due forms and processes of the newly established Church of England, so far as it was known to them both from shipboard services. He gave her the signet ring off his little finger and she wore it on her third finger. She was a strong-willed, comely lass with a dark skin and tawny hair and surprisingly skilled in the arts of loving. But it was not until they buried Killigrew and found that one of his arms was missing that he realized the origin of the wild duck on which he had dined the night they were marooned, and precisely how strong-willed his new wife was. They buried him where the beach joined the forest, at the foot of a candlenut tree, on which Eckford carved the inscription that Ryan had seen. Then the scene was one of lush greenery, but the years had choked the life out of the forest leaving only the lean ashen monument.

Thereafter she ordered him about pretty much as she pleased, and he, far from resenting it, was proud to be the husband of so courageous and ruthless a woman, who could on the one hand disguise herself as a man and run away to sea, and on the other procure needed food no matter what its source. Beyond the fact that she was a West Country girl, and that in her absent moments, he surprised her in the use of phrases proper to the well born, that was all he ever knew of her origin. For within a year their only child, a daughter, was born, and his wife died in childbirth.

He cherished the child, Margaret Elizabeth, and in the crude hut which he built and which he enriched by the art of a sailor's cunning fingers he did his best to bring her up, as he put it, a christian lady. By the time she was seventeen she was strong and lithe and beautiful, with great tresses of tawny gold hair and skilled in all the island lore as well as in the catechism, and what little Latin, Greek, mathematics and history he had been able to teach her. Eckford was now a grizzled fifty-two and immensely proud of Margaret, but he longed with an aching nostalgia that she could never understand, for England. Every day he scanned the horizon for a sail, from a specially built platform on top of the nearest headland, and he hoped that it might come in time to take him and his daughter back to Devon.

In the end it came. But it was in a guise and with a consequence far different from that which he might have expected. Out of the northwestern quarter of the blue immensity came a great Polynesian war canoe. It had no sail and its rowers seemed paralyzed at their oars, for as Eckford and Margaret watched it anxiously, it yawed and drifted ever closer to the reef. But by a lucky chance it found the same entrance that Drake had found and slid into the harbor unharmed. When Eckford and his daughter raced down to the water to meet it, they found that of the twenty men who made up its crew, all save one were dead: maimed and butchered in some inter-island war and then set adrift. The survivor was a white man: a gray-bearded veteran in his sixties. Though badly wounded he was still living. They carried him ashore and cared for him as best they could. He was in a raving delirium most of the time and he only lived for five days, but in his lucid moments he kept talking about a magic fountain, a water that conferred great riches, high up in a crater, on an island known to no man save the ancestral chief of this tribe with which, as a shipwrecked sailor, he had taken refuge. Gradually it dawned on Eckford that the sailor was talking about his island, Margaret's island. The waters, if bathed in, and if drunk, contained the secret of riches beyond belief, said the sailor; and before he expired he gave most explicit directions regarding the position of the crater on the island and the dangers from volcanic eruptions and rock slides that attended the search for it.

They buried him near Killigrew, but without an inscription, said a simple prayer over him and, leaving the canoe load of dead warriors to the gulls and the fish and the cleansing sea, set off to find the magic crater. They found it by following a route similar to that taken by Ryan, and the paradisiacal greenery of the inner cone, after the passage through the blackened and cindery outer crater, smote their senses with the same vivid surprise. Having found it, they bathed in the waters and drank them and were happy.

Eckford finished his tale, planted his leathery elbows on the table and gazed quizzically at Ryan from his smoky cavernous eyes. Ryan scratched his head and arched his brows. Conventional gestures, yet he honestly did not know what to think, what to make of the man's story. At length he asked,

"But what about the cultivation and the English plants around this cabin?"

"The cultivation is of our making—over an unconscionable period, I'll not gainsay. The hut, which we call the bower, was made by me and has been renewed many times. The English trees and shrubs were what we had, and what the good Captain-General left behind for us on the beach. For mind you, though he would brook no slovenliness in the matter of time, he was a man of gentle feeling and knew our needs would stretch for a lifetime ahead."

"And when did you say you came to this lake, Eckford?"

"It would be in the year of Our Lord 1596 and the thirty-eighth year of the reign of our Sovereign Queen Elizabeth."

"She was indeed a great queen. She reigned, as far as I recall, for forty-five years. She died in 1603; the year of Our Lord, that is to say."

"Say you so?" said the sailor thoughtfully. "There is much you will have to tell me, for I have been out of this world for more than three hundred and fifty years, to my reckoning."

Ryan's mind tried to grasp the enormity of Eckford's statement.

"You mean you have stayed the same age since you came here?"

"That was the secret of the water," he said testily as if Ryan had questioned an obvious truth. "The fountain of great richness was in truth richer far than that of Eldorado sought vainly by the Spaniards in my time."

The strange grizzled man rose up to his full height and stretched out his arms.

"It was the water of eternal youth!"

Ryan blinked stupidly.

"Do you not yourself feel the surging in your veins of new blood?"

Ryan too rose to his feet.

"Yes, I do. I felt it earlier this morning when I came to consciousness again; but I thought it must be the air of this place."

"It is not air. It is the water of life that Margaret gave to you."

"The wine?"

"The same. It comes in the guise of a wine to those who taste it for the first time; but to us it is the water—the water of youth."

Ryan laughed uncertainly.

"And shall I become young?"

"Nay, that is beyond the water's power, but you may stay the same as you now are while the years roll by."

Ryan still felt stupefied, but the wild abandon coursing in his limbs brooked no denial.

"Mistress Margaret gave me the water?"

"That she did."

"I wonder why?"

The old sailor gave a grunt.

"To my eye, it could be because you look fair to her, and she would fain have you as her own. For my part," he laid a sinewy hand on Ryan's arm, and then withdrew it with a half smile, "that is a proposal that will bear some thought."

· 16 ·

RYAN walked down to the edge of the little lake and stood looking at the crater's mirror-image of shimmering greens. Unshattered and silent, the looking-glass land led downward in a riot of flowers and rich damp foliage to its floor of watery sky. Through it all, like lost vessels in a fog, the bodies of small gray fish made their sinuous way. The cool green world at his feet and the warm green world sloping upward above him to the crater's edge were as sharply at variance with his own mood as with the black and cindery landscape beyond. The magic elixir coursed through his arteries, and along with it the knowledge that Margaret had handed it to him. He was beside himself with mingled happiness and dread. He felt—as he had not felt for twenty-five years—that exciting sense of apprehension and joy, that ecstatic fear with which, as an adolescent boy, he had awaited, in a suburban drugstore, the arrival of the girl across the street, and the prospect of a clandestine hour or two holding hands in a movie.

He was surprised; but he was wildly happy. He sucked in great gulps of the fragrant air and then, as if to make the cool mirror world match his own turbulent thoughts, he shattered its calm with a stone, and watched the dancing pattern rush to the shore in a series of concentric circles. Yet even as the image of Margaret, which his mind's eye imposed on the dancing waters, fused, parted and rejoined in liquid movement, he was aware of a gnawing doubt.

Did he wish to live forever, even with her? Even supposing that Eckford's tale were true? Against the possibility of youthful passion on an enchanted island, he must set the bleak perhaps literally endless life of looking forward to—what? Once again the beckoning fingers of familiar things drew his thoughts away.

What of the dine and dance joints, the corner drugstores, the wink of traffic lights and the clash of gears at the intersection? What of the Philharmonic on the radio, picnic hikes to Pali, to Arrowhead Lake, to Banff, to the Laurentians? What of the hot grease from a fish fry, the deep roar of steamer sirens at the foot of the Aloha Tower; the blessed weight of musty old volumes from the public library; or the sparkle of after-dinner conversation with a good liqueur? What of his work? What of the cold and complex precision of the logarithms whereby he calculated his lows and his highs: his journeyings alone over vast horizons and among the cosmic forces of the mind, where he was king of all he surveyed?

"What of it," he said aloud. "What offer?" came from the sloping wall of greenery beyond the little lake.

But he knew, far down in the deserted whispering galleries of his mind, that the choice had been made for him: that at the opposite pole of his desire for Margaret lay the negative pole of his isolation, reinforced by the chances against rescue which must be at least ten thousand to one. For if the story were true which he was slowly piecing together from Margaret and Eckford, what chance could there conceivably be that an island which had lain undiscovered on the naked bosom of the ocean for over three hundred and fifty years should be discovered now, simply because he was on it? Yet even in calculating such a remote chance, he was denying the attractions of the island—and of Margaret. He was admitting to a rift in his lute.

Ryan sighed and felt the nostalgic pain of all men who realize that the pursuit of happiness is a vain ambition. But this bittersweet reflection was soon suffocated by a rising tide of excitement. On an impulse, and clad in his torn and begrimed shorts and his unspeakable shoes, he leapt onto a nearby rock and from it dived deep into the cool inviting depths of the little lake.

He plunged down until the water turned from lemon to green to dark brown and his ears were bursting and the blood pounding in his throat. Then he slowly rose to the surface through a world of waving fronds till he broke water out in mid-lake and lay on his back, his skin tingling, while he looked round at the green flower-scented slopes with the great plume of steam trailing its tattered way across the sky. He swam slowly across to the other side of the lake and sat down on a moss-covered stone. Physically he had never felt so fit. Then a chill thought struck him. What of his mental processes? If he stayed young, would he lose his intelligence as his physical vitality increased? A cloud of foreboding darkened his mind, and loomed far more menacing than the possibility of the rescue he dreaded. He rose, trying to shake the mood off, and noticed, half hidden by the dark undergrowth, a footpath starting upward from the water's edge until it was lost among the trees. On the damp mold through which the path left the edge of the lake he saw the imprints of small neat feet. The toes were dug in sharply and the heels left scarcely a trace, as of someone running. The grasses still straightened stiffly, as he watched, from the edge of the prints. With his heart racing, Ryan bounded up the track. He twisted and turned through the undergrowth and entered into a narrow cleft between two rocks.

He scrambled upward over a ledge of tuff. The ground opened at his feet, falling away in a sheer precipice to the dense rain forest far below, and thence to a thin belt of yellow sand, the green girdle of the lagoon, the white foam of the reef and finally the blue of the Pacific unflecked by a single wave. It was a magnificent vista. It was also a highly strategic vantage point. Framed in the enormous twin cleft rocks, as in the backsight of a rifle, was the little point where he had made his landing, and beyond it the landlocked bay where the *Golden Hind* had careened and watered. Anyone approaching the island from this direction must come under the scrutiny of the watcher at his cleft in the mountain tower. And since the prevailing set of the winds and currents was ENE, it was almost certain that those who approached must do so from this direction. For how many months, years, perhaps centuries even, had a young girl and a tough old man sat gazing out over the purple sea, poised like watchers in an eagle's eyrie, while far below the great ocean, unfurrowed by a single wake, had denied them the hope without which life becomes a mere existence?

A sudden heady scent drifted past his nostrils and every

nerve in his body became alive. He leaped lightly down from the rocky shelf into a tiny cup of springy sward lying at the base of the great cleft. In it grew an apple tree and beneath it lay Margaret on the soft grass. He stood quite still and drank in her beauty. The silken grass caressed her smooth thighs and grew up in the cleft of her bosom now lightly pressed against the sward. The narrowing of her lovely body between curving torso and firm smooth hips was a poem; her honey-colored hair lay in a cape over her shoulders and trickled like tiny runnels of golden sand from her back to the grass below. Her chin was cupped in her hands and her great gray eyes looked directly at Ryan.

Directly, and yet even as he stood there half dreading and half yearning for the reproof that might greet this invasion of her privacy, he realized that she was not looking at him, was not in fact aware of his presence. He tried to follow the line of her sight past him and out to sea, but the vast and somnolent ocean gave up no secret to him; its broad bosom remained blue and enigmatic. Then he spoke: "Margaret, forgive me."

She did not move, she made no attempt to shield herself, but the gray eyes filled with tears. Ryan moved a step closer, and with a simple dignity which he could not have mustered before he began his lonely life, he said slowly:

"Margaret, my dear love, you are more precious to me than anything in this strange new world of confined space and endless time. I offer you all that I have, my love for you."

She stirred slightly and her voice trembled.

"Oh Francis, that you should come upon me unawares, not for my modesty but to see me in tears."

"They are the most beautiful tears I have ever seen."

"Yet I should not so easily show my inmost feelings." She raised herself on one elbow. "I love you, I'll not deny it. And yet because of my love I have condemned you to eternity."

"With you it is no unjust sentence, but a joy."

"You speak fair, my love. Come close and let me feel your arms: strong, I'll warrant, that could withstand the buffeting of the winds."

She rose as lovely as Aurora. Her hair hung almost to her knees. Suddenly he felt ashamed of the pitiful remnants of civilization to which he so stubbornly clung. With a brusque gesture he kicked off his old shoes and ripped from his body the tattered strips of cloth that up till now had covered it. She stretched out her two hands to meet his, and for a few moments they stood silent and apart, strength and love flowing into their two bodies through the impulses of their locked hands. So might Adam and Eve have stood in Eden in the age of innocence when the world was young. Yet as the tautness between them mounted like thunderclouds in a monsoon, she cried out.

"Oh Francis, my love, my own! I have given you the fatal water; the water that has kept me young and my flesh firm, whose bones should have moldered on the beach years since."

"Why is it fatal if my fate is to be with you?"

She moved a step closer to him and clasped his elbows with her hands. Her great eyes, clouded with tears, looked deeply into him, through him, past him and with infinite sadness she said:

"That is a metaphysical thought; and you shall indeed be with me. But you come to me still a stranger; let me feel your dear face."

Ryan moved close to her until they were separated only

by the zephyr that wafted its way through the cleft of rock. She reached her hands up to his face, feeling and caressing its every plane and fissure with supple, healing, impulsive fingers, strong as death, yet vivid with life. Ryan clasped her tenderly in his arms and protested:

"Your eyes will tell you that I am no longer young."

For answer, she threw her arms round his neck, held them rigid, and withdrew her lovely head so that he could look deep into her own eyes. Then in a low trembling voice she said:

"My eyes? I am blind, stone blind. You too will lose your sight. God forgive me."

· 17 ·

LATER, when passion had turned into deep affection, they sat one day side by side, looking out over the purple crags and bottle-green verdure of the island to the blue immensity of the ocean. Sometimes they were silent, deep in their own thoughts which wove a web of trust and comradeship about them; more often they talked and through their talk slowly discovered each other. One of the first things Ryan found was that time had given her a serene wisdom about her blindness. The tempest of tears had only been the release, through his presence, of the pent-up feelings of the years.

"Oh Francis," she said, lacing her arm in his as they sat on the sward high above the setting sun, "do you think because you are the first man I have known in these endless years that my struggle against your love was not hard?"

"With me there was no struggle."

"But you are a man. If I had been a villainous hag alone on this island, the story would have been the same."

"No, I swear it."

But she turned the gray misty eyes up to him, so poignant now that he knew they were sightless.

"No, Francis, do not deny it. For though my experience of men is brief, I have a woman's knowledge." She sighed. "When first I heard your voice, and listened to your tale, and felt with the unseen fingers of the blind your special virtue, my heart was lost. When I asked about your wife, you knew in your heart how I felt, and then—"

"And then you poisoned me so that you might keep me for yourself."

"No, that was my father's notion."

"Sailor Eckford?"

"The same; and never had a daughter a more devoted parent. 'Margaret,' he said, 'if the man finds favor in your eyes, as mayhap he will in mine—' "

"But is he sightless too?"

"Oh yes. That is the special quality of the water. 'If he finds favor,' says he—and with my heart afire and my limbs turned to water, who shall say you did not?"

"My darling."

"So my father said that if I wanted you, and if I did not wish you to leave the island, I should give you the magic water. That was noble in him, for never has there been another man on this island."

"I know," said Ryan, "and I am anxious. Yet the water has made me young again; it has made me worthy of you. I am well content, dearest; but shall I also lose my sight?"

"Listen to me, my lover. This sightlessness is in some

sense a thing of the mind. I was twenty-five when I drank the waters, encouraged by the strange islander. That was in the year forty-six of Gloriana's reign."

"Or 1604 of Christ in our reckoning?"

"Yes. You say it is now the year nineteen hundred and fifty-four. Well then, by the notches in our tree at the bower I have been stone blind these ninety odd years. Yet long before that my vision began to fade. It was as if there floated patches of mist before my eyes, and as the years passed by, so these patches of mist grew larger and mingled together till in the end I lived, as now I do, in a world of mist. Save that the mist is now dark, and I cannot see you. Oh my womanly weakness! It has borne these sightless years, yet it now cries out for eyes to see you. Let me feel again your dear face."

Ryan was overcome with a sense of deep pity, and yet the new feeling of power in his body was so strong that he found he could look at her sadness almost objectively.

"When did the mists start to appear?"

She stirred beside him.

"Ah when; if I could but recollect. For twenty-five years I saw no change: then slowly the mists gathered. By about 1700 or so in your reckoning, I could still see, but with difficulty. Within the next forty years the mists closed in. But I could see the sun until about the year of your calendar 1800, and the night did not finally claim me till, as you would say, 1862 or 1863. So you see, though the end is sure, we have plenty of time. And yet . . ."

"And yet, my sweet?"

"And yet," she said pensively, "sometimes I think that there is no beauty that can restore to us the loss and pain we feel when the world before our eyes fades away. Though the mists have surrounded me all these sad years, yet I can see as vividly as ever, in my mind's eye, the picture of our little world here as I knew it before the long darkness began."

Ryan heard her and felt a thin cold finger of fear probing at his heart. He sighed, and she in her turn heard him, and clasped his hand.

"No, Francis dearest, do not sigh. For look, I can tell you even now in words so colored that they could paint a picture of what lies now before us. See how the rugged cliff slips steeply from our lovers' nest, and how it falls in cascading music to the swift green river of the slopes below. Then this river flows to the white sand set like an archer's bow taut against the skirts of the hills. Beyond, the lagoon lies like a green scarf about our island: it breaks in a white mane on the reef, and beyond this again I see—yes I see in my mind's eye as surely as you—the blue of the great sea stretching out to meet the arch of the sky."

"Margaret, my love, it is pure poetry."

"Poetry! In the country of the blind the one-eyed man is king," she said bitterly. "You are my king now, and only through you can I truly bear this new blindness that will not let me see you."

The sinking sun was an orange ball suspended on the horizon and once more Ryan broke the blessed silence with the unanswered question of an enquiring mind.

"What made you know that you were immortal? When did you know that the waters had begun to make you live longer, live forever?"

She turned her great clouded eyes to his.

"I do not know. The dying islander had said that it would be so, and life on the island was becoming so tedious that my father and I were of a mind to believe anything. And who knows: perhaps belief is the test of the soul? But I knew, I think, when my hair ceased to grow."

Ryan nodded vaguely, but in his mind was forming, like a puddle in the rain, the notion that she might be lying. Perhaps she and her father—if he was her father; there was a gnawing doubt there, too—with their strange accents, outlandish garb and tales, might have been wrecked on the island at any time in the last twenty years. Or they might deliberately have sought this life for purposes not yet revealed to him. Instinctively his grip tightened on Margaret's arm and she whispered:

"What ails you? Does my story seem so wild?"

"No, no," he said hurriedly and felt the ashy discomfort of the self-confessed liar, "it is only the strangeness of it."

"It is a strange world."

He thought: these doubts are very simple; they spring from jealousy and of a desire to hate and injure what one loves. But nevertheless he went on probing.

"Margaret, my love," and already the endearment held in his ears a faint savor of falsity, even though he tried to keep the prosecuting counsel's tone out of his voice. "How in your blindness did you see me? How did your eyes give me the feeling that you were looking at me? How was it that, until you told me, I did not know that you could not see?"

She sighed.

"Ah, Francis, my love, you doubt me? Dearest one, when a woman has been sightless for so long as I, when she numbers the darkness not in days, or years, but in scores of years, she learns to do a thousand things which sight denied her. Each sense becomes more sharp. Look."

She rose to her feet, her tawny hair falling over her shoulders and her figure trim and proud under the rising moon.

"Look, I can find my way like an antelope in this rocky defile where a false step may bring me death."

She darted off in the dusk, and to his alarmed amazement ran with sure-footed ease along the brink of the precipice, leaped lightly over the rocks and boulders, and stopped in full career a hairsbreadth from the jagged wall of the cleft. Ryan held his breath. She called laughingly: "Do you see my skill?" But he remained silent. She hesitated and turned with her body held in a lovely line of nervous hesitation like a gazelle sniffing the wind. Then she started to move swiftly, but uncertainly, darting hither and thither and suddenly coming up short. After a few moments she pleaded with him in the gathering darkness.

"Francis, Francis, my love, do not tease me so."

Silently he began to tiptoe toward her, intending to come up behind her and put his hands over her eyes, but even the very slight rustle which his bare feet made on the grass brought her like an arrow to his side, and the next moment she was crushed against him and in her warmth he forgot his doubts.

"Do you believe me now, Francis?"

"I do believe you, my dearest."

Now the moon had risen behind the rocky cleft, a great gold soap bubble hanging in the damask sky. They heard Eckford come wheezing up the path and begin to light a fire. "I have a brace of fine birds that have lived too long," he cried.

Ryan shouted back. "In your dark world, Eckford, how did you know of my coming? How could you foretell and watch over my every movement?"

Margaret gave a delightful laugh.

"That is my father's affair. Will you tell him our secret?"

Eckford straightened up from the fire where two fat duck-like birds were spitted on a stick of green wood. He grinned in a wide gristly smile and the fire struck weird lights from his gray eyes.

"There's no harm in it, I daresay. Well, then, watch now, while I summon my messenger. A strange messenger to you, no doubt," he chuckled.

The old sailor turned toward the landward side of the cleft and gave vent to an eldritch howl that chilled Ryan to the bone. A few moments later he repeated the uncouth noise. He waited with his head cocked expectantly. There was a slight scrabbling sound in the underbrush over by the cliff edge, and the next instant there bounded into the light cast by the fire an enormous cat, perhaps the same one that had given Ryan such an unpleasant moment back at his camp, or perhaps its cousin. As soon as it saw him, it arched its back, bristled and retreated towards Eckford.

The sailor gave a short laugh, and stroked the animal's back. It nuzzled his legs and started a purring like a dynamo in a transformer station.

"There's my messenger," said Eckford with pride, "and I have more than fifty such all over the island. They roam at will, but they come at my bidding. They are my eyes, my ears too. What do you think of them?"

Ryan could not help laughing.

"Did these animals tell you what I did and where I was? Do they speak?"

"No, sir, they do not," replied Eckford, with a brief flare of temper. "I would not fill your head with such green notions. They do not speak. But they hear, they see, they smell, and they feel. And upon their return—though they are not seen by me—they are felt, heard, and smelled." He emphasized the last word with a vigorous shake of the finger. Ryan accepted the rebuke.

"I'm sorry, Eckford, but I don't quite understand."

"These cats are progeny of two cats that Drake left with us when he cast off that sunlit autumn day, so many years ago. They are not all. The full progeny roams the island. Some are killed by birds and animals; some by crabs; some by each other. But of those that remain I have trained fifty."

"How long did this take?"

"When Margaret and myself felt the long night begin to close in on us, I chose two cats, and mated them here. Their direct progeny now unto many generations—but always to the number of fifty—have been trained to return to me always for cooked food, which they prize beyond all other."

"I see all that," said Ryan, "but I do not see how they can tell you of my presence."

Eckford smiled shrewdly. "For scores of years my daughter Margaret and I have waited for someone to come to this island. Is it likely, do you think, that we should miss our chance? And it is more simple than you suppose. I know this island from stem to stern; I know the set of each current, the strength and direction of the prevailing wind. If anyone is coming to this island, it is to Drake's Harbor that he will come if he can get alive over the reef."

He paused to give a deft turn to the spit.

"I trained my cats to go to that little harbor, every day as long as my sight was with me. Afterwards they led me there. I trained them to scavenge and explore, to search every strange object. By heaven, sir, you had lain on the sand less than a day and a night when I knew. One cat came back and it smelled of a smell I have not smelled for centuries, but one I shall never forget; human blood sir, and human sweat. That told me; and within a day I was down by your encampment. I could not see you, being sightless, but I could tell by these ears, nose and fingers, where you were. Thereafter the cats did so. You wonder why you did not see me? For all my blindness I know this island as the palm of my hand and am also swift and utterly silent. For all your knowledge, you were clumsy and noisy in movement. I kept out of your way."

"I don't doubt it at all." Ryan laughed. "In fact I shouted and yelled at first so that you must have heard me. And I remember too that I saw one of your cats when I was crossing the inlet, and your foot-marks once I saw too in some damp sand. But if you knew that I was there and sick and lost, why did you not help me?"

Before replying, Eckford took the birds off the spit and split them open with deft strokes of his knife. Then he rose solemnly to his feet.

"I knew full well that the first man to come to this island would seek Margaret's hand. To seek it, he must be worthy of it. I will be honest with you. I was not to know whether you came alone, or with others, perhaps with evil intent. I was determined that you should make your own way and, if you could, make it here alone. You have done so, and you are worthy of Margaret's hand. I welcome you to our small company. Had you been unworthy, I should have slain you. Should you ever prove unworthy . . ." He paused, then added with gruff cheerfulness, "But now sir, to supper with a will, for tomorrow is . . ."

"Our wedding day," said Margaret with a charming blush.

"So it is indeed," said Eckford, bringing over the succulent birds. "We shall have a wedding breakfast, and with the rich wine of our youth."

"Our endless youth," said Margaret, her gray eyes lustrous under the moon.

Ryan could only say, simply and from the heart, "I thank you both. You I respect, Eckford, and your daughter I love with all my heart."

Eckford nodded and smiled a little grimly. "It is well."

After supper the old sailor left them, with many a hoarse and pointed jest, to return to his quarters by the hut on the edge of the crater lake below. Ryan and Margaret were alone once more, in the arms of a soft and warmly scented breeze with the sward for a bed, and for canopy the deep throat of the sky. Far below, the mountain streams gave out soft music as they fell down through the rain forest to join the sea. The moon shone low, warm and yellow, and sent a golden swath of shimmering light across the blue-black infinity of the great ocean. Sea and sky met, as they had met today and would meet now for eternity perhaps, without a single accent to ruffle the perfect edge, the hard line of a perfect circle.

Their happiness seemed complete; yet Ryan still had a feeling of sadness. If only the perfect chord, the great arc of the globe, could be broken by a sail, a smoke smudge—anything. Once more his mind recoiled from a present paradise without end. Despite the woman at his side, he who had always been afraid of death now thought: I am condemned to live forever. I cannot die. But with a flood of reassurance came the knowledge that he was still the master of his fate: the knife, the pistol . . . Immortality could slip from his fingers at his own will—if ever the will to live was less than the will to die.

· 18 ·

RYAN could never become wholly at his ease with Eckford, despite his outward friendliness. While Margaret gave unstintingly of affectionate companionship and expected little in return, the grizzled old salt always seemed to hold something in reserve. Ryan sensed that the sailor's pride had been injured by his own arrival on the island. Much as Eckford might have longed for a visitor from the outer world, much as he might have hoped that Margaret would find a husband, it was clear that the arrival of a new and younger man on the island had ruffled his self-importance. He had been the guide and mentor of his only child; loved, adored and looked up to. Now a stranger had begun to assume his place. It was a familiar situation for a father to be in, but nonetheless painful for that; and Eckford, though he was correct and polite—almost cordial indeed—did not unbend as much as Ryan would have wished.

Eckford, on his part, began to nurse a modest but growing sense of grievance. The lonely life in the timeless land had made him forget the clashes of character, the rubbing of the edges of personality which form the warp and weft of social intercourse. The desire, never entirely stilled, for a return to the faraway land of Devon, had become as green as yesterday when he felt Ryan's unconscious body lying on the sand. But the stranger who was to rescue him from his exile, who was to bring with him memories of Dartmoor hills and cottages of lichened stone—had they changed so much, he wondered, since his boyhood?—had become the pretender to the kingship of the island. Eckford found himself displaced and something small and venomous began to sprout inside him.

Ryan tried to humor the old sailor by praising his skill as a craftsman, but it was uphill work. Eckford was certainly not unfriendly but he was also decidedly difficult. Ryan at first thought it was foolish to worry over the old man's personal feelings when his own life was now so happy, but one day something happened which made him think that he did well to be vigilant.

Though he had lost count of the days and had little wish to return to life as he had known it before he found Margaret, her intense admiration for his exploits when he had come alone to the island made Ryan think anew of whatever prowess he may then have possessed. He saw himself in a fresh perspective and in due course became filled with pride to the point where he had an irrational desire to re-visit his old camp.

He had not left the vivid green confines of the crater and its little lake since he had first discovered them, and the thought of wandering, even for a few hours, among the old familiar haunts far below, grown strange now through the passage of time, had its appeal for him. His little camp in the sand dunes; was it still there? His notched tree on which he had so carefully kept the days? He smiled to himself: it seemed so long ago now. His big dollar sign in the sand; would it have drifted over? Did it matter if it had? Ought he not perhaps to obliterate it entirely now that every day took him further from the wish to be rescued?

Margaret, gorgeous with pink hibiscus in her red-gold hair, took time from her household work—in this case weaving a new rug for the earthen floor of their bower—to come with him as far as the crater's lip.

"Be careful, beloved," she said as she pressed his hand. "Remember the earthquake and tread carefully when you come to the narrow passes."

"Have no fear. I am not as sure-footed as you and the sailor, but I shall take care."

"Will you destroy your sign in the sand?"

The question was deliberately provocative and as she asked it, she wooed him with her eyes. He decided that he too could temporize.

"What would you have me do with it?"

"Why," she said after a pause, "what you will," and with a rippling laugh she waved goodbye and ran back down the slope toward the lake. He turned from her with a smile and the next moment found himself looking down once more on the blackened lunar landscape of the *caldera.* A few brief steps down the rocky slope and the island paradise was just a green memory, a vivid burst of color along the edge of the crater behind him. In front all was a cindery waste of ashes and congealed lava. But now that he knew it, the landscape had lost something of its strangeness, and he picked his way easily among the cinder cones until he came to the outer edge of the *caldera.* Here he scrambled up the brief rocky slope and stood looking down at the hair-raising series of giant hexagonal steps by which he had ascended so many weeks ago. He wondered how he had ever climbed them; then he remembered that he had been spurred onward by the voice of the echo. How he was now to get down became for the moment an even graver problem. While he studied it, he raised his eyes and was struck anew with the wonderful vista before him.

He had lived for so long in the cloying confines of the green crater and lake that he had forgotten how wonderful it was to feel the trades bruising his cheeks and ruffling his hair; to see the island spread out below him in a cascade of frothing forest and grass, girdled by the blue lagoon and beyond it the surf creaming over the half-submerged reef. The thunderous roar came to him faintly, ebbing and flowing as the trades picked it up and swept it back and forth in the blue. The little beach where he had landed and which contained his first camp and his sign in the sand were still hidden from him by the swelling curve of the descending hill; but he had all day before him and he stood drinking in the beauty of the scene, feeling the salt breeze in his nostrils and wondering how on earth he was to negotiate the steep rocky steps down to the grasslands below.

He was aware of a shadow between him and the sun. It was close and hard-edged; the shadow of a man. Ryan knew without turning that it was Eckford, but he thought it well to encourage the old sailor—an easy prey to flattery where his physical prowess was concerned—in his belief that he moved and walked as deftly as one of his own trained cats. It was an effort not to turn, but Ryan remained gazing out to sea, waiting for the sailor to make the next move. He nevertheless experienced, for the first time since coming to the crater, the same vague pricking between the shoulder blades that he had felt when he reconnoitered the boat with the flag of Saint George. Presently the sailor spoke.

"A goodly step down that slope, Master. He who essays it incautiously may suffer a broken neck."

Ryan nodded, turned and smiled at the old man.

"I was thinking the same thing myself, Eckford."

The leathery crinkled face stared back at him from unwinking eyes. Eckford was standing a little above him with his left foot up on a boulder. Beside his right foot squatted one of his enormous cats: scarred, fierce and intent. Ryan spoke with an ease he was far from feeling.

"I was also so bold as to think you might show me the way down, Eckford. You know the island so much better than I do."

The compliment cleared the air and Eckford smiled.

"Come, Hodge," he said to the great cat which arched its back and purred sonorously. "Let us show the Master our private path, shall we? Follow me, sir."

He snapped his fingers and the cat ran on ahead among the loosely strewn rocks, tail pointing high in the air. Ryan fell into step beside the sailor and they began tramping along the edge of the crater, bearing steadily south and keeping the slopes below always in full view. Ryan noticed—though he was determined not to notice it officially—that no matter how often he tried to change their position, Eckford always managed to keep him on the outside. They walked in silence for some time. Once Ryan caught Eckford in the act of shooting a sidelong glance at him. It was an eerie experience; for he could not tell whether malice or good nature lurked behind those curtained gray orbs. He felt as though he were passing before a row of faces rendered both featureless and menacing by heavy dark sun glasses. But the sailor's mouth—a thin line of displeasure—gave him away and as they dropped below the lip of the crater Ryan was on his guard.

Unexpectedly Eckford's rolling gait ceased. With arms akimbo he turned and faced Ryan. At the same time a smile as spurious as a counterfeit note irradiated his tough, pleasantly ugly visage.

"Well sir," he said with a toss of his head, "you can remember so far back as the day you climbed this hill?"

Ryan nodded and wondered what was coming next.

"You mind that when you reached the bottom of the great columns there were two paths, and you took that leading left?"

"It looked more promising."

"I little doubt it. Besides you wished to see the cause of an echo, did you not?"

Ryan made no attempt to conceal his interest.

"Why, yes, so I did."

"Ha-ha!" The old sailor roared with laughter while the cat beside him bristled at the sound. " 'Twas I called to you. I! Old sailor Eckford. And where do you suppose I was hid?"

Ryan shook his head and Eckford permitted himself the ghost of a sneer.

"Had you come up the other path," he said, "you would have seen *me*, and what is more," here he lowered his voice and crouched conspiratorially, "you would have seen my cats. This is my bestiary, my private bestiary. Would you see it now?"

Ryan hesitated. As he did so there was a rumble of distant

thunder and lightning split the far-off sea. A cloud passed over the sun and a gust of damp wind reached for his hair and beard.

"Come now," roared the sailor, "you doubted my word the other night! When you see my cats, doubt no longer. Are you ready?"

As Ryan still hesitated, fearing to put the sailor's offer to the test lest it reveal a trap, the sky suddenly opened, and rain began to stream down: heavy and sudden as a kona storm in Hawaii. In the few seconds it took them to reach the shelter of an enormous scarred boulder, both men were wet to the skin. Against the roar of the rain—streaming from the firmament, smashing down bushes and grasses, scouring the sides of the bare hills with deep gullies of liquid mud—Ryan heard the sailor's voice.

"Ahoy! Ahoy, ahoy, ahoy," he shouted in in derision, "aye, it was good sport. But bless you, I mean no harm to you, Master. Come now to my bestiary. At least we shall be dry."

Though he feared both for Eckford's sanity and his own safety, Ryan had little choice, for the sailor gripped him by the wrist and pulled him helter-skelter through the streaming rain. They slipped on wet stones, grazed their legs on sharp boulders, but like Mazeppa tied to his horse, Ryan could not let go. They leaped, ran and jumped their way down a narrow ravine and when Ryan was almost at the end of his tether and gasping for breath, the old man relaxed his grip and they stopped before a sheer face of rock about forty feet high. At that moment the rain ceased as sharply and completely as it had begun and there they stood breathless, eyeing each other as they steamed in the reborn sunlight.

"Inside, Master," said the sailor, not unkindly.

Eckford gave Ryan a shove, but as he turned with an angry word on his lips, his outstretched hands felt the adamantine rock before him yield. Soundlessly a rocking boulder moved to one side. He felt Eckford's hand in the small of his back and then he was being guided through a brief passage whose walls streamed with viscid lime. Ryan had a strange sense of powerlessness as he heard the sailor's laugh in the darkness behind him. Yet it seemed a friendly laugh and when, a moment later, they rounded a sharp curve and came into a rocky cirque about a hundred yards in diameter, with a floor of beaten sand, he was too surprised to worry about the expression in his host's face. Had he looked back, he would have found that it was one of self-important triumph rather than of evil intent.

For this was the bestiary. There were cats everywhere: huge grizzled creatures as gnarled and almost as large as a jungle panther. They basked on the sand; they gamboled together in heavy play; they sat licking themselves in the sunshine. Some leaped from branch to branch of a stripped casuarina tree rending the air with mock whines; some sat sedate and mysterious like Egyptian cats of onyx disinterred from some musty tomb; others growled in sinister fashion over a pile of rat carcases in a noisome corner. As soon as the two men entered the compound, Eckford gave a low clear whistle. At once each group of animals ceased its particular activity and made for the sailor in a crowd of purring, whining fur and flesh, tails high, whiskers alert, topaz eyes flashing fire and bonhomie. In a few moments Ryan and the sailor were stranded like two lighthouses in a sea of jostling animals. Ryan was uncertain whether to laugh or remain tense. The situation was grotesque, almost ludicrous, and yet the animals and their unpredictable keeper posed a very real threat to his safety. The old man started to boast.

"What think you of my cats, sir?"

"Well, Eckford, I'll not deny that I'm impressed."

"Aye? Yet these, you may recall, are the animals whose exploits you doubted when I told of them."

"Of course, man, but that was before I had seen them."

The great beasts nuzzled his legs, growling in friendly ferocity. Eckford looked up at the sun. It was reflected from his occluded eyeballs like sheep's eyes in the headlamps of an oncoming car. When he dropped them, his voice was invested, for Ryan, with a note of challenge.

"They are fierce, these beasts."

"I don't doubt it."

"You may not believe that one of them, with a well aimed sweep of its claws, could lay open a man's face?"

"I don't disbelieve it."

"Yet you do not believe it?"

"Yes, Eckford, I find it possible."

They were sparring now for some kind of opening in a context whose purpose and future he could not foresee. The sailor stamped his foot on the ground, and the cats receded, lurking and crouching at a distance.

"My word is their law," said Eckford, with a pride which Ryan would in other circumstances have found ridiculous. "They would spring forward as quickly as they now retire."

Ryan felt his hands tighten and his muscles start to tense. He heard his own voice, artificially calm and pernickety.

"Precisely what do you mean by that?"

The leathery face broke into a hundred wrinkles and the

old man laughed: a theatrical Elizabethan laugh full of fustian and bravado.

"You love my daughter!" he jeered. "You love her? It is well. What price then do you set upon your head? Name it, and I shall consider whether my spies here"—he indicated the jostling cats with a wave of his arm—"will be content."

Ryan was now convinced that he had to deal with a stark eccentric; and he paused, wondering whether he should essay a trial of physical strength with the tough old salt, or whether he should rely on a battle of wits. He had scarcely made up his mind in favor of the latter when a high clear voice cut across the bedlam of feline noises like acid through grease.

"What does this wrangling mean? Down! Quiet, you importunate beasts!"

Ryan saw Margaret stepping lightly down from a narrow defile at the far end of the cirque. She was dressed in a leathern jerkin and skirt; her legs were clad in boots of tough woven rushes; her hair was unbound and her tresses cascaded to her shoulders in a shower of red gold. In her left hand she carried a pistol—one of those same richly chased weapons with which he had seen her the night they first met. She fingered it idly as she advanced toward the two men. Ryan's emotions were mixed: relief, admiration for her poise, shame at her intervention, chased each other through his mind, and as he waited for the girl to approach, he cast a surreptitious glance at Eckford. The old salt seemed to be in a curious state of indecision. As Margaret came toward him, he dropped his eyes almost as if he not only expected but actually feared a rebuke from her. Ryan thought: this man is crumpling under the pressure of a timeless monotony; he can no longer respond to a challenge. But this, he realized, made the old salt doubly dangerous because he might now possess the cunning of the weak.

The cats had dispersed and Margaret, casting a brief, smiling glance at Ryan, walked slowly up to the old man. With great firmness but with infinite tenderness she grasped his shoulders with her hands.

"Father! What is it?"

Eckford leaned toward her as if seeking physical sustenance from her body; as if in a crisis, it was the child and not the father to whom strength had been given and from whom strength flowed; as if, in the challenge to his authority by Ryan, he sought strength in the flesh and blood of that other fearless woman who had died in childbirth centuries before.

"Father, you are not yourself. Get you gone to the bower while Francis and I follow behind." She spoke with great affection but with a ring that brooked no argument.

Eckford nodded obediently and sighed.

" 'Tis well," he said. He turned briefly to Ryan but the clouded eyes were genuinely blank, like fish scales, and no longer throbbing vibrantly behind the translucent curtains.

Eckford walked slowly across the sandy compound to the rock wall at its far end, turned and waved and then went out of their sight. When he had gone, she sighed in her turn.

"Alas!"

"What is it, my beloved?"

"My father means ill to you; I felt it and that is why I came. And yet for all my knowledge of him I cannot reason it. For he must know that though I have a new love in you, him I love and revere always. That is something that can never change."

"Do you think he led me here with evil intent?"

"I am sure of it. These animals of his—marvelous messengers though they be—would tear a man to pieces at his word."

"Then I should count myself lucky."

She slid her arm through his and walked him slowly over towards the exit through the rocky ravine.

"Yes indeed," she said very seriously, her great gray eyes full of apprehension. "He is jealous and might perhaps have harmed you."

"And you have saved me. I owe my safety—perhaps my life . . ."

"Nay, not your life. To think thus were to think too curiously."

"Well at any rate my safety—to you."

She squeezed his hand. "It is a small thing." She turned, he with her, and they looked down for the last time on the strange training ground for the voracious cats over which Eckford had ruled for so many decades. Margaret was pensive.

"I fear for you, Francis. I must keep watch with these sightless eyes of mine lest you be taken from me."

"That will never happen," said Ryan evenly. The knife, the pistol; there might be other uses.

But she remained silent all the way back to their home by the lake and silent during the night, while Arcturus shone pale and cold out of a rain-washed sky and the old man in his sleep grumbled and muttered in the hut fifty yards behind them. Was this the rift in the lute of his happiness? It seemed too external, too circumstantial. As long as his love for Margaret and hers for him ran deep, what did the sailor matter? Yet he felt a twinge of uneasiness and when during the night he awoke to see the stars pale before the lime green of approaching dawn he realized that though he was safe, he owed his safety to the intercession of a woman. He reflected that were he not so much in love, he would regard that as a somewhat degrading circumstance.

As the pre-dawn wind scudded across the pewter lake he found himself, for the first time since he had discovered the green crater, wondering a little about the future, and about his relationship with the father of the woman who was now his wife.

· 19 ·

THE cyclops eye of the sun swept high over the battlemented tors of Elizabeth Island, and discovered in the midst of the cindery waste the green slopes and the limpid elliptical lake. The harsh light which could spell a scabrous death to sailors adrift on a raft in the Pacific, no more than gilded the surface of the little lake; for at six thousand feet the sun's rays are cooled by the whispering winds of the trades. At the southern end of the lake the hot springs boiled and bubbled, sending their trails of white vapor scudding seaward. Seen from an immense height the whole island revealed itself for what it was: a series of extinct volcanoes grouped round a tall dormant volcano. The hot springs could then be seen as a surge of steam rushing from the safety valve of an immense boiler whose unbanked fires roared and trembled deep inside the earth. From this height one might imagine the whole world shuddering like the walls of a giant powerhouse, and kept from exploding only by the slender spout of steam wafted seaward from the mountain top.

It was on one of many such days that Ryan, now completely engrossed with Margaret, followed her from the rustic hut at the edge of the lake towards the springs. They were bound for a fresh supply of the life-giving water to be siphoned off carefully from the glistening rock walls which hemmed in the gushing jets of steam. Then they would collect the condensed water in gourds and carry it back to the bower where it was buried in a small cellar beneath a trapdoor covered with a mat of woven grasses. Ryan was alert and expectant, for in addition to the acute pleasure which her company always gave him, she had promised today to show him what she called the "secret of the springs." As he stepped along behind her on the narrow mountain path, watching the swaying music of her walk, he was astonished at the distance he had come both in time and space since that day—so many years ago, it seemed—when he had landed on the island.

They lived now together as man and wife in the rustic hut and her blindness never troubled either of them. Centuries of deft motion in her circumscribed world had made her sure and delicate in her movements; while for him the magic of love would have blotted out deformities or deficiencies far worse than this. The great gray eyes seemed to him full of love, and when they turned upward to him—as they so often did—it was impossible for him not to feel the thrill and sparkle of the desire that lay behind the cloudy orbs, and in the body whose shuttered windows they were.

Ryan was now deliberately shut into his own new world. He lived from day to day and from sensation to sensation. Happy in the adoring worship of a woman who seemed to him perfect in both mind and body, the vain regrets which he had felt earlier at the shackling of his creative spirit were now numbed and dulled. He saw in Eckford, despite his doubts, all the bluff male companionship which he might need; and as for imaginative and intellectual pursuits, he had begun to scorn them. At first he had been unhappy about this, for to the vanity of the male the marriage bed and the production of children rank as experiences common to all men. It is in the intellect and the imagination that a man fully realizes himself and that he lives through the praise of after ages. But it takes a most exceptional man to resist the adoring flattery of a beautiful woman, and Ryan was not one of these. Indeed, propinquity had undermined whatever purpose he might once have had; and in any case did not Margaret have for him much more than mere physical attraction? Was she not for him something more than the external symbol of man's inner guilt?

She had taught him history. With her he had relived the thrills of the great morning of the Renaissance; had breathed the fresh salt air with those of the *Golden Hind* who, for all they knew, were to sail off the edge of the world into space. He had learned from her the strange terrors, the bittersweet memories, and the delicious anticipations of her mother who had shipped before the mast disguised as a man: her breasts tightly swathed in muslin, her waist padded and her nimble feet clad in heavy leather boots. He had learned, too, something of the toughness and cold inhumanity which possesses a girl who, at the age of twenty, has seen men keelhauled, impaled on cutlasses and disemboweled.

Margaret had heard tell of all these things; yet in her long life—her incredibly long life—she had also learned all the feminine crafts and accomplishments that she could coax from the island. She wove and plaited the grasses and ferns, and even the wool from the cats' fur into mats, curtains and covers for the chairs and tables. She it was who, with Eckford's help, had constructed the funnels to catch the water as it condensed off the rock walls from the jets of steam. She had made the pipes of pan with which she entertained him as the night was in its first youth. She had designed and painted the earthenware jugs and tankards; had made sweet-smelling unguents from the herbs of the crater; turned into a score or more of tasty dishes the fruits of the English trees which Eckford had so carefully planted and tended.

Only one thing puzzled him about her immense and unceasing industry; the sense of the eternal passage of time. How could she, so vital and alert, so aware of the poignancy of the fleeting moment, how could she not have had her senses dulled by the knowledge that eternity lay before her? Could the desire for suicide be withstood, and why had she and Eckford never made an attempt to escape from the island? How had she remained inviolate throughout the long centuries while time stood still and the bloom of youth lay eternally soft on her cheek?

The answers to some of these questions came slowly, as time went by, from her own lips.

"Time in your sense has long ceased to exist for me," she said, "and for my father also. God was kind to me, for it was many scores of years after drinking the waters that I became blind. And during those years, my sense of the passing of time changed. At the beginning a day seemed to me as it now does to you: tedious if I were out of humor, joyous if I were in humor, but a day. Soon though, a day and a night became to me as no more than the flapping of a dove's wing, and the passage of the sun through the arc of the heavens no more than a bright splash of saffron on the blue: and a year was gone."

" 'A thousand ages in Thy sight are like an evening gone.' "

"What words are those?"

"The words of a priest who lived long ago, though after your time to be sure, beloved."

"Of whom did he speak? In whose sight?"

"The sight of God."

"No, Francis, that is not right. We should not be compared to gods, my father and I, for we are not immortal."

"But the springs gave you eternal life."

"The springs kept us eternally youthful, but they did not cure us of disease. Those we cured with herbs and with rest. And they could not cure us of accident. We are lucky not to have been bruised or broken by the rocks; and, my beloved, in the days when we were going blind, that was a hazard always before us."

Her lovely gray eyes became subtly softer and more faraway as she saw in her mind's eye the hazards of two centuries ago.

"Did you never become exhausted and bored with life?" he asked. "Did you not sometimes *wish* to kill yourself to escape from an eternity of barren years on an empty island?"

"Oh, Francis, how little you understand me. For me life was vivid and wonderful. The waters filled me—as they have filled you—with a tremendous desire to live. And when the days turn to minutes, and years to days, the passage of time is forgotten. The visit of the islander, which you say, according to your reckoning, took place in 1653, seems only yesterday to me. My father marked the years by carving on the rocks, but for me life has been one glorious afternoon. Once though, I did try to escape."

"When was that, beloved?"

"It was before I became blind, but when the vapors were already starting to swim before my eyes. I began to think that the island was the cause of my loss of sight, as indeed it was, though in a way which I did not comprehend. My father built me a boat out of the hollowed logs of a candle-nut tree, lashed together with the tendrils of the liana vine. I tried to escape."

"But the reef would have smashed you to pieces."

"Of course. My father stopped me. He was even more blind than I was, but I could not keep the secret from him. He raced down to the shore after me and sprang into the water as I paddled across the lagoon. He caught me as I was nearing the white water. But not before a shark caught him."

"Poor devil."

"It was a horrible sight. He cried out and great streams of blood stained the green lagoon. But I rammed my paddle into the mouth of the shark and then I towed the canoe, with my poor father clinging to it, to the shore."

"You are brave as well as beautiful."

"I had no time to think. It was all over in perhaps ten minutes, and I was on the beach and dragging my father with his bloody torn leg up the sand like a wounded beast."

She spoke in a low whisper, but Ryan felt little beads of sweat start from his forehead, and for a moment it seemed as if he were tied to a Medusa, to a Lady Macbeth, rather than to Atalanta or Venus. She had stopped speaking and turned to him, in a gorgeously feminine appeal.

"Ah Francis, do not make me speak of it. It is two hundred

years behind us now, and I had rather not remember. Will you forget, with me?" Then she rose and stood up strong and straight in the moonlight, a perfect figure of mature womanhood at its apex.

Now, walking behind her along the mountain path, he was unwillingly reminded by her lithe swinging, masculine gait of her steely strength as well as her womanliness.

The fragrant undergrowth, dripping with the morning dew, thinned as they neared the crest of the sloping green crater. A moment later, as the path turned and ran along the rim of the *caldera,* he saw once more the strange cindery land lying between his paradise and the edge of the rocky tors that dipped steeply to the small coastal plain and the sea beyond. As she reached the lip of the crater, she beckoned to him.

"You see yonder crag?" She pointed to a steep jagged rock that rose on the near side of the great vaporous plume. "There lies our secret. Follow me."

They slid and slithered along a narrow track down the seaward side of the crater. Soon the feathery greenness that lipped it was all that remained of their private world and they tramped across a hundred yards or so of charred rock, and congealed lava. Ryan seemed to feel the ground tremble beneath his feet. As they neared the other side of this desolate inferno, the jagged rock above them loomed large and sulphurous red, in violent contrast to the black and ash-gray landscape at its feet. They were now in the shadow of the white drifting plume and great banners of steam scudded between them and the sun. A fine spray, falling on the congealed lava and stone, made walking precarious. Gusts of wind blew the spray in Ryan's face, and as he followed Margaret, he marveled at her sure-footed grace. They picked their way—she leaping lightly, he stumbling and slipping—right to the very base of the rock. Here the spray fell like rain and the noise of the gushing steam was the hiss and roar of locomotives.

Ryan kept his eyes on the treacherous rocks, seeking to find a firm foothold. When he lifted them he had a moment of panic; for amid the roar and hiss of the great steam cloud, Margaret had vanished. He came to an abrupt halt, and his heart almost stopped beating, as he imagined her sucked to her death in that steaming cauldron; but a moment later the silvery music of her laugh cut through the rumble of the great vents. Looking up, he saw her waving a honey-colored arm—as it appeared, incredibly—from a slit in the rock almost directly above his head. He took five steps forward and the mystery was solved. Easing his body through a narrow cranny in the rock he found himself at the foot of a rough natural stairway leading into the center of the rock itself. It curved upward steeply in a sudden silence. Taking a 180-degree turn in semi-darkness irradiated by a strong smell of lime, he caught up with Margaret who was leaning on a small slit in the rock, which seemed much like an ogive window in the circular staircase of a Norman keep. She put her hand in his, and led him upward into the curving darkness. As they mounted, he became aware of a muffled roaring, and of a shuddering and clanking as of a bank of high-speed dynamos in an enormous generating station. The sound reminded him of the titanic roar of controlled power which had assaulted his ears when, as a boy, he had visited the great power stations on the Niagara River.

They ascended in narrower circles. The path became steeper, the noise more stentorian. All he could feel in the pitch blackness now was the firm clasp of Margaret's hand

and her slow but steady upward pull. Then the darkness was suffused with a faint greenish light. The pressure of Margaret's hand seemed to be pushing him back; he felt her firm warm body close to his, and as his eyes became accustomed to the roaring gloom, he saw that they were standing together on the slippery edge of a gulf whose appalling depths he could only guess at. Roaring past them at incredible speed mixed steam and water surged upward from the very marrow of the world. As he peered forward, he could feel the hot breath of the earth's molten center searing his face. He leaned backward against the damp walls of the rocky niche in which they stood. At once the trembling and shuddering of the earth were transferred from the rock to his own spine, and thence through his arm and hand to that of Margaret. She motioned to him to descend.

Turning his back on the raging inferno of steam and heat, he picked his way carefully down the steps and out of the slit in the rock into the daylight shining on the congealed landscape of the burnt-out crater. Here she took the lead. Wordlessly, they retraced the same path which they had trod an hour earlier, climbed the slopes of the *caldera*, grasped at the fragrant greenery on its lip and threw themselves exhausted on the flower-strewn meadow of their own little Eden. It was not until then, with the roar of the steam vents a dim memory, and with their view confined to their familiar world of lake and grass, tree and flower, that either spoke. It was Ryan who broke the silence.

"What a terrifying cauldron!"

Her gray eyes shone behind their dusky curtains.

"When first I went there I had my sight, even as you have now. I was rooted to the staircase with fear, and yet my fear had in it something both of awe and of excitement."

"What first made you go there?"

"The islander told us of a god living in the slits of the high rocks, a god who roared his anger at the world, and who spat in the face of the sun. He told also of another strange legend among his people." Her voice held a curious unresolved note, and Ryan pressed her.

"May I hear of it?"

"You may not wish to," was her enigmatic reply; but he laughed.

"More conundrums, Margaret?"

"Very well then, I will tell you. The legend said that if those great vents were ever to be stopped—even for an instant—the earth itself would explode."

"And that is your secret? The secret of the cave?"

"That is my secret. Do you not find it worth knowing?"

Now her tone chilled him and he asked: "Why? Why is that worth knowing?"

"Listen, beloved, if that vent were to be stopped even for an instant, even by someone's flesh . . ."

"What do you mean?" he asked her almost roughly. But she said in measured tones, "If I should ever lose you, Francis, my life would be useless to me."

"Useless? What nonsense! What folly is this?"

"I am with child."

His vague unease shifted to a wan tenderness. He lifted her chin and she turned toward him with an indefinable expression on her lips of mingled coquetry and shyness. Then she rose, pulling him upward with her.

As they stood in close embrace, a sound, at first no more than the distant buzz of a bee on a summer afternoon, slowly obtruded itself on Ryan's consciousness. Reluctantly he raised his head. At once every nerve was alive with tingling alarm.

The girl in his arms now raised her own head; she too had caught the sound, the faint insistent throbbing drone. His alarm became hers.

"Francis! What is that?"

But he remained rigid and deaf, his arms locked tightly about her. He was striving to hear, and yet not to hear, the sound which would have meant rescue and relief, but which could now mean only the end of his happiness, poignant in its briefness. An airplane.

· 20 ·

THE Admiral had the search party airborne out of Rotifanga at first light. This was unfortunate for Tom Griffith, who had spent the previous evening carousing with the press to expiate his failure to obtain accreditation on the final expedition for more than three of its members: the AP man, one correspondent for the radio networks and one cameraman with a couple of hand-held Eyemos for the newsreel pool. He had tried. Spurred and jabbed by the press he had tried very hard; but the Admiral used the shortage of plane seats to reinforce his natural aversion to newspapermen (though not to publicity) and in the end the best that Griffith could do, with a lot of pleading, was the three seats. However, they knew he had tried, and because he had done his best they joined him in a farewell party at the community hutments, with the co-operation and indeed the splendid availability of the cellars of their French allies and hosts. Griffith lurched home a little before half past two, knowing they had to be airborne in three hours.

Now with the bustle and excitement of the departure behind him, he looked down through the port of the plane that was carrying him; down past the trailing edge of the big flying boat's wings; past the jet pods, hanging like giant chrysalises, down, down sixteen thousand feet to an ocean ruffled as faintly as a bird's wing by an evening zephyr: looked and felt good. His big plane was mothered by an aircraft carrier that dragged along far behind them now at a steady thirty knots, leaving a trail of white spume in the blue-black ink of the Southeast Pacific. The Admiral had decided to send the big flying boat, with its maximum range, direct to the point where, so he judged from the scanty information at his disposal, the target lay. Should it fail to find any island, the plane was to start cruising in target areas A-left and A-right, keeping in constant radio contact with the carrier. Should the flying boat sight the island, it would anchor in a convenient roadstead, if one existed. The plan depended on the weather. A high pressure area with winds of a maximum of force 3 and long easy ocean swells had been predicted for the next seventy-two hours. This was important, for though the flying boat could manage the estimated 1800 miles in perhaps six hours, it would take the aircraft carrier at least two days and three nights at full steam. The Admiral had therefore sent the ship out forty-eight hours ahead of the big flying boat.

Griffith's plane had come abreast of the aircraft carrier about fifteen minutes earlier. At first she was nothing but a smudge of smoke on the horizon, which from their height was about eighty miles away, and looked as curved as the moon seen through a telescope. Then, as they crept up on it, the ship became the narrow spearhead of a trailing lance of foam. Looking down through his glasses Griffith saw that it was lifting at the bows as if a moderate sea were running. He walked up to the front of the big plane and checked with the navigator. Latitude 34°52′ South, longitude 105°42′ West. They were getting down towards the roaring forties, and he wondered if the disturbance of the sea was due to this. The navigator shook his head in pitying but good-natured contempt. Griffith wandered back to his seat, picked up his glasses and searched again for the carrier. To his surprise he found it miles astern. Then he remembered that the plane was traveling at ten times the speed of the ship and wondered no longer. The plane was probably not much over an hour away from the island now: that is if they were on course, if the course was correct, and if all the information given them by the original sighting plane was reliable. Tired of looking at the sea, Griffith put down his glasses, closed his eyes and mused awhile.

As he dozed in the drone of the great plane, he realized it was the front seat at a new adventure. Griffith's nature was prosaic, but the possibility of finding some remote and undiscovered island, of being perhaps the first pair of eyes to see it since the dawn of time, held for him a strong and sudden fascination. He found himself dimly remembering the books about islands which he had read as a boy; how he had lain curled up on an old camp bed in the attic for hours, reading *The Swiss Family Robinson,* while his mother searched for him in vain to do the household chores. There was *Coral Island* too. He couldn't remember the number of times he had followed Jack, Ralph and Peterkin on their adventures with wild boars, sudden squalls in a skiff, cannibals and pirates. Or *The Lonely Island,* with the sad and savage tale of the mutineers of the *Bounty* and how they had loomed out of the sea on Pitcairn Island and planted their flag on Adam's Peak. So lonely: perhaps as lonely as the island they were trying to find. Perhaps as nonexistent, save in the world of romance and fiction.

His barrel-chested body slumped deeper into the bucket seat, and his thickening, slightly petulant leathern face relaxed and softened as he dredged up from the sluggish curds of a mind unused to reverie, the images of boyhood. The camp bed in the attic creaked as he shifted his position on it. From the rafters and the roof shingles came a hot musty smell, stale yet exciting. Perhaps behind the disused highboy a pirate lurked. The broken washstand with its china ewer and basin made a wonderful cave for Jack, Ralph and Peterkin. The old tin cabin-trunk, its sides a kaleidoscope of faded labels, was full to bursting of treasure trove: doubloons, louis d'or, gold mohurs, pieces of eight. From the street outside came the faint noise of children playing beneath the deep pools of violet shade cast by the maples; the sun threw a slowly moving gold bar on the attic floor as it shifted through the hot, lazy, endless afternoon of boyhood.

He was jerked upright by a shout on the intercom. "Well, here we are. Where the hell's this island of yours?"

It was the pilot. As he waited for the navigator's reply, Griffith looked below him. Ocean. Nothing but the featureless face of the empty Pacific. He heard the navigator's laconic reply.

"This is 35°16′ South and 105°23′ West. No land in sight."

"Commencing eastward sweep A plus One."

He saw the horizon tip beneath the trailing edge of the wing and felt the side of his seat press against him as the plane started to bank. Griffith's stolid stomach tingled at the pit with boyish excitement. He moved up to the front of the plane, past the dozing forms of the marine landing party, and sneaked into the vacant space behind the navigator's seat. The navigator looked up at him with marked distaste and the copilot mouthed, against the overwhelming roar of the great craft, something that looked very like: "Get the hell out: we're busy." Griffith gave him a bar of candy and settled down in the tiny bucket seat behind him. The copilot shrugged his shoulders and returned his gaze to the bewildering array of dials and indicators before him. Griffith inserted a wad of gum in his cheek and sat munching contentedly, looking out at the immensely increased horizon which the curving perspex revealed. He had never seen so much sea and, he mentally noted, didn't care if he never saw it again, at least in such volume. The droning plane was suspended in a bowl of light blue vapor above a circular horizon of endless cobalt. From this height not a streak broke its even immensity save for a faint deepening of the blue where some cold current welled up from the abyss. Griffith kept his eye roving in a 180-degree arc through the perspex, as if he would conjure the island from the sea by the sheer intensity of his gaze. The plane droned on headed due east along the base of the arc. Twenty minutes went by. Griffith got tired of looking, leaned back, curled himself over on his left side, pulled his cap down over his eyes and prepared to doze.

Then, out of the extreme corner of his left eye—almost over his left shoulder—he caught a glimpse of something that jerked him wide awake. He grabbed the collar of the navigator's shirt and shook him vigorously. The airman turned round with a snarl, but when he saw Griffith's face, it modified to a frown. Griffith leaned down to the man's ear and shouted:

"By God, this is it. Take a look over your left shoulder. About five o'clock." As he shouted he pointed, and both men turned their eyes and craned their necks toward the northwest.

Rising like sentinels out of the ocean, and looking twice their height because of the extreme unexpectedness, were two purple cones of land, the lower to the west, the higher to the east. From the higher, a plume of whitish-gray vapor trailed towards them through the empty sky. The cones looked purply and mysterious in the afternoon light. At this distance it was impossible to tell whether they were rock or earth or forested. The navigator nodded excitedly and touched the pilot's shoulder. He looked up wide-eyed. He had expected, like his colleagues, to hit the island head on from the north and was disconcerted at finding it off his port quarter, and almost astern. Another fifteen minutes and we'd have lost it, he thought. By now the navigator had spotted the island and was plotting a fresh course.

The plane swung and banked in a wide arc of almost 140 degrees, so that it was on a course approximately northwest by north. The island now lay directly ahead. Word had spread throughout the plane and the doorway from the fuselage into the pilot's cabin was crowded with curious sailors and marines, peering to get a first look at the object of their search. Approached from the southeast, the island's two cones at first stood out in startling isolation, joined by their narrow neck of land. But as the plane drew nearer, the larger of the cones, which Griffith estimated at roughly six thousand feet in height, began to obscure the smaller, save for a small narrow spit of land which projected into the sea like a curving sword. They came closer and Griffith heard over the intercom the pilot signaling the carrier and receiving instructions to come in low for a reconnaissance.

The island now stood dead ahead and a little below the oncoming plane at a distance of perhaps eight miles. It filled over a quarter of the horizon. Griffith looked down with absorbed interest as the battlements of the larger cone, and its trail of white vapor, came steadily nearer. So this was the island no one had ever discovered? This was—conceivably—where Ryan and the scientists had fetched up? Impossible. Their plane had gone into the drink. Ryan and the others were dead; they must be. The island was at least 370 miles, even according to Griffith's rough calculations, from the place where the plane was supposed to have ditched. Supposed to have ditched? Yes that was it. But no one really knew where. He thought of Ruth and the old flame flickered unwillingly to life. He wondered what she was doing; who she was with. She's probably with nobody, he thought; those last farewell words on the porch had rung true.

The plane was almost on top of the nearer cone and banking to begin its circuit of the island. Griffith scrambled over to the perspex to get a better view. The plane swept in above the shallowing water that shaded from cobalt to green and then to white. They were across the fringing reef of coral where the white waves boiled, and skirting the slopes of a typical "high" island. He saw the plane's shadow rippling and bubbling on thick forest vegetation. Over on the starboard beam a smaller barren island shot momentarily into view, fringed on the seaward side by the reef and on the landward side by the yellowish-green water of a wide lagoon.

Now the plane was flying close to the rock turrets and

about a thousand feet above them. He got out his glasses. The forested slopes shuddered abruptly to a stop: the rocky minarets shot by. Then Griffith saw the interior of the crater, a region of gray-black ash and rock. He gave an exclamation and the copilot heard him over the roar of the plane and looked down. Within the large crater was a smaller one, its inward edges covered with vivid green and at its bottom a tiny lake. He saw the copilot's lips forming a "Well, whaddya know?" and he raked the green slopes and the lake with his glasses. There was no sign of human habitation, unless it was a path, which might be a goat path, threading through the trees. The green of the inward slopes looked unhealthy to him, a sort of chemical metallic green, and the lake like a dull plate of pewter. The plane swept on. He raised his glasses to the rapidly disappearing trail of vapor. Seen in magnification it looked like jets of steam, escaping from an immense cauldron. A pretty powerful force, he thought, driving that steam up from inside the earth. He wondered when the island had last erupted, but since he was no seismologist, the blackened crater and the *caldera* yielded him no clue.

The land slipped away and the plane flew above a narrow isthmus joining the two unequal cones. It looked low and sandy as if it had been built up in fairly recent times. Then the land curved away to the north again, rose to a modest wooded height of a couple of thousand feet and opened up into a little elliptically shaped landlocked bay. Griffith beckoned to some of the landing party to come closer and get a better view. Navigator and pilot were interested too and started the great machine circling at half throttle over the bay, while expert eyes gauged its suitability as a seaplane anchorage. Griffith judged the bay was about a mile deep and from half to three quarters of a mile across: but its neck was extremely narrow, not more than perhaps a hundred yards. Then it opened out into the main lagoon and dead opposite was a passage through the barrier reef; but much narrower, perhaps less than thirty yards across. A skillful pilot, he reckoned, could set the plane down on the bay and there, completely sheltered from wind and gale by sloping wooded hills two thousand feet high, could safely ride out any storm. But it would take a very skillful pilot indeed to get the plane airborne, particularly if it were fully loaded. To make things tougher, the bay curved slightly which meant that a pilot would have to gun the plane on a curving course, and unless he was airborne before he reached the narrow channel, he would stand a good chance of being swung toward one point or the other by ocean winds blowing across its mouth. Quite a problem, Griffith thought. The Marine next him bellowed in his ears. "Dinky little harbor, but what the hell's that on the shore? Do you see what I see, sir?"

Griffith gave a dazed nod. Like the marine, he too had seen, on the broad crescent beach near the harbor, an incredible sign drawn in the sand.

Having circumnavigated the island and examined the harbor the pilot veered off to northward while the radio officer sought instructions from the mother ship. The carrier told the craft to rendezvous at its side at a point about one hundred and eighty-five miles north-northwest of the island and to come down and tie up. The seas, it repeated, were almost flat calm with only the long, slow, even ocean swell. They would consider making a landing and perhaps a reconnaissance in force the next day. The carrier noted that the plane had observed no signs of life on the island.

Dusk was falling as the plane headed north to rendezvous with the carrier. The navigator had drawn a rough map of the island as they passed over it and Griffith leaned across his shoulder to take a look. The island looked rather like a caricature of a cockatoo; the main volcano a stubby body, the landlocked harbor a beak and the long sandspit the comb. A bit like Walt Disney's Joe Carioca. A couple of Marines nodded agreement. The plane droned on into the soft evening sky and the men returned to their accustomed seats. Griffith strolled back to the rear perspex bubble between the giant tail fins, to take a last look at the island through his glasses. The beach would have vanished, but perhaps there might be other signs.

The island was already about six miles astern when he took up position in the rear-gunner's seat. The cones were reversed now; the large one on his left and the smaller on his right. Even from this distance the cloud of vapor stood out from the peak, like a tuft of pink cotton-wool in the after-glow flying from the top of a purple tower. Suddenly he sat upright, focusing his glasses with extreme care. A faint light was blinking high up in the rocky fastnesses of the larger cone. It flickered on and off like a firefly in the gloaming of the tropical night and Griffith sat glued to his seat trying to make some kind of mechanical rhythm or identifiable code out of the light. But even with the aid of glasses he was unable to do so, and with each minute the plane drew further away and the light more dim.

He dashed back up to the fuselage, got hold of the sergeant of marines in charge of the landing detail and whispered excitedly:

"There's a light sending signals on the island. Come back and help me identify them."

The burly leatherneck raised incredulous eyebrows, but heaved himself up out of his seat and lumbered back with Griffith toward the tail. Together the two men crouched on the gunner's seat, their faces close up against the perspex. Griffith was tense with excitement. They waited for the light.

But no light came. They sat there until the two cones of the island were dark blots on the fading horizon; until the smaller cone, and finally the larger cone vanished beneath it. When nothing was left but sea and sky, the big marine turned a ruminative eye in Griffith's direction, his unspoken question shouting as loud as a parade-ground command. Griffith felt himself coloring.

"I tell you, sergeant, I saw it as plain as the nose on your face."

"Yes, sir?"

"A small yellow light—high up on the big mountain, blinking—fitfully—but in some kind of code."

"Yes, sir?"

"As if some guy was trying to signal us." He realized he did not sound very convincing. The sergeant cleared his throat.

"Do you think there's folks on the island, sir?" His voice held a polite irony.

Griffith shut his lips, then opened them.

"Yes sergeant, I do, and I shall so report to the Admiral."

"Okay sir," he replied, as who should say: The poor guy's nuts.

But Griffith was certain that the light he had seen had a human origin and his heart beat just a little faster. What a story it would make: what a scoop! What a feather in the cap of Lieutenant Commander Tom Griffith, U.S.N.

· 21 ·

RYAN'S grip on the girl remained rigid and unrelaxed. Out of the void of the sky the insistent drone seemed to be pointing at him like a poised sword. Now it was a sharp distinct buzz like the bitter acuteness of pain when it is first felt. But as the machine approached, its droning rumble began to fill the air and flood the senses like the throbbing assault of pain when it has flowed through all the chambers of the body. The sun dipped below the crater edge and the cool evening air seemed chill and comfortless.

Margaret's cloudy gray eyes were full of wonder, but not of terror or alarm. She shook him by the arm.

"Francis, what is it? What is that sound? Why are you so stiff and silent?"

"It is the flying machine I told you of."

"Is it coming here?"

"I'm afraid so."

"But why are you afraid?" Her lips were parted in eager excitement. "May it not come with some of your people?"

"That is what I am afraid of."

"I do not understand."

"Listen, my darling, how can I explain to you what contact with my world would mean? If this machine comes, then men of my world have discovered this island. It would be only a matter of days, perhaps even hours, before they make a full-scale landing, perhaps a military landing and take the island as their own."

"But the island belongs to me. They can do nothing without my permission."

"I wish that were true, best beloved. But this is not the sixteenth century or even the middle of the nineteenth, when the queen of an island might hope to bargain with a foreign invader. If this is a machine bringing men from my country, or from the United States or Britain or France, they will land first and ask questions afterwards."

"The cats will stop them!"

"My dearest, if they encounter the slightest opposition, there could be machine guns, perhaps even flame throwers; all sorts of ghastly devices of which you have no conception." He paused. "But I don't think they will act in this way."

"But why?"

"Because, if they are my people, they may be looking for me."

"Oh Francis!" She whitened. "Will they take you away from me?"

He pursed his lips grimly.

"Not if I can stop it. Oh, they would be quite polite to you too, darling, don't worry about that. But you'd be absolutely powerless. They would never leave the island alone again."

She nodded, as if dimly comprehending.

The sound of the plane was now loud and throaty. It filled the southeast quadrant of the sky and already they were having to raise their voices to speak against it. To Ryan the noise sounded at once familiar and menacing. But on the girl, to whom the sound was entirely new, it was still producing an effect of excitement, though mingled with a certain amount of apprehension. She stood looking upward with eyes, nose and mouth twitching and on the alert. Then as the oncoming plane changed course, its sound was caught by a gust of wind and ricocheted off the stony crags. The throaty bay became a sullen, ringing, metallic roar. Suddenly she spoke.

"Francis, I do not like that noise. It seems to me evil."

He nodded. "It is evil. Far more evil than you can ever know."

He paused for a moment, sensing the plane's distance and direction. It was nearing all the time, but it was hidden from them by the high tors and the stream of vapor from their summit. It could not be more than five miles off now and judging by the sound it was at least a four-motor job, and flying low. He was prepared to bet that a four-motor job would be either United States, Canadian or British, but he was determined not to be seen when the chance came to verify his judgment. He was thankful for the westering sun and the oncoming dusk, but he knew that those in the plane would have glasses, and that on the green lawn-like slope Margaret and himself would be pinned like two butterflies on a baize cloth. He grasped her firmly by the arm:

"You don't want them to see us?"

"No Francis. Heaven forbid. I am frightened. I—I . . ." For the second time since he had known her, tears came to her eyes.

"I wish I could see!"

Without a word he picked her up in his arms and ran, traversing the slope to a little wood of rhododendrons. Here they lay on their backs, side by side, while he peered upward through the leafy canopy. The noise grew deafening, and she gripped his left arm with both hands in something close to real terror. A moment later he saw it.

It swept out from behind the tors roaring like the last trump and seeming to cover half the sky with its vast wingspread. It was scarcely five hundred feet above them and flying fairly slowly, not much more than two hundred miles an hour he estimated. He could feel the girl trembling at his side, but in the few seconds that the enormous craft was overhead, his powers of observation, schooled to function under stress, performed at their smooth and competent best. He saw four piston engines, and two turbo-prop—a typical B 64 flying boat. He saw the huge five-pointed white stars beneath the silver-gray wing, and as the tail fin shot by, the radar antennae and even, he fancied, someone looking out through the perspex. A United States Navy plane, and a flying boat. That might or might not argue a carrier—those big aircraft could come down in calm seas by themselves—but on the whole, he thought, a carrier. Yes definitely a carrier, for any kind of reconnaissance of the island was bound to involve supplies, communications and possibly transport.

The great plane was now heading toward the smaller cone and the area of his first primitive camp. The girl had stopped trembling and was sitting up staring sightlessly before her, her hands pressed to her ears. He wanted to stand up and shake his fist at the great blundering, cumbrous man-made bird: his-made bird, the symbol of his own civilization which he had renounced. With the clairvoyance of desperation, he saw the train of events: a landing on the island, the discovery of their idyllic quarters and the horse-laughs and catcalls of the irreverent navy; himself recalled to make a report; Margaret exposed to strange ways and possibly to grosser familiarities; bulldozers and "off limits" signs; empty Klim tins and Coke bottles. He saw it all. He had built himself a new life; he had made the fairy boyhood dream come literally true. to live happily ever after. It was within his grasp. Now he knew he had been living behind a paper hoop which this flying spearhead of civilization had shattered in a single uncaring thrust.

Margaret spoke in a low tense voice, recalling him from his reverie.

"Francis, I am afraid. That is a hateful, terrifying noise, and still it goes on."

He patted her arm, but was abstracted and did not immediately answer her. The plane was about four miles off now and seemed to be making a leisurely circuit of the smaller hill beyond his camp. He wondered if it would come back, but dusk was gathering fast, the plane had its lights on, and he scarcely thought it would return. Perhaps it would never return. His heart surged with joy. The plane had soared over the island at two hundred miles an hour and he was certain they had not been seen. He was equally certain, from his knowledge of the position of the hut and other works of human hands, that these too had not been seen.

"Take me back to the bower, Francis."

"Yes, darling, I . . ." A sudden thought smote him. Where

was Eckford? Supposing he had been seen? Supposing he had wished to be seen? He jumped to his feet.

"Darling, can you find your own way to the bower?"

"Of course, but . . ." she looked startled.

"I want to find your father. The aircraft may have seen him."

She gave a low cry. "Oh, I hope not."

He swallowed. "I must go. You understand, don't you?"

"Yes."

"I shan't be long."

"Meet me in the bower, dearest."

"I shall. Try not to be anxious."

He leaped down the path, whisked through the rhododendron bushes and between a couple of small deodars at the edge of the lake, and ran as fast as he could along the green sward beside the water till he came to the hut. He shouted, "Eckford! Sailor Eckford!" several times but received no reply. The table was set for the evening meal, and as he entered, two cats jumped to the floor and scurried out the door. Nearby on the fire, fish was frying in a skillet. Eckford could not be far off. Ryan paused to look and listen for the airplane. It had completed its circuit now, and, having seen all it wanted, was flying leisurely away to the north like a great raven in the dusky gloom.

He left the hut by the sloping path that led to the precipice over which they threw their refuse. Some unexplained instinct made him tread warily and cease his cries as he peered over its lip. Squatting on his haunches was Eckford, his back toward him. In one hand he held aloft a great flaring torch of faggots dipped in the pitch of the blackened *caldera*. In the other he held a large wooden bowl, and alternately covered and uncovered the torch with a sweeping irregular motion.

Ryan paused a moment then raced down the path. Eckford heard him come and turned with a crooked grin, but before he could speak, Ryan burst out hotly:

"Eckford! What the devil do you think you're doing?"

There was no mistaking the anger in Ryan's voice and the old sailor reacted sharply. In a voice heavy with sullen resistance, he said: "Signaling. That's what."

"You damned fool. D'you want them to know there are people on the island?" He stood panting with his fists clenched at his side. The sailor felt the atmosphere and his hand went up to his leathern jerkin. Ryan wondered if he had a knife there. But the sailor was between him and the precipice. The drone of the plane became fainter in the night sky. He decided to adopt a more conciliatory line.

"Listen, Eckford. Do you want this life of ours to go on, or don't you?"

The sailor spat on the ground. "It's right enough for you," he said.

"And not for you, after all these years?"

"If I had a woman to share my bed, perhaps I should feel the same, my fine young buck. But I lack one and I want now the company of men."

"Men? Aren't we three enough?"

"I said men. Men of Devon."

There was no mistaking the slur; but Ryan chose to ignore it. He tried another tack.

"You're blind, Eckford. You'd be prepared to wander in a world whose ways you don't know? And what about the magic waters: how would you take them?"

Eckford looked up at him in the half light. There was on his bearded face an expression of sharp ferocity.

"I don't care if I die," he snarled. "I've lived long enough. I wish for the company of my fellows and I'm going to get what I want."

Ryan looked down at the man who now stood between him and happiness. He felt rather desperate.

"What do you want?"

"No interference, Master."

"Did you signal the plane?"

"I did."

"You know what that means? The plane will come back—maybe with a ship and men."

"That's what I want."

"It's not what I want, and it's not what Margaret wants. That plane's not coming back, Eckford. Or if it does it's going to find that this island is uninhabited."

He paused to let the threat sink in, though uncertain as to how he would follow it up. His hesitation almost proved his undoing for it goaded the old sailor to desperation. There was a quick movement of Eckford's arm, a blue flash of steel in the gloaming and Ryan felt a sharp and violent pain in his left shoulder. Almost at the same moment he charged downhill at the sailor.

Eckford stepped nimbly aside to let his opponent go down over the cliff, but Ryan had foreseen this move and despite his pain was ready to counteract it. As Eckford side-stepped, Ryan stiff-armed him in the throat, with the full force of his downward rush. The next moment the two men were grappling on the steep tussocky slope, digging with their toes to prevent their slipping and feeling desperately for each other's windpipes. Ryan was in acute pain from the knife wound in his shoulder, but he was younger and stronger than Eckford. He felt with his fingers on the sailor's thick sweaty neck, found the windpipe and began to press. The sailor was wiry and struggled violently, at one point grabbing the hilt of the dagger which still protruded from Ryan's shoulder and jerking it free. Ryan almost fainted from the pain, but he did not relax his grip and soon the sailor's struggles grew feebler. After they had stopped, Ryan still kept his fingers clutched to the man's windpipe. He wanted to make sure that he was completely unconscious, though beyond this point his mind had done no calculating.

When he was quite sure that the leathery old sailor would give no more trouble, he relaxed his grip and stood up. He would tie the old man up with liana vines and leave him to cool off while he and Margaret formed a plan. But as he turned to fetch the vines, the unconscious man began to roll forward towards the brink of the abyss. Ryan clutched frantically but failed, and the next minute his ears were filled with a sound that he hoped he might never hear again: the soft reverberating thud of a body smashing from crag to crag as it careened madly down the cliff to destruction. Finally it ended and there was silence save for the clatter of sand and small stones as they slipped and slithered down the cliff.

Ryan sat on the slope sick and trembling, with his face in his hands. He had killed his lover's father; and he knew that he could not face her and tell the truth. Almost as bitter was the realization that whether or not Eckford's signals had reached the aircraft, nothing on earth could prevent it from returning to the island. For he remembered now that his dollar sign, dug with so much difficulty long months ago, still stared at the sky from the empty beach.

22

WHEN Ryan, on leaden feet, finally reached the threshold of the rustic hut, the darkness was complete, save for the feeble gleam of the little vegetable oil lamp which Margaret had lit against his return. He approached like a thief in the night for he was heavy with guilt, and he did not want her to hear him until he had stilled his heart and decided what he should say to her. But he had counted without her sharpened sense of hearing, and as he stood irresolute in the darkness he heard her voice.

"Francis, Francis. Is it you?"

It cut across the heavy night and he knew that he had no course but to answer. He did so with a weariness that he could not keep out of his voice.

"Yes. It is I."

He stumbled forward into the pale glow of the lamp. She

came to meet him and, clasping his hands, looked up into his face. He was reminded poignantly of her beauty the night of their first meeting, weeks, months, years ago. He had forgotten, for in the meantime he had entered the timeless land. In the ensuing silence she sensed his unease and went to the heart of the matter.

"Where is my father?"

Her question was gray and without emotion.

In times of crisis the simple way is often the inevitable, unconsciously arrived at and as natural as the drawing of breath. Now in this crisis, when he could see with the eyes of a clairvoyant the end of the new life which he thought he had built so soundly, he saw also that he could tell only the truth. With a sense of relief he said:

"Your father is dead."

The passage of centuries may have dulled her sensibilities, or perhaps it was that the steel and sinew inherited from the mother who had died so many long years ago enabled her to withstand the shock; or the timelessness of her life may have given her the strength to look philosophically on all happenings. She said simply, "Perhaps it is better so," and then, loosing his hands with a sigh, turned away and lowered her lovely head. But he, full of the nervous tension of the civilization in which he was raised and which he thought he had left behind, could not let well alone. He wished to be forgiven.

"I killed him."

She turned her great gray eyes full on him and in their pewter depths he detected for the first time a small irony.

"What else would you have me think? Of course you killed him."

"He was signaling to the airplane."

"That does not surprise me. He would wish to be rescued from a life which no longer has so useful a place for him."

Used though he had become to the ruthless strength inherited from her mother, her calm acceptance of the tragedy both chilled Ryan and stung him to protestations.

"But you don't understand," he cried. "I didn't mean to kill him. We fought, I grounded him. I meant to pick him up, but . . . he rolled over the cliff . . . I . . ."

"Did he not attack you first?"

"Of course."

"With a knife?"

"Yes, with a knife."

"That would be his weapon." She smiled sadly. "You must understand, dearest, that I am an Elizabethan; I look at such matters somewhat differently. He betrayed us. He is dead. Perhaps . . . perhaps he had been my father long enough."

She put her hands on his shoulders again, and her voice sent a shiver through him.

"Do you not think, my best beloved, that we too may have been lovers for long enough?"

Though she called direct to his own deep-seated doubts, he was uneasy to find them given such blunt utterance. He hesitated, but she pressed him.

"What have we to live for?"

His answer, in its sentimentality, in its appeal to basic instincts, should perhaps have been hers.

"There is our child."

She shook her head and disengaged herself.

"I do not wish him to live in the world you have described;

nor one which is ruled by the terrible machine which I heard tonight."

He found himself trying to justify mid-twentieth century civilization.

"Dearest, it is not like that. There may be fierce and terrible weapons, but we do not use them all the time. And there are riches, both of the body and of the spirit, which we miss here on this island."

"What are they?" She was oddly cold and withdrawn.

He started to think of them, but as he reeled over in his mind the endless string of devices with the description of which he had delighted her when first they were in love, they seemed now inadequate. Against the background of the somber mountain and the infinity of the ocean, and in the context of their passion, words like radio, refrigerator, television, automobile, motion picture, diesel locomotive, sounded vapid and hollow.

He thought of the marvels of medical science, of surgery and antibiotics, but of what use would they be to a woman who held in her body the secret of eternal life? He imagined a hundred subtly blended sensations of his civilization: exquisite food and ambrosial wines; the richness of tended fields; the soaring steel and concrete and chrome and aluminum of modern cities. But the images were curiously out of focus and faraway. He wondered if this paralysis of the memory were one of the by-products of the magic water of youth. He heard her voice again: cold and passionless now.

"What are they? What are the gifts of your civilization?"

It was a voice that he scarcely recognized. It throbbed with command, and he felt once again the irresistible attraction which had first drawn him to her. But under the influence of the water of forgetfulness (perhaps, he thought, these are indeed the waters of Lethe, the river of oblivion) his ability to recall the sights and sounds of his own world was fast disappearing. The memory of the life he had once known was becoming blurred round the edges. He made a final effort.

"I will tell you. My world has things undreamed of in our narrow life. Great music for instance: the noble, sturdy faith of Bach; the somber triumph of Beethoven and the liquid fantasies of Debussy; the exquisite performance of a great symphony orchestra when the audience is hushed. It can give you the immortal paintings of Rembrandt and Goya, of Rubens and Constable, of Cézanne and Van Gogh. It can show you the architecture of Wren and Palladio and Wright, the town planning of Hausman and l'Enfant: names to you perhaps, but their works endure through centuries. It can offer you the poetry of Milton and Racine and Goethe, and the prose of Dickens and Stendhal and Mark Twain. My world can provide vivid spectacles: concerts and grand opera, the theater and the ballet, painting and sculpture; the thrill of racehorses rounding the bend or of a circus come to the city; the word of great philosophers like Spinoza and Kant and worship in soaring cathedrals. It gives you trade and plenty and individual liberty and the sacredness of the person. It gives you the rule of law and a knowledge of the stars. It gives you the three hundred and fifty years that have passed since you drank the waters and entered the timeless land."

He paused breathless, his face flushed. Margaret nodded as if in appreciation, but her face wore a faintly ironic smile.

"The world has indeed wrought wonders in the years since

I left it, Francis, my beloved. But to me who have not seen these wonders, the terrors seem less remote. You speak of great music, but what's that to the memory of Byrd at the virginals? Your great painters cannot compare with Michelangelo, and I come of a race who worshiped his name. Of your architects I do not know; but what poetry can compare with that of Chaucer and Dante? Of these my father often told me and indeed they are more real to me than my own life, I sometimes think. We had the rule of law in Tudor times, and all these other vague names mean nothing to me as compared with the end of my happiness which I assuredly heard in the roar of that machine."

He nodded, for his conscience was ill at ease. She slid her hand into his.

"My beloved, I have lived too long in this island. I have become too accustomed to its ways. I fear change. Oh, I do not mean that I fear the change which you have brought. You are my life and my light. But, to change to another land, another world—I could not do it even if your world were an Utopia like that of Sir Thomas More."

"Then I shall stay with you."

"Yet this other world is your world; truly, is it not?"

"It was, but is so no longer." And yet even as he spoke he was conscious of a corroding doubt. He cast it aside and repeated:

"No. I shall stay with you."

"Oh Francis, I do not want to cheat you of your long vanished world, but you are a part of me now. And," she added ruefully, "I could not see these miracles you speak of even if I would."

Again he gyrated toward the old world he knew.

"But through me, you could see them! I should describe

them to you. I should tell you about them, and we would be in love . . ."

"No. It will not do. To go back in your metal machine would be the end of my life. The end of everything I have known. Besides, the war and destruction—this atomic bomb of which you speak—would darken our lives."

She rose and clasped his hands once again. When she spoke her voice was charged with emotion.

"There may be yet another way. I have seen the centuries roll by and I am ready for their end. We have had supreme happiness together. Tonight we shall share it again and tomorrow . . . we may exchange one kind of eternity for another."

Unexpectedly she dropped her tone to a most womanly beseeching.

"Say you will come with me?"

His answer was immediate and automatic.

"I shall follow you to the end of time."

She kissed him and sighed. Then she moved over to the table and poured some of the magic wine into gourds. He watched her with a vague feeling of unease.

"Why do you do this? Have we need of wine?"

"I feel a sadness, my beloved," she answered. "Such a sadness as I have not felt since I first heard from my father the story of Drake's white ship leaving him and my mother alone that afternoon so long, long ago."

"Do not be sad. We shall be together soon." He put his arm about her shoulders.

"Yes," she said without emotion. "Yet for the first time in my long life, I should like to drink—as a rite and as a sacrament."

She raised the gourd goblet to her lips and looked at him over it with her great gray eyes. For a brief instant he had an extraordinary feeling that the cloudy curtain had lifted. The next moment she was in his arms and they were both whispering incoherent words of endearment.

· 23 ·

GRIFFITH stood on the foredeck of the carrier, watching the mysterious shape of the island disengage itself from the pearly gray of first light. He was not ordinarily an imaginative person, but the purple island with its double cones held him fascinated. He gazed at its now familiar shape, trying to conjure up the winking light he had seen last night. But to no purpose. The great cone with its tuft of steam, grayish now in the half light, remained cold and withdrawn. Griffith had been up for the past hour, ever since the carrier's radar had located the island looming up from beneath the sea's great saucer into the ken of man. He had tripped over retractor wire, bumped into half-clad figures, been cursed in the dark in his trek from his amidships cabin up to the square stubby bow end of the flight deck. But he had shambled on with the slow purposeful lope of a sleepwalker, completely engrossed in the island before him.

Now that the light was paling, the rock lost something of its mystery. In a few moments the sun, with the incredible swiftness of a Pacific dawn, would explode over the edge of the great cobalt saucer and explore the high crags. As the moment approached, his certainty about the island ebbed; and yet it was on this certainty that he had staked his reputation as a man with a nose for news, and on which the Admiral had decided to beach a landing party this pearl-gray and expectant morning. Only he was not to be a member of it. That was the sad fact which gnawed at his vitals and prevented his complete enjoyment of the slowly unfolding scene before him. As he gazed at the island he chewed the cud of his bitterness: to be close to a story, and yet not to be allowed to go there to see it break. In a sense though, he grudgingly admitted, it was his own fault. For when the great aircraft had taxied smoothly up to the side of the carrier the previous night, heaving gently in the Pacific swell, he had been one of the first to scramble up the boarding net and seek an interview with the Admiral.

The old man was at first skeptical, but sitting there in his little cubicle of white-painted steel, with a single bulb overhead encased in a vapor-proof glass dome, he ended by believing and by calling in his staff captain to listen. Griffith could hear even now, the Admiral's sharp bark, as his story unfolded.

"What's that? You mean to say there was a light and it was worked by human agency?"

"Yes sir. A system of dots and dashes I'm not familiar with."

"Couldn't have been the wind, blowing branches in front of a fire?"

"No sir, it was man-made."

"Trying to communicate with us?"

"Yes sir. About 1950 hours this evening. I followed it for ten minutes, but couldn't make head or tail of the signals. Then it stopped."

"Did you have your glasses on it?"

"Yes sir, and to me it looked like a lantern."

The Admiral leaned back in his tight little swivel chair and hitched up his belt. Then he swung around, pulled down a map from the roller case behind him and studied it briefly. He shook his head.

"On the face of it, it's ridiculous. According to the information I have, this island has never been charted. It's inconceivable that someone should have landed there and still be alive."

"Pardon me, sir, but I understood that was one of the things we were supposed to clear up."

"Yes, yes, yes, hell, yes," said the Admiral testily. "But you and I know very well that it's not castaways we're after, but strategic raw materials. The rest of it's moonshine."

Griffith leaned forward slightly on his feet and placed the tips of his fingers on the Admiral's desk.

"Do you know what else I saw, sir?"

"What? Of course not. What *did* you see? For God's sake, stop being mysterious, man."

Griffith paused and let his words drop into the ensuing silence like stones into a pool.

"A dollar sign."

"What?"

"Yes, sir, a dollar sign, a great big dollar sign dug in the sand."

The Admiral smote the desk with the flat of his hand.

"That settles it! Either you're completely crazy, or there's an American on the island."

"Or maybe a Canadian sir."

The Admiral glared belligerently.

"Or maybe a Canadian, Griffith, or a Mexican, or a Cuban, or conceivably a follower of Chiang Kai-shek. But most likely an American." He stood up. "We'll put a landing party ashore in the morning."

"Yes indeed, sir!"

"You will brief them as to whereabouts."

"Yes, sir."

"No story, Griffith."

"Sir?"

"I'm sorry to disappoint you, but no one has the faintest idea of what's on that island. There may be savages, there may be men from Mars. There may be no one. There may be representatives of an unfriendly power. There may be chattering monkeys. I want the first landing to be a reconnaissance by the marines, and I want you to observe the exercise from the ship, through glasses. When we know more definitely how the land lies you can go ashore. After all," he added with a twinkle, "even a P.R.O. has to get background material first."

Griffith swallowed his disappointment.

"Yes, sir."

"Not that I think a Public Relations Officer's skin is too damned precious," the Admiral added, with a grin, "but I want you for the big show, when we land in force."

He nodded to terminate the interview and Griffith saluted and marched from the stuffy little white steel sepulchre into the companionway and thence up on deck.

Now, twelve hours later, he was on deck again, and with the coming of the light, resentful of the passive role he was to play. As he fumed and pondered, the sun burst over the water like a thunderclap and sent rays almost level with the ocean, reddening the tips of wavelets as they came. The rosy fingers had already started probing the crannies of the rocky tor, and the wisp of steam was a puff of pink cotton-wool against the awakening sky. The hum of the power winch lowering a boatload of marines from the center-port davits filled the morning air. Lucky devils. He went over to the side and looked down at the men as they sank from view beneath the huge sweep of the carrier's gray hull.

With the usual good-natured contempt of the leatherneck for the sailor—in fact, for everyone on earth, and specially the P.R.O.—they catcalled from the descending boat. "Where's your steno—sir?" "He ain't never had nothin' tougher than a deadline, eh, sir?" and similar pleasantries. Griffith gave them an ironical half salute as he gazed at these men of action with unfeigned envy. Then the operators let the winches run full out and the boat hit the water with a smack that produced a chorus of protests and oaths. The next minute the little vessel was cleaving a white parabola of churning foam as it sped from the ship's side and bounced across the gold-tipped waves toward the island. Griffith leaned his elbow on the taffrail, his chin moodily in his hand and stared after them for several minutes. Then, with a sigh, he turned to go below for breakfast.

Ryan had awakened with a start at first light: awakened to a feeling of vague apprehension. The little room in the bower was filled with Margaret's lingering fragrance and the place next to his was still faintly warm, but Margaret herself was not there. In the triangular opening of the reed-curtained door a few stars still shone in a sky changing now from mauve to gray. The wind that heralds the dawn brushed fitfully through the trees and there was an uneasy stirring in their upper branches. Ryan leaped to his feet shivering a little, from a chill presentiment rather than from the wind of the waning darkness. For he remembered now her strange mood of the vanished night, and he sensed even as he called her name that he must seek her at once, and yet, that his quest for her might be fruitless.

"Margaret!"

He waited while the magic name billowed across the little lake and died among the trees. The possibility of a terrible truth was hardening in his heart, but he called again, his legs astride, his hands to his mouth as the dawn rushed nearer.

"Margaret!"

But the sound echoed and died and a moment later he started to run along the edge of the lake to the track that led up the inner slope of the *caldera* toward the blackened waste outside. There was not a doubt in his mind that she had gone to the roaring cavern where the great jets of steam plumed skyward; nor did he need a guess at the reason. As his feet bore him upward to the brink of the *caldera* he remembered vividly her words—was it only the day before? An age which now seemed so long ago, when the illusion of their perfect world had not yet been shattered by the noise of an aircraft engine. In his mind's ear he heard the echo of her voice.

"If I should ever lose you Francis, life would be useless to me."

Now he knew, and the knowledge drove him nearly frantic. She had decided to rid him of the encumbrance which she now dimly felt herself to be. She was preparing to let him return to his own world, and was on her way to almost certain destruction, unless he could prevent her. It never occurred to him that in preventing her he might himself be destroyed; for since he had drunk the waters of youth he felt immortal. But he panted hard to breast the slope at top speed for he knew that she must have a sizable start, and that though she made the journey in her own private darkness, her foot would be just as sure as his. As he reached the crest of the *caldera,* the dawn came up in full battle array and he saw the cindery wastes of the crater floor bathed in reddish light so that it looked like a set piece in a scene of ancient carnage, and the huge plumes of vapor were suffused with pink.

Then he saw something else, and it gave him pause. Far below him and to the north of the island the freshly illumined ocean was streaked with smoke and darkened with the shapes of men o'war. With the naked eye he could make out quite easily an aircraft carrier, and two destroyer escorts as well as a scattering of smaller craft maneuvering busy wakes round their parent ships. Though the flotilla lay from eight to ten miles off the island, it seemed to fill the whole arc of the horizon, so long had it been empty of anything save sea and sky.

So the Navy was here. Instinctively Ryan gave a gesture of despair. He felt trapped by the conflict of his own emotions. He longed to reach Margaret so that he could prevent her useless sacrifice and take her with him back to his world; yet at the same time he did not wish her to be defiled by contact with that world. He longed to remain forever living in an island idyll; and yet he wished at the same time to show an Elizabethan the delights of the twentieth-century world. But while he strove with himself in an agony of uncertainty, events were narrowing desperately his margin for decision; and he who had become timeless now burned with a futile desire to arrest time in its flight.

He was not given the chance. In the few moments that he paused to scan uncertainly the movements of the fleet far below, Margaret reached her self-appointed goal in the roaring cavern. As Ryan's eyes turned back from the flotilla to the surging jets of vapor, he saw them turn in an instant from white to a dirty gray, and the earth heave. But long before any sound could reach him, light and life had been blotted out: this time for them both; this time forever.

While Ryan was striding half-demented from the green crater to the steam vents, the carrier was standing about eight miles offshore, for the Admiral did not wish to risk his craft in uncharted seas. It was almost opposite the smaller cone, and with his glasses Griffith could pick out the narrow opening between the sand dunes that marked the landlocked harbor he had seen from the aircraft. Off to his left the larger cone reared its forested slopes about eight to ten miles off. The keystone of rocks, against which the forested slopes surged in vain, looked in the morning sunlight like the crown of a king who had held sway over a race of gods. The little boat with the marines in it chugged merrily away from the carrier. The dawn wind had dropped, leaving the air heavy and humid. He noticed that the tuft of smoke or steam jetting from the mountain top seemed a little larger and a little dirtier than when he had seen it yesterday. Then he went below. That was what saved him. For at the bottom of the companionway his world was suddenly blotted out by a flash of blinding light and something smote him in the chest with the impact of an express train.

Minutes later he awoke to see a bulkhead stove in, smashed furniture protruding from a nearby cabin and a rating lying in the blocked corridor with his shoes blown off. He saw that he was alive by a miracle. The ship had been subjected to the force of a tremendous, perhaps an atomic explosion. Griffith's thoughts were confused, but lingering at the back of his mind was the belief that the expedition might have been drawn into a trap by an enemy power bent on its destruction, or else that the island which he had thought uninhabited was a secret atomic testing base and that whoever owned it had chosen to annihilate possible spies. He stumbled about in a daze at the base of the companionway; his left arm had begun to hurt abominably, and he found that he could not raise it. He wondered vaguely if it was broken. Then he became aware of a muffled shouting in the bowels of the ship. Stepping gingerly over the unconscious rating he squeezed past the edge of a buckled watertight door and found himself in one of the hangars. Through acrid smoke that swirled in great eddies by the open doors on the port side, he could see a fire burning fiercely. Dimly he descried figures dancing round it. One of the mechanics rushed up to him. His overalls were torn and his face smeared with a mixture of blood, oil and grime.

"What happened?"

"Jeez, I dunno, sir. Can you give us a hand with the foam extinguishers? One of these is on fire."

"I've only got the one arm, sailor, but I'll do what I can."

"Thanks a lot, sir."

The man rushed back across the ribbed steel deck, Griffith tramped after him, his loose arm hanging uselessly by his side. The gray paint had peeled off in huge blisters on the port side. When they got within twenty-five feet of the burning aircraft, the mechanic handed him a foam extinguisher. Holding it between his feet, he directed the spray with his right arm. In a few minutes the fire was out. He was faced by the charred carcass of a fighter plane dripping browned foam like icicles, while round him stood and squatted a small circle of begrimed ground crew. He found his voice and breath.

"Whatever happened?"

A tall sandy-haired fellow wiped the grime from his eyes.

"It's like this, sir. I was working on this craft with Spud here," he indicated a squat taciturn companion. "We're both inside the craft, our eyes turned to the metal, like—guess that's what saved us."

Griffith nodded mechanically.

"All of a sudden there's a tremendous flash of light—like lightning's hit a power cable, only more so, sir. We duck and next minute there's a roar like a furnace and a blast that knocks us off our feet and sends us skiddin' over to the starboard side of the hangar." He gulped and paused for breath. His companion interjected.

"Next thing you know, fires have started and we're trying to put 'em out with carbon tet and foam extinguishers. That's when you came, sir."

Griffith nodded dully. His arm was paining fiercely now.

"What happened to the rest of the ship?"

"Don't know, sir. There's a couple of guys hurt bad back in the stockroom, but the ship seems to be okay. I'm staying here till I get orders."

The squat man spat agreement into the buckled carcass of the fighter plane.

"Sure, we'll be okay. It's the poor guys that was goin' ashore that's had it, if they got that far."

"You mean the marine landing party?" said Griffith sharply. The taciturn man looked at him curiously.

"Sure. Who else? Have you taken a look outside?"

Griffith shook his head. The little man jerked a thumb in the direction of the port hangar door.

"Take a look out there."

Griffith lurched over to the edge of the huge doors which opened flush with the main decking. He propped himself up against the steel jamb and looked out.

The island had vanished utterly and completely. In its place a dense pall of greenish-gray smoke hung like a curtain from the horizon to the zenith. At its base the troubled waves churned and boiled in great discolored surges, shot with bits of charred pumice and stippled with jets of steam. At its skyward edge the curtain twisted and turned its way upward, creeping toward the focal point of the heavens and turning the sky a dirty green. The faint sound of rumbling explosions came to him dimly through the smoke. Tongues of orange flame flickered and flared uncertainly in the murk. The sky was leaden-green, the sea like tarnished pewter.

Even as he watched he caught the slight wash and ripple of water sliding past the side of the ship. The Navy was in control again. The vessel was being slowly moved away from the scene of destruction, out into the cleansing waters of the Pacific. Griffith heaved a great sigh of relief. Then he passed out.

· 24 ·

THE story of Elizabeth Island, delayed until the return of the expedition to Rotifanga in the Tuamotu Archipelago, burst upon the world over the by-line of Lieutenant Commander Tom Griffith. In Honolulu it made a 42 point flare headline in the *Aloha Times*, where it occupied the entire front page to the exclusion of an atomic explosion in Nevada and the eruption of Mauna Loa. To Ruth, as she lay on a rattan chaise longue in the garden behind her apartment, it came in the guise of a blessing. After a wry smile at the by-line she knew would give Griff so much pleasure, she read the terse, tightly worded, but exhaustive account with a sense of mounting excitement and of tremendous relief. And when she had finished, she lay for over an hour with the paper loose on her slender knees.

MYSTERY ISLAND EXPLODES

U.S. SHIPS DAMAGED

"LUCKY TO BE ALIVE"

by Lt. Cdr. Tom Griffith, U.S.N.

ROTIFANGA BASE, FRENCH OCEANIA, June 23 (AP). One minute the island was there; the next it had vanished in an earth-shaking roar that made an explosion in Nevada seem child's play: vanished behind a five-mile-high curtain of smoke and flame.

One moment I was walking down a white painted corridor in one of Uncle Sam's largest aircraft carriers; the next I was unconscious.

The explosion took place at approximately 5:43 A.M. on Tuesday, June 15, in latitude 35°16′ South and longitude 105°23′ West. That's where this mystery island is located. I was P.R.O. in a joint U.S.-U.K.-France expedition sent south from Pango Pango in American Samoa and Rotifanga in the French-owned Tuamotu Archipelago, to prove the existence or otherwise of this island never sighted before by seamen or explorers.

I can report that it existed all right. I saw it with my own eyes and so did a lot of my buddies. I can also report that it now exists no longer. It was blown to smithereens—the whole shooting match—in this greatest explosion of all times: greater than Krakatoa, greater than Mt. Pelee, so the scientists with our expedition claim.

When I came up on deck after the explosion all I could see at first was a boiling curtain of sulphurous murk blotting out land, sea and sky from view. It was lit from inside by great orange flashes and a noise came from it like an artillery barrage. The air was pea-green and the sea seemed to be seething with streaks of foam and bubbling like a cauldron. We were about eight miles off the smaller cone of the island at that time and about ten miles from the explosion. After a while I fainted.

When I came to the ship had moved about five or six miles astern. My arm was paining me badly. I stumbled down to the sick bay to get it fixed. Oil and grease was everywhere and here and there a plate was buckled or stove in. The sick bay had a few walking wounded; it's amazing to me that no one was killed, but I guess we were too far off. Even the marines in the landing boat who were a mile closer in escaped with a bad ducking. The surgeon found my arm was broken but he gave me a knock-out drop and fixed me up with splints and a cast.

By this time I was forgetting about myself and anxious to see what was happening topside. I went up on deck. You could have knocked me down with a marlinspike. The great murky curtain had lifted. It hadn't disappeared. It had simply raised its lower edge about eight degrees above the horizon and it hung suspended between earth and heaven like a great swath of yellowish-green crepe. Beneath it the air was clear and you could see a swatch of blue sky between the curtain and the ocean. The ocean was an untroubled line of blue-gold in the morning sun. But that was wrong. I blinked my eyes. That was where the island should have been. But there was no island. All I could see were a couple of black splinters and white foam, and the sea all round us red and yellow with volcanic mud and ash.

I went below and got my glasses, strung them around my neck and clambered up on deck. It was hard to use them properly with one arm, but finally I got them focused and looked through them. This is what I saw. For miles around the sea was like a muddy river in spate, swollen with great streaks of red, black and yellow. Over where the island had been steam was still bubbling up from under the sea and the ocean was boiling like a kettle over the place where the big volcano used to be. Away to the right I got my glasses on the two jagged splinters. Close up they turned out to be two teeth of black basalt surrounded by churning water; all that was left of the little cone. As I watched the water mushroomed and a great spurt went skyward. A minute later I heard a terrific roar, and had to hang onto the rail against the blast. When the water sank back into the ocean even those two splinters had gone.

It was eerie. Early that morning I had seen an island, shaped like an hourglass, about five miles long, with its larger peak about 6000 feet high. I'd flown over it the day before in a plane. Now it was gone, and not a rock, not a stick, to mark it. The Admiral kept us standing by for two days until all our flotilla was with us and we'd radioed Rotifanga to say we were coming back. During that time we kept a sharp lookout for any further explosions, figuring that if an island can disappear that quick, it could be shoved up again from the ocean bed in nothing flat. But nothing happened and there were no more explosions.

By the third day the curtain had gone. It hung there a long time and for several hours each day it blotted out the sun and made the light yellow and theatrical like a partial eclipse. Finally a trade wind came in from the southeast and whipped it away, but not before it had covered all our ships to a depth of about two inches with fine volcanic ash. When it had gone and the sea looked quiet, the Admiral called for volunteers to go in a cutter and cruise round where the island had been. It was too dangerous to send in a larger ship, not just because of the possibility of further explosions, but because the destruction of the island must have created a whole complex of submarine shoals and ridges, sandbanks and rocks, and a shallow draft vessel was needed.

Though any mission would only have a fifty-fifty chance of success and might be blown up by another explosion, there was no lack of volunteers. Twenty-four marines went off in a cutter across a choppy sea to where the reef and shoals were, about ten miles away. I followed them with the glasses and saw them cruising around, backing and filling, tacking and turning about for the best part of a couple of hours. Then they came back. They reported extensive shoals round the edges of what had been the two cones of the island, conforming roughly to the contour. But in a brief survey they got nothing less than four fathoms over the shallowest parts. As for the big crater itself, they went right over it. They reported the water still at about 140 degrees; but no bottom after reeling out 200 fathoms. Then they tried again with a portable fathometer that's worked on the sonar principle. They set it for 1200 fathoms, but still no bottom. I guess that hole must lead right to the center of the earth and unless its plugged, the whole Pacific may drain away through it!

We left the day after for Rotifanga and we shall have

to leave it to our successors in the Allied navies to chart fully the strange new underwater profile of this vanished island. I understand that it's to be called Marine Shoal in honor of the leathernecks.

Two questions remain. Was the island inhabited, and why was it not discovered before? The answer to the first is simple. It was inhabited, but whoever lived there is dead now and we shall never know who they were. All I know is—and I'm authorized by the Navy to say this—when we flew over one of the beaches we saw a huge dollar sign scraped in the sand. It may be that some ancient race we know nothing of had such a sign which may have meant something quite different to them from what it means to us. Saul Sample, the anthropologist with our expedition, says all the known evidence is against it. So we're left with the hypothesis that it must have been an American, or someone who knew the dollar sign. That might mean a national of practically any country in the western world and quite a few in the eastern. All I know is the mark, seen through glasses, was recent. Sculpture in sand doesn't stand the test of time very well. I leave it to you.

Why the island was never found is anyone's guess. The Navy thinks that the most logical explanation is that it's far away from any sailing routes of the 18th, 19th or 20th centuries and that the great explorers, like Cook and Byron, Roggeveen and Bougainville who charted this part of the Pacific, never came within a hundred miles of it. Certainly a study of their routes in the navigational charts of the U.S. Naval Hydrographic Office confirms this.

So that was it. Ruth lay recumbent on her rattan chaise longue and tried to reconstruct, from Griffith's staccato and slightly self-important prose, the essential truth of what had really happened. Yet she was vanquished before she started; for long ago, when the news had come of the loss of Ryan's plane, she had wanted to believe him dead, so that now she was incapable of sifting objectively in the quicksands of her mind the evidence for or against his connection with the lost island. The vivid and magnificent story flowed past her and drained untouchably away, while the busy backwater of her mind teemed with small and petty notions, personal to her. As a result she saw the story in terms of her own emotional entanglements with Ryan and Griffith. And since she could not, or was unwilling to conceive of Ryan ever having had any existence at all since the crash six months ago of the B 77, her immediate reactions were in terms of what she should do with Griffith.

Throughout the long steamy afternoon, heavy with the promise of a kona rain, she lay somnolent on the chair and distilled appropriate images of herself and her future, toyed with them, discarded them, or put them aside into the disordered lumber room of her brain for further use. The fact that loomed largest in her limited horizon was that Tom Griffith would now be on his way home and that, on the whole, she did not wish to see him. She did not want to reenter a relationship from which she had freed herself. But as the afternoon shadows lengthened and the honey-peckers began to sing in the casuarina tree, she realized there was a stronger reason: she did not want to appear to be asking any favors from Griffith. To have cast him off, to have failed to provide herself with a suitable alternative outlet and to admit this by returning to him: that would be unthinkable.

Searching for a retreat in which to rebuild her life, her thoughts now turned to Canada. As she cast back in her mind for memories of the dry wind-swept streets of a city in the foothills of the Rockies, the lush Polynesian honky-tonk of Honolulu and her six years in it seemed to quiver and become insubstantial before her eyes. She saw instead the dun-colored rounded hills near Calgary, their grass burned bare by the killing frosts of November. She saw the treeless corridors of cement and steel that made the downtown section, and to her they no longer seemed cul-de-sacs of ferocious gloom, but gay many-peopled thoroughfares down which the damp warm chinook swept along, bringing the corrupting smell of azaleas and melting ice into a land still held fast in the grip of winter. She thought of gnarled and twisted cedar poles holding their arms aloft with a network of power cables and telephone lines; darkening the stretch of high noon outside the Palliser hotel; placing the people in a cage—cement under foot, bricks and concrete for walls and wires for a ceiling—and she threw back her head, arched her throat and laughed for the first time in several months.

Because she was so engrossed in her private affairs she gave scarcely a passing thought to the headline below Griffith's story.

MAY BE DRAKE'S VANISHED HARBOR:
ELIZABETH ISLAND—SAYS NAVAL HISTORIAN

Instead, she rose, stretched languorously and went inside to start packing. The debris of the past few years could be tied up in a neat little package which she could stuff under her arm and bring out again in Canada, completely made over and with fresh frills and exotic embroidery on it. As she moved toward the house the new story of the new Ruth was already beginning to take shape. The hill breeze sent a cooling tentative finger across the lawn and whisked up the paper where she had let it drop. It skated across the neatly groomed grass and wrapped itself round the ridged and cracked bole of papaya tree.

> WASHINGTON, D.C., June 25 (UP). The island which blew up in the face of the U.S.-U.K.-France Naval expedition to the South Seas may have been the long lost Elizabeth Island of Sir Francis Drake, according to Captain A. B. Mittra of the Hydrographic Office of the U.S. Navy.
>
> Captain Mittra states that when Drake returned from his famous voyage round the world of 1578–1580 he told of an island which he had named Elizabeth Island in honor of the Queen of England and where he had spent the 24th to the 25th October 1578 while running before a southeast gale after rounding the Horn. In this unexpected haven Drake went ashore, procured wood, water and fruit and named the landlocked harbor Port Sir Francis Drake.
>
> In his voyage Hakluyt tells how Drake's expedition "entered into the haven of an island and ankered above the length of the shot of a great peece from the land at twenty fathome deepe where they stayed three or foure dayes and the wind coming southward they weyed anker . . . having found fresh and very good water with herbes of singular virtue."
>
> The chaplain of Drake's expedition, Fletcher, drew a

map of the island and had this to say of it. "In this Island were growing wonderful plenty of the small berry which we named currants, or as the common sort call them, small raisins. I went on shoare with such tooles as I hadd of purpose ever about me when I went on shoare, and had graven Her Majestye's name, her Kingdom, the year of Christ and the day of the month. I returned again in some reasonable time to our company."

Despite the evidence, says Captain Mittra, which must have been secured from Drake himself after his return to Plymouth loaded with between $50 to $60 million worth of Spanish treasure, no subsequent navigator had been able to find the island, and in the year 1748 it was removed from the navigational and hydrographic maps of the world.

The present island which has just exploded may therefore well prove to have been the original Elizabeth Island of Francis Drake. How the island remained undiscovered for close to 400 years Captain Mittra was unable to explain, but suggested that those who followed Drake had not made due allowance for the set of the Cape Horn current and that for the last 200 years, since it was taken off navigational maps, no one has been particularly interested in its existence.

Upstairs Ruth was humming to herself as her story took shape. She had already telephoned the Canada-Australia line and secured passage on the old *Ruapehu* for Vancouver. Already she could picture her arrival in the city of the foothills still wearing a widow's weeds; not perhaps dramatic in themselves, but inspiring pity, and to her male friends a pleasurable suggestion of accessibility. The drama would lie in her tales of adventure in far-off lands. Though pedestrian and tawdry in themselves, they would not appear so to her simple and simple-minded friends in Calgary, the raw sweet city uncorrupted by the smell of frangipani or the taste of the custard apple. She smiled to herself as she brushed her thick chestnut hair.

· 25 ·

LOST IN a melancholy waste of waters two ships, six thousand miles apart, briefly furrowed the bosom of the Pacific. A passenger vessel with black hull, white superstructure and red funnels bucketed briskly northward through gray lumpy seas off the coast of Oregon, where the cold currents that seep down from the Aleutians shroud the continental shelf in fog. A gray warship steamed through tropical waters of deepest cobalt away from the translucent green lagoons of the Tuamotu Archipelago. Yet both were linked by over sixty million square miles of water—more than all the land in the world combined—which rolls from Bering Straits to Antarctica and from Panama to the Philippines, covering half the globe.

On the poop deck, the one reserved for tourists, sat Ruth Ryan prim in a deck chair, shooting a sidelong glance from beneath her lashes and behind her sunglasses at any male prospect. But it was a grim business, for she was traveling off season when unattached females are at a discount. Snug in a cocoon of self-satisfaction she wove in ever brighter colors the story to which her friends and relatives would listen for many a week to come: glamorous nights beneath tropic stars, days dedicated to the pursuit of the exacting social round, iced drinks in tall tumblers, the crisp profile of white sharkskin. Then the tragedy of widowhood and the little woman with the stiff upper lip. Tomorrow they would reach Victoria and late the following afternoon would sail beneath the spidery threads of the Lion's Gate into the skyscraper jaws of downtown Vancouver, crouched at the foot of snow-covered peaks. She had scarcely a passing thought for Griffith and none at all for Ryan.

Down in his little cabin on C Deck, Griffith listened to the rustle of the oil-smooth water through the open porthole and conned once more his official report of Expedition Treasure Trove and its astonishing ending. He was a good enough P.R.O. to know that his exclusive story, filed the day the *Dragonfly* had sailed into Rotifanga for running repairs, would make headlines all over the world and would associate his name with one of the major news breaks of the century. Yet he was enough of a sailor not to let it turn his head and to know that his arm, broken in the explosion, and his ability as a firefighter demonstrated later, had won him a warm place in the hearts of those among whom he hoped to serve. Also—and this was a cause of particular gratification—the old boy had undertaken to recommend him for his third stripe. As the *Dragonfly* wallowed slowly across the fifteen hundred miles of sea separating Rotifanga from Pango Pango he had no thought of Ryan and no more than a twinge of regret over Ruth. There were other fish in the sea.

Besides, he remembered his last conversation with the Admiral. The old boy had called Griffith into his cabin to check over the first draft of his statement for the press. After bending bushy eyebrows for a few moments over the foolscap, the Admiral had given him permission to sit down, a most unusual privilege. Griffith sat at first somewhat on the edge of his hard metal chair. The Admiral fussed with the paper, dropped cigar ash on it, and wiped it messily away with too flowing a hand. Then suddenly he peered up from beneath his thatched brows.

"Funny business this, altogether, Griffith."

"Yes, sir."

"I notice you didn't put in the part about seeing the light signals?"

"No, sir—I . . ." he stopped. He was going to say that he wasn't certain he had actually seen the signal; but he knew the old boy would snort at that, for they had already spoken of it together. Instead, he said:

"I didn't think it was much use talking about a signal that couldn't be deciphered, sir. Too many people might have asked why we didn't find out what it meant."

The Admiral gave a grunt. "I agree with you. Best to leave the ends all tidied up. Who do you think it was?"

Griffith hesitated. "I don't know, sir."

"Do you think it might have been this fellow Ryan?"

"It's possible, sir." Griffith paused reflectively; then, encouraged by the Admiral's gruff smile, he plunged on. "But so many things are possible in this exercise, sir. For instance, I sometimes wonder, was this really the island we were looking for, or could it have been, maybe, some other island?"

"Great heavens, man, the latitude and longitude, the compass bearing; they were all precise enough." But there was an edge of uncertainty in his voice.

"I know, sir," said Griffith, "but that cruising airplane's original fix could have been an error. And besides, we've seen so little of the island. We flew over it once—at dusk. It was there, and then—it wasn't." He gave a foolish little laugh.

"Good job those leathernecks didn't get too far from the ship," mused the Admiral. Then abruptly, "Any other ideas, Griffith?"

Griffith hesitated again. "I'm wondering whether maybe this other island, if there *is* another . . ." His voice trailed off. The Admiral nodded his head.

"The same thought has crossed my mind too, Griffith."

They sat, trading hard looks for a moment; then the Admiral broke the silence.

"D'you know what I think, Griffith? I wouldn't breathe this to another soul in the world; but I think it's conceivable—just conceivable, mind you—that we may have missed our target."

Griffith looked across at the old man, feeling suddenly nearer to him than the bonds of discipline normally allowed.

"D'you know what I think, sir? I think maybe someone lost a dream."

"Who? This fellow Ryan?"

"If it was him, sir, yes; if not, well—someone."

The Admiral sighed. "Maybe we've lost a dream too, Griffith. And it was so real," he added half under his breath.

"You can still dream, sir," said Griffith with a grin. The Admiral smiled.

"I know, Griffith, I know. That is just possible, even in the Navy."

Instinctively both men glanced out of the portholes at the disappearing smudge of acrid cloud far astern.

Far to the south, the great ocean swells, blown by the trade winds, roll round the bottom of the earth, unshackled, unimpeded and untamed. Only the albatross, high in the biting freshness of the sky, or the occasional blue whale, sounding up from the depths of the abyss, may mark the insignificant patch of discolored water on that enormous waste of seas: all that is mortal of Elizabeth Island.

But to those who believe in them, all islands are immortal.

About the Author

Graham McInnes was born in London in 1912, was educated in Australia, and has lived in Canada for the past twenty years. His activities have not been limited either geographically or in their variety. He has been, successively, Art Editor of the Toronto *Saturday Night*, Canadian Correspondent for *The Studio* of London, Commentator in Toronto for the Canadian Broadcasting Corporation, Lecturer in Art for the Extension Department of the University of Toronto and for some years a producer of documentary films, including many films on art, for the National Film Board of Canada. Since 1948 he has been a Foreign Service Officer in the Canadian Department of External Affairs in which capacity he has served in Ottawa, in New Delhi, India, and in Wellington, New Zealand.

While Graham McInnes has published books on Canada and on Canadian art, *Lost Island* is his first novel. Married, and the father of two boys and a girl, he is himself the son of Angela Thirkell, the nephew of Denis Mackail, a cousin of both Rudyard Kipling and Stanley Baldwin, and the great-grandson of Edward Burne-Jones.